3 0132 02247771 0

D0358207

MURDER ON PAGE ONE

Since retiring from a law career which included sitting as a judge in High Court murder trials, Ian Simpson has been writing crime fiction. In 2008, one of his books was shortlisted for the Debut Dagger by the Crime Writers' Association. He has also written newspaper articles on legal topics.

MURDER ON PAGE ONE

IAN SIMPSON

Copyright © 2012 Ian Simpson

The moral right of the author has been asserted.

Apart from any fair dealing for the purposes of research or private study,
or criticism or review, as permitted under the Copyright, Designs and Patents
Act 1988, this publication may only be reproduced, stored or transmitted, in
any form or by any means, with the prior permission in writing of the
publishers, or in the case of reprographic reproduction in accordance with
the terms of licences issued by the Copyright Licensing Agency. Enquiries
concerning reproduction outside those terms should be sent to the publishers.

This is a work of fiction. Any resemblance between the characters
in this book and real people is coincidental

Cover design by Tayburn

Matador
9 Priory Business Park
Wistow Road
Kibworth Beauchamp
Leicester LE8 0RX, UK
Tel: (+44) 116 279 2299
Fax: (+44) 116 279 2277
Email: books@troubador.co.uk
Web: www.troubador.co.uk/matador

ISBN 978 1780880 624

British Library Cataloguing in Publication Data.
A catalogue record for this book is available from the British Library.

Typeset in 12pt Minion Pro by Troubador Publishing Ltd, Leicester, UK

Matador is an imprint of Troubador Publishing Ltd

Printed and bound in the UK by TJ International, Padstow, Cornwall

For Annie

Times are bad. Children no longer obey their parents and everyone is writing a book.

Cicero, circa 43 BC.

1

The body lay on the floor, as warm as the blood that seeped through the plush Wilton carpet or trickled down the white walls.

A clean, deep cut had caused that blood to spurt in spectacular quantities from the left side of the neck until the heart was still.

Glassy-eyed, brain-dead, finished, Lorraine McNeill's high-achieving life was over.

Her black skirt had bunched up round her hips, revealing long, shapely legs – legs to die for. Like a butcher arranging the shop window, the killer lifted a slender ankle and put underneath it a sheet of plain A4 paper. One character had been typed at the foot: the numeral 1.

'Well, you wanted a murder on page one,' the killer whispered, then left to be absorbed into the anonymous crowd.

2

His shabby chair gave a painful creak as Detective Inspector Noel Osborne threw his eighteen stones into it. Before he could open the baker's bag he was clutching, his phone rang.

'Oh, good morning, ma'am ... yes ... just following a lead ... nothing exciting ... oh ... another one? ... yes ... I will ...' He pulled a face at the receiver before slamming it down. He turned to the other two officers in the Wimbledon CID room. 'So, another literary agent. Lorraine McNeill.' He swilled the name round his mouth. 'She's not Scottish by any chance?' he asked hopefully.

His back turned as he made coffee, Detective Constable Bagawath Chandavarkar, 'Baggo' from his first day in the police, grinned. Inspector No was incorrigible. Since giving up their national drink, he had not had a good word to say about the 'sweaty-sock jocks'. The previous June, Baggo had wound him up repeatedly by calling Henman Hill 'Murray's Mound'.

Detective Sergeant Flick Fortune scowled. 'She lived in London all her life,' she said sharply.

Osborne reached into the bag and drew out a cream doughnut.

'The SOCOs and the photographer finished an hour ago, so I told them they could take the body away. Sir.' Flick made sure Osborne saw her looking at the wall clock in the CID room. It showed half past eleven.

Fifteen – love, Baggo thought to himself as the kettle came to the boil.

Osborne swung a brown shoe, darkened by muddy slush, onto the papers littering his desk and bit into the doughnut. Cream squelched out, some dropping on his shirt. 'What do we know?' He wiped the cream from the crumpled fabric and licked his finger.

Flick said, 'Yesterday, Ms McNeill worked late. She was the only person in the office. *Rigor mortis* was complete when she was found this morning at about nine. Her throat had been cut and she'd bled to death.'

'So time of death would have been some time yesterday evening. Any sign of forced entry?'

'None. She may have known her attacker.'

'Or they barged in as she left for the night. Had she arranged to meet anyone?'

'Don't know. Chandavarkar has her i-Phone.'

'Anything interesting there, Baggo?' Osborne asked.

'Nothing yet, gov.' He put the mugs down and resumed his seat. 'This lady did not have a big social life, if her contacts are anything to go by. A publisher was her last caller, at half past five yesterday evening. I've ordered up the phone records for her and her office. I will tell you more tomorrow.' The classical sing-song of Mumbai was over-laid by the flat whine of the English capital.

Osborne turned to Flick. 'What's happening at the scene?'

'I left Peters there with the receptionist. She's been told not to touch anything and not to use her computer. Do you want to see for yourself?'

'Never saw the point of rushing to a crime scene, Felicity. I need to think …'

Fifteen all.

'Flick, please. Sir.'

Thirty – fifteen.

'Felicity's your name, and you can't belly-ache when I call you that.'

Thirty all. The game is warming up, Baggo thought. Two days previously, Flick had complained to Superintendent Palfrey that Osborne called her 'doll', 'pet' and 'my love'. He had been summoned to the station head's office and spent quarter of an hour with her before storming out, his face red; angry, not ashamed.

Flick glared. She despised everything about Osborne: his slobbishness, his idleness, the extent to which he was off-message. He had an addictive personality, smoking like a chimney, even in the office. Years ago, his irregular methods concealed by perjury, he had jailed a lot of East End villains; in the muster room he was still a legend in his own lunchtime. But modern, transparent policing was not his style and he had developed a fondness for whisky that had nearly cost him his job; High Court Judges are not all deaf, and none of them likes being called 'old wanker' in the street outside the Bailey. Now, his mojo long gone, instead of drinking, Osborne ate, mostly curries and doughnuts. His sinewy thirteen stones had ballooned beyond recognition and, motivated only by his pension, he coasted towards retirement. It couldn't come soon enough for Flick, either.

'I need to think,' he repeated, slurping coffee. His mug was so chipped and stained that few tramps would touch it. 'That other literary agent was strangled, with paper stuffed in her mouth.'

'Not just paper, something she had written.'

Forty – thirty.

'Quite right, my lo... Felicity. Made her eat her words.' He looked meaningfully at her.

Deuce.

'Anything odd about the new one?' he asked.

'There was a bit of paper under her. It had '1' written on it.'

'One?'

'The numeral.'

'Interesting.' He scratched his crotch then said, 'Someone must hate literary agents. Don't much fancy them myself, but who's going to murder them?'

'Unpublished authors, I suppose,' Flick said.

'Are there many who can't get published? Bookshops are full of rubbish. With your education, you should see that.'

Advantage Osborne.

Flick had ceased to rise to jibes about her two/one degree in English Literature from Bristol. She sipped her coffee then explained, as if to a child: 'There are good writers who don't get published and bad ones who do. It depends on whether a publisher thinks the book will sell. Thanks to computers, anyone who wants can write a book these days.'

Deuce.

'What do you mean?'

'A book has to be typed. Before computers you had to type out every page yourself, or get someone else to do it. If you made a bad mistake, or wanted to change something, you had to re-type the whole page. Sometimes pages. Now you can alter your work easily. Bit like you and your statements,' she added pointedly.

Advantage Fortune.

Osborne ignored the dig. 'So you put all your imaginings on the computer, then print out your book when you're finished?'

'You don't even have to do that. You can e-mail your work round the world.'

'I see. But why blame literary agents if no one likes it?'

'It's probably the literary agent who doesn't like it. Most publishers look only at work sent to them by agents, so, if you want to get published you need an agent. Good agents reject hundreds of books every week. Yes, hundreds.'

'And if they do take a book on …?'

'It still may not get published.'

'And there's another reason to blame an agent,' Osborne said, wiping his mouth with his sleeve. 'But a writer wouldn't have the one eating her own words …'

He nodded towards the whiteboard, where an asymmetrical, botoxed face, clarted with make-up, had the word 'victim' beside it in green ink.

'Jessica Stanhope.'

'I know. And this new, sweaty-sounding one …'

'Lorraine McNeill.'

'Representing them, would they?'

'I doubt it.'

'So if there's a wannabe that both agents have turned down, we have a suspect for both murders.' Osborne looked triumphant.

'I'd worked that out. Sir.'

Game Fortune.

'Well, Felicity, what are you waiting for? We need two lists, soon as you can manage. But we'll do the usual personal checks as well. Don't want to overlook the bleeding obvious. I wonder if this one got up to as much hanky-panky as Jessica.'

'Are you going to visit the crime scene at all? Sir.'

Osborne screwed up the empty bag and missed the bin with his throw. 'Suppose it'll fill in the time till lunch. You drive.'

'It's just round the corner. Off Worple Road. I thought I'd walk.'

'We'll take the car in case it snows. You drive.'

Baggo waited till they had left. 'The match will resume later,' he announced to the empty room. 'New balls, please.'

* * *

'She was such a lovely person,' Aline-Wendy Nuttall sniffed as she struggled to re-attach her false eyelashes. Tear tracks spoiled her heavy make-up, her silver-grey hair was askew and her nose was red. It was only a few hours since she had reported her employer's murder. 'I can't face anything till I have my eyes on,' she confided to Flick as Osborne rummaged in a filing cabinet and a bored Detective Constable Danny Peters looked on.

Flick raised her eyebrows. 'What exactly do you do here?' she asked.

'Anything I can to help. Ms McNeill is … was so busy. I answered the phone, opened the post, kept her diary. Sometimes I saw people she was too busy to see. "You're my shield," she would tell me. Some people can get quite nasty, you know. Excuse me.' Seizing tissues, she swivelled her chair and buried her face in her hands.

'We'll just look round,' Flick said. The McNeill Agency's premises were compact. Osborne had already moved from the poorly-heated hallway, where Aline-Wendy's simple pine desk was situated, to what had been Lorraine McNeill's office. No one else worked for the agency.

Trying to think of the blood as paint, splashed extravagantly about the room by a crazy artist with a bucket and spray-can, Flick stepped over the soggy, coagulating stain on the carpet to the right of the door and inspected the walls. Alongside the likes of Tony Blair, David Cameron and Stephen Fry, the dead woman's superior smile shone out of numerous photographs. Anyone with her who was not a recognisable celebrity clutched an award, a plaque or a dagger. Flick presumed they were writers she had successfully represented. The huge, laminated black desk held only a crystal vase containing a dozen red roses, a telephone and a small laptop. Osborne sank into the leather swivel chair behind it and started going through the drawers.

'Go and get the receptionist to open up this computer, will you?' Osborne said. 'We'll have to take it away, but I'd like a sniff round it first. And try to find out who sent the roses. You're a woman,' he added.

Shaking her head, Flick willed herself to be patient.

'I organised the flowers,' Aline-Wendy admitted after some probing. 'Ms McNeill thought it important, professionally, you know, that people should see how much she was loved. I know very little about her private life, she kept that to herself. When someone did send her flowers, she was so pleased, so happy. Anyway, at the end of a bad week I organised a delivery. I put on the card: "From you-know-who", and she just winked at me. But I could tell she liked them. From then on, every Monday, I phoned in an order. These were fresh yesterday. She commented on their deep red colour.' Her voice dropping to a whisper, she added, 'I even started taking the money out of the company account.'

'Sergeant! I haven't all day,' Osborne's voice was raised.

'Sorry,' Flick whispered, then added, 'We really need to see what she had on her computer. Could you get us in?'

A look of panic passed over Aline-Wendy's face. 'But

Ms McNeill is … was very strict about security, erm, confidentiality, that sort of thing.'

'This is a murder,' Flick said softly. 'Did Ms McNeill have any enemies you can think of?'

'Some agents didn't like her much, I believe, but she always said that was envy. Almost everyone loved her …' She reached again for the tissues.

'Felicity!'

'Coming,' Flick snapped. Putting on a severe face, she said, 'We need to catch who did this. Please, now.'

Aline-Wendy responded to a firm tone, as Flick sensed she would. She glanced at her face in her hand-mirror and sniffed. Then she marched into her employer's office, doing her best to ignore Osborne, who lolled in the chair and watched as she bent over the desk.

'There, that's her e-mails. You'll be able to see most of her documents, too. I don't know the passwords for a few files. That's all I can do. And we don't have ashtrays in the office.' Aline-Wendy straightened herself, sniffed again and left the room.

Osborne pinched the butt of his cigarette and put it in his pocket then spent the next ten minutes reading e-mails. A pile of hard-backs sat on a coffee table. Flick selected one and began to read. It was a 'whodunit'. On the first page, a pensioner was garrotted. She picked up another. It opened with a traffic warden being hung, drawn and quartered. She saw the significance of the page under the body but didn't rush to share her insight.

'Nothing here,' Osborne sighed. 'Still, you'd better have a gander.' He looked out of the window. 'Give me the car keys. I'll pick you up here in a couple of hours.'

Trying not to imagine the aromas she feared he would return with, Flick brushed fingerprint powder and cigarette ash from the desk then sat at the dead woman's computer, eating the muesli bars she had packed in her briefcase.

An hour later, she reluctantly agreed with the Inspector. It was the computer of a busy and successful businesswoman, with no frivolity anywhere and surprisingly few unpublished books in the documents.

'Did Ms McNeill get a lot of approaches from people who wanted her to represent them? New writers, I mean?' Flick asked when Aline-Wendy brought her a coffee.

'Hundreds. Every week.'

'I see no sign. There's nothing on the computer and there are no piles of manuscripts in this room.'

'We don't keep them here. I'll show you if you like.' She led the way to a cupboard in the corner of the hallway. With an apologetic shrug, she opened it.

The space from floor to ceiling was crammed with thick bundles of paper, all white A4. Flick pulled out one at random and disturbed some dust. The thick rubber band which held it together had perished and fell uselessly to the floor. On the front, in large bold type was the title, *A Bath Full of Blood*, and the author's name and details. At the back was a large, brown, stamped addressed envelope. Spilling it and some of the typescript, Flick checked the first page. As she expected, a body was found in a bloody bath. She put the bundle down and selected another: a gamekeeper was shot on page one.

'Ms McNeill liked a shock opening,' Flick commented.

'She insisted on it. For crime.'

'Was it mostly crime she dealt with?'

'Yes. There's a huge international market. If you get a hit, it can be very lucrative. We've had quite a few best-sellers.'

'I see from your website that wannabes are asked to e-mail their submissions. What happens when they do?'

'They come to me. I look at them. If the first chapter seems well-written and there's a murder on the first page, I e-mail the author, inviting them to send the full manuscript in hard copy, with a stamped addressed envelope. The manuscripts go in the cupboard.'

'And did Ms McNeill …?'

'She was so busy. She concentrated on her existing clients. "They're our bread, butter and jam," she would say.'

'What about the wannabes?'

Aline-Wendy pulled a face. '"Nevergonnabes", she called them. I felt sorry for them. Some had tried very hard. I usually took a couple from the cupboard home at weekends and, if I really liked them, I put them on her desk, but it's nearly two years since we've taken on a new author. Mind you, today he's a best-seller.'

'Can you give me a list of all the wannabes who have approached you in the last year?' Flick was thinking needles and haystacks.

Aline-Wendy shook her head. 'The e-mail rejections

get a standard response then I delete the submission and our reply. Once we've had a look at the manuscripts we send them back. We don't keep records. You could look through the cupboard, of course.'

Flick, who had pictured herself writing detective stories in her retirement, was downcast. 'If they send in their manuscript and don't hear back, do they not get impatient?'

'Sometimes, but I just tell them we're very busy and we'll let them know when we can. About once a year, I go through the cupboard and send back a whole lot even if we haven't looked at them.'

'Can you think of anyone who has responded angrily after being rejected?'

'They just seem to accept it. Sorry, I can't think of anyone right now.' Aline-Wendy shook her head then brightened. 'But I have an idea. You should contact the Crime Writers' Association. They run a competition for aspiring writers. It's called the Debut Dagger. If Ms McNeill's killer wants to become a crime writer, they're sure to enter. I think the closing date is early February.'

'Just a week or two away. A lot of the entries will already be in. How do I find them?'

'I don't know. They're in England, somewhere. You'd probably be best Googling them.'

As Flick thanked Aline-Wendy, the door flew open. Osborne rolled in, pungent wafts of spices and nicotine in his wake. Flick took the air freshener from the desk and gave a five-second burst.

3

'You're 'aving a laugh, pet … Felicity. Why should crime writers associate? To plan murders?'

'As we can't compare lists of both agents' rejects, the Debut Dagger has to be the next best thing.'

'We're sticking in the real world. I'll solve this with old-fashioned police work, not by consulting 'Ercule bloody Poirot.'

'They say that all writers reveal more of themselves than they think, and if we're looking for disappointed wannabe authors …'

'Bollocks. You cannot be serious.' They were driving past the All-England Club on their way to Lorraine McNeill's flat, and Osborne mangled the vowels of Brooklyn and Whitechapel as he delivered the famous McEnroe line.

Flick shrugged. It was no more than she had expected. She would wait till old-fashioned police work hit a dead end before raising the subject again.

Lorraine McNeill had made her home in a modern luxury block standing back from a road containing expensive houses. Four-by-fours, or 'Wimbledon tanks' as Sharon, Flick's friend in traffic called them, guarded many of the driveways, ready to close in on the local

Primary School later in the afternoon.

Flick had the keys. Once through the outer door, the two officers gazed round the marble-floored foyer, silently asking themselves how much a flat here would cost.

A ping announced the arrival of the lift. Over his shoulder, Osborne said: 'You said the second floor? Check out the stairs and I'll have a look at the lift.' As the door slid open, he barged in before a smartly-dressed woman could get out. Flick had noticed that, in the presence of wealth, the Inspector became more than usually pugnacious. She smiled apologetically at the woman, who ignored her.

The stairs were spotlessly clean. Flick saw nothing remarkable as, deliberately slowly, she made her way up. Outside the flat, Osborne scowled at her, an unlit cigarette between his lips. Enjoying his impatience, she selected the correct key, put it in the lock and turned it.

Cautiously, she pushed the door and peered into the dark hallway. There was a screech and a scrabbling noise. A light brown cat sped past and down the stairs. Both officers pretended they had not been startled. Osborne switched on the light and they went in.

Immaculate was the word Flick first thought of. Clinical was the second. It was like a show flat until Osborne left muddy footprints behind him. Even the cat's litter tray and basket, side by side on the floor of the gleaming kitchen, had a designer appearance.

Flick went to the desk in the living room and began to search through the drawers, unsure what she should be looking for and hoping that she would recognise something significant if she saw it. It did not take her long to bag the financial papers and scan the holiday brochures. Luxury was the constant theme, but from the pages that had been marked it was clear that McNeill had been a single holidaymaker. Flick went through utility bills and boring letters about insurance and concluded that the dead woman had been well-organised and rich, but lonely. The only thing in the room with personality was the bookcase. It occupied an entire wall and most shelves held two rows. There were lines of bleached and battered Agatha Christie paperbacks. Dorothy L Sayers, Ngaio Marsh and Georgette Heyer were well represented. Flick ran her fingers along volumes by Drabble, Du Maurier, Mitford and Austin. A leather-bound Dickens set occupied the top shelf. The sole photograph in the room was above the fire. It showed a family group: a father, mother and two pre-teen girls. Their clothes suggested the late seventies. The CD rack was filled by Mozart and Beethoven. Flick wondered if the preening confidence exuded by her office had been skin-deep, and that Lorraine McNeill had come home seeking the comforts of childhood.

'Life is full of surprises,' Osborne said, making her jump. He came into the room and waved under her nose a pink dildo, which he held by his fingertips, despite the rubber gloves. 'Bedside table,' he explained. 'Hold this bag open, will you?'

Flick could see no connection between the dildo and the murder, but she showed no emotion as she helped bag the exhibit.

'Got to be thorough, Felicity,' Osborne said. With a wink that made Flick's flesh creep, he returned to continue his search.

The retired stockbroker who lived across the landing told the detectives that Ms McNeill had been a quiet neighbour. Pleasant and polite without being friendly, she worked long hours and seldom had visitors. He and his wife were appalled to hear she had been murdered. She had lived there alone for the past three years.

'So, no partner, no lover, success by day, wanker by night. You say there's no children, a sister in Australia and a widowed mum in a home near Slough?' Osborne asked once they were back in the car.

'Right.'

'She drank, you know. She had two gin bottles in the kitchen. And a good few bottles of wine. Chateau this, Chateau that and Chateau the next thing.'

'Were the bottles empty or full?'

'Full, of course, except one of the gin bottles. But you don't buy that stuff to stick it up on your mantelpiece. Anyway, her ex-husband's coming in. When?'

'Five.'

'Do her finances look okay?'

'Can't say for sure, but yes, I think so.'

'Dig deeper, Felicity. This woman had one deadly enemy, and I plan to find out who that was, without blindly interviewing a bunch of crap crime writers.'

* * *

'I hadn't seen her for months, honestly.' George McNeill, a tall man in a shapeless tweed jacket, who reminded Flick of the actor in the BT ads, looked worried. 'We are … were divorced,' he added defensively.

Neither Osborne nor Flick said anything. Faces expressionless, they eyeballed him across the table.

He began to gabble. 'It was a bit acrimonious at the time, but that was three years ago, and we were fine any time we met or spoke on the phone. It was a complicated settlement. Loose ends to tidy up, you know? Lawyers are expensive, so we tried to sort out any problems ourselves. Not that there were many. Or that important, really. No children. Just as well, I suppose … It was a mistake to buy property in Spain. You think our bureaucracy is bad …' With a twitchy smile he looked at the files on the desk. 'It got sorted, of course. She could negotiate, I can tell you. She was a natural for her job. I still can't believe it.' Sitting back in his chair, he looked almost desolate.

'Did she have any other romantic attachments?' Osborne asked sharply.

McNeill looked shocked. 'No. We sort of drifted apart. We first got together at university.'

'No other relationships at all?'

'I don't think she had anyone. I didn't check on her, of course. And, well, I … but she didn't mind. It was after we'd split.'

'What's your lady-friend's name?'

McNeill frowned. 'I don't see how that's relevant, but it's Claire. Claire McNeill. We married three months ago.'

'And your ex-wife didn't resent this?'

'No. She sent us a wedding present. A pile of books, actually.'

'Did she drink? We found alcohol in her flat.'

McNeill screwed up his face. 'Yes, a bit, but not excessively.'

'What about enemies? Maybe writers she'd turned down?'

'Can't think of any names. I suppose there must have been ...' His voice caught.

'When was the last time you went to her office?' Flick asked softly.

'Months ago. Let me see. September, it was.' He consulted a diary. 'Yes, the tenth. There was a document to sign in a hurry for the Spanish lawyer. Not that he ever hurried.'

'Have you seen her since?'

'No.' He gulped. 'I've just remembered. When I was in her office in September, Aline-Wendy argued with someone on the phone. She told them not to be so persistent; it wouldn't get them anywhere. She hung up on them. I remember because it was so unlike Aline-Wendy.'

'And what were you doing last night between five and ten?' Osborne made it sound like an accusation.

'Oh. Yes. You have to ask, don't you?' McNeill put his diary on the table and indicated an entry, '5.30. Snowie'. 'Alan Snow, he's my dentist. Lambeth, St Georges Road. He always gives me the last appointment of the day and we go for a pint afterwards.'

'Where?'

'Pig and Whistle. It's practically next door to the surgery. I got home about eight.'

'And just one pint?'

'Well, two or three, actually, if you want to be precise.'

'Drive home, did you?' Osborne asked sharply.

'No. Tube. Bakerloo then Jubilee. Claire was cross. The toad-in-the-hole was cremated.'

As Flick took a note, Osborne said, 'We need to have a formal identification of the body. Would you mind?'

McNeill shut his eyes for a moment then sat up straight. 'Yes, Inspector. Of course. She could be a royal pain, but I … I'm still very fond of her, in an odd way.' He turned his head and breathed deeply. 'One thing. Do you know what's being done about Stanley?'

'Stanley?'

'The cat. Burmese. He was ours, but she got custody, if you call it that. Erm, I'd like to have him now.'

Osborne said, 'Find him and keep him, as far as I'm concerned.'

Flick said, 'We'd rather not get involved in that.' Neither officer had given the cat a thought after his speedy exit from the flat.

4

'So the ex's alibi checks out, her finances seem okay, and we don't know of anyone arranging to meet her the day she was killed.' Osborne summarised their lack of progress. It was noon on the second day of the investigation, and he had called Flick, Peters and Baggo into a corner of the CID room. He did not want them to be overheard.

'Anything interesting from the phones, Baggo?'

'Not a sausage, gov. It was all dull as ditch-water. Authors and publishers, taxis and restaurants. Same goes for the computers. Nothing for you to get your teeth into.' Baggo's eyes twinkled as he glanced sideways at Peters.

'No help from CCTV, and no unexpected fingerprints at the scene.' Flick said, frowning at them. Long ago, she had ceased to find Osborne's gluttony amusing. 'I suppose you've tried Facebook?' she asked Baggo.

'A very boring entry, Sarge. Mostly about her cat. There were some nice comments from authors she had helped.'

'She seems to have had no lovers, no sins. Well, just the one …' Osborne leered at Flick then continued:

'What do we know about that receptionist, the eyelash woman?'

'Seems okay,' Flick said.

'She was really upset,' Peters said.

'Well let's look at her more closely. My old Sarge, Thumper Binks, always suspected the person who found the body, specially if they were the last to see the deceased alive. Felicity, you do that.'

'What about the wannabes and the other agent? Shouldn't we at least try and find a link?' Flick asked.

Despite Jessica Stanhope's exotic private life, which suggested a number of leads, that investigation had stalled. Like McNeill, she had been murdered in her office. She had been working late and was found strangled the next morning. An article in *Publishers' Weekly*, in which she had deplored the lack of emerging talent, had been scrumpled into balls and put in her mouth. Again, CCTV did not help and fingerprints had been wiped, even off the paper balls.

Six weeks on, Osborne was far from making an arrest, although his gut told him a jilted lover, Frank Lowe, a financial journalist who owned an extensive collection of handcuffs and whips, was the killer. His alibi depended on a Filipino masseuse in a Soho sauna and his photograph had been posted below the dead woman's on the whiteboard, the words 'kinky journo' scrawled beside his nondescript face.

'In the old days, Thumper Binks and I would have beaten a confession out of him, even if he was a bleeding masochist,' Osborne had muttered to Peters, who had gleefully told the rest of the station.

Osborne glared at Flick. 'Always wanting to use your English degree, aren't you? All right. On you go. But no going behind my back to the 'Ercule bloody Poirot Association. Peters, you put the squeeze on the receptionist. See if she stood to gain by McNeill's death. These eyelashes could be hiding something.'

'And don't forget to ask her about the caller George McNeill told us about, and see if she can now remember any would-be authors who were very persistent,' Flick added.

Peters nodded. 'I'll go this afternoon. I didn't get the impression that Aline-Wendy wanted to take over. I heard her talking to someone about other agents.'

'Anything on the techy side for me to do?' Baggo asked. His instinctive talent for IT and a desire to keep his Brahmin complexion out of the sun made a computer desk his natural habitat.

'Go over the computer and phone stuff in Stanhope's case and see if you can find a link with McNeill,' Osborne instructed. 'These cases are not going to solve themselves,' he added unnecessarily.

* * *

Jessica Stanhope had worked for Creech, Haldane and Laughton. They were a large agency with many clients. Their office was off Mostyn Road at the Gardens end. As Flick stepped into the imposing hallway she looked round the newly-installed cameras. Had they been there six weeks earlier, Stanhope's killer might have been arrested and McNeill might still be alive. A lift whisked her up to Carol Edwards' office and Stanhope's former assistant got straight to the point.

'I've prepared a list already, actually,' Edwards said, handing over seven closely-typed A4 sheets listing names and addresses. 'These are the people Jessica rejected during the last year. She was our main crime agent, so she had more submissions coming to her than the others. Our guidelines are strict: first three chapters and a synopsis in hard copy. Once a week, generally on a Friday, I'd take her what had come in. She'd look at them all. Some she'd reject after a page or two, but a few would be asked to send the complete manuscript. A reader would give their view, and if it was positive, Jessica would read the whole thing herself. We took on just two new writers last year.'

'What about the rejected material? Do you still have any?'

'No. We sent it back if they'd enclosed the postage. Otherwise we re-cycled it. If we'd let it build up, we'd have been swamped.'

'But you kept a list?'

'Some people kept sending in the same stuff. I checked each new submission on the computer and if they'd submitted within the previous year and didn't tell us, I'd bin it straight away.'

'Can you think of any wannabes who were particularly persistent or aggressive?'

Edwards thought for a moment. 'There was one man.

He was disabled. An ex-soldier. He kept on going on about that, as if he should be taken on because he was in a wheelchair. I had to be quite firm with him over the telephone. I think his name was Wallace.'

'Could you check, please?'

Edwards reached for the list and ran her finger down the column of names. 'Here we are. Ralf Wallace, Flat 2B, 12 Hope Crescent, Bracknell. He could be seriously objectionable.'

'Anyone else?'

Edwards shook her head.

'You list names and addresses, but nothing else?'

'Correct. I've no idea what their writing was like.'

'Well, thank you very much. I don't suppose you've had any new thoughts about enemies she might have had?'

''Fraid not. I did think the paper in her mouth pointed to someone she had rejected, but your inspector seemed more interested in her private life. Do you think this is connected to Lorraine McNeill's murder?'

'Too early to say yet.' Flick was convinced it was. She returned to the station and pored over the list as she chewed her muesli bars.

* * *

On Mile End Road there was a small, dark pub untouched by designers. In an alcove at the back, Osborne sat beside a thin, gnarled little man whose eyes moved constantly round the bar. He was nearer his patch than he liked, but Osborne had insisted on this place. Two cokes sat on the table in front of them. One was untouched.

'Just 'cos you're off the batter, Noelly, it doesn't mean I can't drink. My tongue doesn't work proper without my usual.'

Osborne couldn't bring himself to buy alcohol. He looked in his wallet and found nothing smaller than a tenner. Reluctantly, he handed it over. His companion got up and returned with a pint and a triple Scotch. If there had been change, Osborne didn't get it. He watched as his old snout supped the pint.

'I haven't all bloody day, Weasel. Have you heard anything about contracts on literary agents or not?'

'All in good time, Noelly. You haven't been near me for years, yet today you want me to jump. What's a literary agent?'

'Someone who sells books before they're published.'

'Oh.' Weasel put on his thinking face and tasted the whisky. 'No, I can't say I have. I can ask around, of course, but that means buying drinks.'

Osborne handed over a twenty.

'A lot of drinks.'

'I'll pay you well when you give me something.'

'Booze is pricey now, Noelly. You'll be able to claim it on expenses.'

While payments to a CHIS (Covert Human Intelligence Source) were regarded as necessary evils in the modern police world, giving drinking money to a disreputable, double-dealing informant like Weasel needed to be justified by results. Osborne handed over another twenty, hoping his claim would not be closely examined. Years ago, Weasel had been one of his best snouts, one of a number who had brokered deals that, if revealed in court, would have straightened the curls of the judge's wig. Now he was the only one on his radar, the rest being dead, in jail or out of circulation.

'That's it, Weasel. You'd better get me something. I'll be looking for you at the start of next week.' Osborne downed the second coke and left.

* * *

'Wallace? Ralf Wallace? That's the man Aline-Wendy has just been telling me about. He was wounded in Iraq and is well into disabled rights. He phoned a few times, accusing McNeill of discrimination.' Danny Peters raised his eyebrows. Back at the station, the detectives were comparing notes.

'Both these women were killed by someone able-bodied.' Osborne sounded gloomy. 'What about her, the receptionist, I mean?'

'She seems totally genuine, gov. She's been left twenty-five grand and she's over the moon. She's no interest in taking over the agency or anything like that. Apparently a friend of McNeill's, who's also an agent, will be approaching her authors, but not all will go with her.'

'Not worth putting up on the board, then?' The space below Lorraine McNeill's photograph was embarrassingly empty.

'No, gov. Don't think so.'

'What about you, Baggo?' Osborne asked.

'I have been working a dry well, gov. Sorry.'

Flick said, 'I tried phoning a couple of people on the list Carol Edwards gave me, but it's no good. One claimed he'd submitted to so many agents he couldn't remember if he'd approached McNeill or not. The other refused to answer my questions. There's three hundred and forty-one on the list. They're spread all over the country, some from abroad.'

Peters broke the silence that followed. 'You know, gov, that crap crime writers' club may be our best bet. We're struggling.'

Flick kept her mouth shut.

'I'm afraid we're running on empty,' Baggo said.

Osborne took a deep breath. 'Right, Felicity. Follow it up. Baggo, you help her.' He got up and left abruptly. It had been a bad day, and the fumes on Weasel's breath had unsettled him. He had to find something to eat.

5

The next morning, Flick and Baggo drove down the M2 to Sandwich, where Lavinia Lenehan, the organiser of the Debut Dagger Competition, lived. Although it was still January, there was a touch of spring in the air. Tightly-wrapped buds swelled cold, bare twigs, and clumps of pure white snowdrops penetrated the frost-burnt remains of last year's grass. The outside temperature gauge in the CID pool car didn't work, but the heater soon became redundant and the low sun caused Flick to put on her dark glasses.

'Do you read much, Chandavarkar?' Flick asked.

'Yes, Sarge. Today should be very interesting. But please call me Baggo. Everyone else does.'

When he had arrived at the Wimbledon office a year earlier, he had been met with barely-concealed mockery. He had taken this as teasing, not bullying, and readily answered to Baggo. Within weeks, his cheery nature, IT skills and hard work had made him universally popular. But Flick, uncomfortable about his initial treatment, always called him Chandavarkar.

'I don't think Baggo is a, well, dignified name,' she replied stiffly.

Baggo frowned. 'I know there is a lot of racism in the

police,' he said slowly. 'But I expected that sort of thing when I joined up. To tell the truth, at home we have a good laugh at you Native Brits. You have lovely pale skin which you try to burn off every summer; you eat Vindaloo till the sweat comes out of the top of your heads; you have no extremes of climate yet you moan about the weather; you drink yourselves silly so you can't enjoy the weekend with your families; and you talk constantly about football, which you can't play for toffee. We laugh at you more than you laugh at us.'

'That's nothing to be proud of.'

'It's life, Sarge. As long as I'm treated fairly, I'm not going to get upset over a little racism. Mind you, if anyone calls me a Paki, I'll kick his bum. Or hers.' He grinned.

Sensing that his reaction to being called a Paki had nothing to do with political correctness, and disliking his reference to kicking a woman, Flick tightened her grip on the steering wheel and stared at the road ahead.

The uneasy silence which followed was broken by Baggo. 'Do you read detective stories, Sarge?'

'Yes, I do actually.'

'Which writers do you like?'

'My favourites are the Kay Scarpetta books. I also enjoy Karin Slaughter. Barbara Cleverly too. And you?'

'To me, Dorothy L Sayers is the Queen of Crime. Of the modern writers I like David Baldacci and Ian Rankin. I'd love to visit Edinburgh. It sounds so gritty and cold. I model myself on Rebus, you know.' He looked for her reaction.

'Do you?' She sensed he was testing her. It was probably a joke. She forced out a chuckle.

* * *

Aided by a sheaf of Googled pages containing both directions and pictures of the route, they easily found Lavinia Lenehan's home. Set back from the road in an exclusive cul-de-sac, gravel crunched expensively as they parked in front of the mock Tudor detached house. Long-established rhododendrons and mature, waxy-leafed camellias obscured the neighbouring houses. The doorbell gave a musical chime and a dog barked. The door opened a fraction and a woman peered out.

'Detective Sergeant Fortune and Detective Constable Chandavarkar. We phoned earlier,' Flick said, her warrant card in her hand.

'Just a minute.' The door closed, there was the noise of canine protest, then the woman opened the door wide. She was fifty-ish, tall and elegantly dressed. Half-moon specs perched on the end of a large nose. She smiled.

'Ms Lenehan?' Flick asked.

'Mrs Smith, actually, but yes, that's me. Please come in.' She led the way into a spacious, south-facing room, brightened and warmed by the midday sun. Bookshelves occupied two walls and a Chippendale carver sat in front of a large mahogany desk covered in papers. The detectives sat side by side on the chintz-covered sofa. Their hostess sat on the carver.

'Do you organise the Debut Dagger Competition?' Flick asked.

'Yes, I do. Perhaps I should explain. I wrote for ages without any success, then I got my wonderful agent. She told me that Jane Smith, my true name, would never sell books, so I changed it for literary purposes. I've been lucky since then.'

'I like crime books, but I regret I haven't read yours,' Baggo said. 'I must correct that deficiency soon.'

'My stuff is set in the nineteen forties. My protagonist is an aristocrat, and he has a pretty girl barrister as a side-kick. I actually sell better in America than here.'

'I shall look out for them,' Baggo said. 'I think Lord Peter Wimsey is the bee's knees.'

'We're here because we're investigating the murders of two literary agents in London.' Flick got the conversation on course. 'We believe that the murderer may be an aspiring crime writer who would be likely to have entered your competition, and we would very much like to have access to all the entries.'

Mrs Smith wrinkled her nose. 'I'm delighted to help if I can, but you must be short of clues,' she said. Taking the answering silence as agreement, she said, 'Do you have a warrant?'

'No, but I can get one.'

'I'd prefer it if you did. Data protection and so on. But I don't want to be obstructive. What do you think you might learn from the entries?'

'Well, both killings show imagination. Not all the details have been released, but we have reason to think that the killer may have wanted revenge on agents who rejected him or her, and killed them in a way that reflected their anger. So entrants showing a strong sense of revenge or describing bizarrely appropriate killings would be worth investigating.'

'Writers do give away quite a lot about themselves, particularly if they're inexperienced,' Mrs Smith mused. 'How soon can you get a warrant?'

Baggo produced his i-Phone and looked at Flick.

'May we go somewhere private?' she asked.

A quarter of an hour later they returned, confident of having a warrant e-mailed to Baggo's i-Phone by four that afternoon. The detectives prepared to take their leave and return later.

'I wouldn't hear of it,' Mrs Smith exclaimed. 'It would be wonderful to talk to real police officers. When you phoned this morning, I knocked up a lasagne. My husband comes home for lunch, and he'd love to meet you too.'

Mr Smith turned out to be a local solicitor with a frosty manner that was soon mellowed by a glass of claret. While Flick ate sparingly and drank water, Baggo took advantage of the hospitality, earning his meal with tales of life in the police. He described how Prawo Jazdy became the most wanted man in Ireland, although the words were not a name but meant 'driving licence' in Polish. At this, Mr Smith choked alarmingly on his lasagne. As his wife patted his back and fussed over him, Baggo avoided Flick's glare.

Having survived lunch, the solicitor drank his coffee and returned to his office. Mrs Smith re-filled their cups, lit a cigarette and leaned back in her chair. 'Agents are powerful people,' she said. 'They say everyone has a book in them, and maybe they do, but very few can keep the pace of a story going for long enough. That's why fiction writing is more demanding than factual stuff. You have to keep on flogging your imagination, keep the reader engaged. It's a craft, you know, and it can be taught. A good agent will spot someone they think has talent and guide them: what to write, and how to write it. If you can get a good agent, you will almost certainly succeed one day, but it can take an awfully long time, and an agent will want to really believe in an author before taking them on. The publishing business is going through challenging times at the moment, with e-books and Kindle, so there are a lot of writers with real talent who will never get published, conventionally anyway.'

'That must be very frustrating,' Flick said.

'Yes. I'm lucky to have such a good agent, and to have got in when I did. Of course, it's like most other things: the more you do, the better you get, and I feel my latest book is my best. Most reviewers seem to agree, I'm glad to say.'

Back in the sitting room, they discussed practicalities. There were over five hundred entries for the competition, about half in e-form. With less than a fortnight before the closing date, more were expected. Each entry consisted of the first three thousand words of the book plus a synopsis, about fifteen A4 pages in all. Mrs Smith had dismissed nearly three hundred entries as hopeless, but the rest awaited the selection of a shortlist. She was happy to give the officers the three hundred hopeless ones as soon as they had the warrant, but wanted to give them copies of the rest later, in dribs and drabs, with the competition going ahead as scheduled.

Flick pursed her lips.

'We don't want to tip anyone the wink, and it'll take us a fortnight to check three hundred,' Baggo whispered in her ear.

'All right. Since you've been so cooperative,' Flick said.

'Splendid. Now I suggest you should sit on the sofa and I'll bring you some reading material. Unofficially, of course. You'll see that a lot of entries come from abroad or from distant parts of Britain. You might be able to whittle them down geographically.'

'Will they know that they are among the rejects?' Baggo asked.

'No. We acknowledge each entry but reveal nothing until we announce the shortlist. So all these poor devils will think they're still in with a chance.'

'When does the shortlist come out?' Flick asked.

'About the end of March. We do some checks before we make the announcement. We couldn't allow the Crime Writers' Association to be conned, could we?'

'Quite,' Flick said, not understanding why Baggo was sniggering.

Two hours later, with only thirty-five entries read between them, the warrant came through and they drove away, the boot weighed down by two heavy mailbags. Mrs Smith promised to start sending the e-mail entries the next day.

'Before you go,' Mrs Smith said, her voice catching. 'Jessica Stanhope was a friend. Do you think she suffered terribly?'

'It was probably quite quick,' Flick replied. She was lying. The room showed signs of a struggle and the dead woman's face had been horribly contorted. As Flick drove up the M2 she wondered if she had said the right thing.

'Some character, Mrs Smith,' Baggo commented. 'Quite up-to-date yet reassuringly old-fashioned.'

'Absolutely. It must be a challenge to write historical novels. If you find one of hers, could you lend it to me?'

'Of course, Sarge.' He glanced at her. 'Er, talking about the past, did you see that there's a season of old Hitchcock movies showing in town? In colour, now, but with the magic of the big screen. All my friends are away this weekend, but I was thinking of going anyway.'

Flick showed no reaction. 'Well I hope you enjoy yourself.'

'Might you go?'

'Doubt it. Do you have many friends in London?'

'Yes. I spent three years at school in Slough, and most of my contemporaries found jobs here. One of them is getting married, but I didn't know him so well, and I have not been invited.'

Flick did not comment. She had smooth skin and a good figure. Baggo wondered what she did at weekends. Whatever it was, she showed no interest in making him part of it.

6

Osborne watched morosely as the clear fat that had dripped from his two pies congealed into a white, glacial skin on the plate. He stubbed out his cigarette in the middle and tried to make the butt stand upright in the greasy sludge. He had waited in the alcove at the back of the pub in Mile End Road for over an hour and there had been no sign of Weasel. The investigation was going nowhere, and Palfrey had been giving him grief. Peters was checking and re-checking ground already well-covered, while Fortune and Baggo spent their time reading Debut Dagger entries. Osborne knew he needed a break, and hoped one would come soon. Most of the villains he had caught had made stupid mistakes, and confessions had been more easily come by in the days before interviews were recorded. This killer, assuming it was one person, was almost certainly clever. Too clever, perhaps.

Retirement couldn't come quickly enough. Alone at his table, he closed his eyes and imagined easy days in Spain and a pension. Would he jeopardise that if he gave Fortune's pert arse a playful slap on his last day? Not worth the risk, more's the pity. He checked his watch, got up and left. The barman pointedly ignored him.

Hunching his shoulders against a biting wind and

sleety rain, he had nearly reached his car when he heard a familiar voice behind him: 'Where do you think you're going, Noelly? You're going to like this.'

* * *

'That's old-fashioned police work for you,' Osborne gloated, as he wrote 'Willie Johnson' on the whiteboard. 'No photo yet. But before Peters and I go to see him, just check to see if you've been completely wasting your time, Felicity.'

Trying to conceal her annoyance, Flick went to her desk. Baggo made coffee then scanned the e-files Mrs Smith had sent.

It took Flick nearly quarter of an hour to find what she was looking for. Osborne put his feet on the desk, opened a bag of doughnuts and embarked on one of his Thumper Binks stories. If Peters was bored, he hid it well. Baggo looked from narrator to audience and smiled.

'Willie Johnson is on Stanhope's list,' Flick said, cutting across Osborne's punch-line. 'He's also one of the Debut Dagger rejects. He entered in hard copy: paper, not e-mail, as you'd expect. Revenge is the theme of his book.'

'Give us the short version,' Osborne snapped.

'Well the first part is set fifteen years ago. A CID sergeant goes to a murder scene and takes an ornamental box and smears it with blood. He plants it on the victim's business partner. The rest of the book is in the present. The business partner is serving life. He admits the murder to impress the Parole Board. When he's released he takes his revenge on the victim's wife, the real murderer, and the corrupt policeman, who was sleeping with her. Not a bad story, really, but the writing's terrible.'

'Let's have a gander.' Osborne seized the sheets of paper and began to study them.

'What did he give as his address, Sarge?' Peters asked.

Flick consulted Stanhope's list. '1 Makepeace Road, Littlepool, near Harpenden.' She smiled. 'Of course there will be only one place on Makepeace Road: Littlepool Open Prison. Is there anything wrong? Sir?'

Osborne's face had fallen and lost some of its colour. He grimaced. He did not look like a detective who had just cracked a case.

'You go and see him, Sergeant. Take Peters. And if he asks about me, don't tell him anything. That devil's supposed to be in for life. Christ knows why he's in an open prison.' When they had left, he turned to Baggo. 'Can't make an omelette without breaking eggs, Baggo. Always remember that. Johnson was a villain, no doubt about it. He used to be known as Johnny. I'd forgotten his name was William. I'll murder that Weasel for not properly telling me who he was talking about. And I never fancied his tarty wife, whatever the evil bastard thinks.'

'You think he now wants you to have your chips, gov?'

Scowling, Osborne left without a word.

* * *

Rush hour traffic was heavy and it was evening before

Flick and Peters arrived at Littlepool. Twenty-five years ago it had been a small, quaint community few had heard of, the solid ramparts of Makepeace Castle a benign, reassuring presence on raised ground beside the village. Flurries of summer visitors boosted the shop and the pub trade and Sir Geoffrey Makepeace's erratic driving caused affectionate tut-tutting. After he had failed to take one bend too many, inheritance tax and dry rot defeated his heir, who sold up and went to live in Spain with the pub landlord's daughter. The Home Office bought the ancestral pile and turned it into an open prison. Soon, Littlepool became known for all the wrong reasons.

The officers passed through the listed façade into a state-of-the-art modern prison. There was nothing streamlined about the procedures, and there was a delay before they were allowed to see the records they wanted. An hour after their arrival they sat in a small, glass-walled interview room. They felt dirtied by the stench of prisons, the blended odours of male bodies, preserved as if in a bottle with a dash of antiseptic. It seeped into their lungs and stuck to their clothes.

Willie Johnson came in and looked at the two officers sitting behind the formica-topped table. He drew back the chair opposite, sat down and crossed his legs and arms. Nearly six feet tall, thin and bony, enough of his white hair had escaped the cutters to show that he still had a full head. His dry, colourless skin was wrinkled. A vertical scar extended up from his right eyebrow and his nose looked as if it had seen a few fights. Primitive blue tattoos adorned his neck, arms and hands. He gave Flick and Peters the sort of look a talent show judge might give a poor act.

Flick broke the silence. 'I'm Sergeant Fortune, and this is DC Peters. How have you been spending your time in jail, Mr Johnson?'

'Where are you from?'

'London. Can you answer my question?'

'How do you think I've been spending my time?'

'Well, I understand you've been writing.'

'Is that a crime?'

'No. But have you?'

'What if I have?'

'Have you tried to get your work published?'

'So it's work, is it?'

'Writing a novel is certainly work.'

'So I've been writing a novel, have I?'

Peters snapped, 'You know you have, and we know it too.'

'So you've looked at my Facebook page? But hot tottie, here, has just said it's not a crime to write.'

Flick wished she could control her blush. 'Mr Johnson, we are investigating the murders of literary agents. We know you sent part of a crime novel you had written to Jessica Stanhope and that she rejected you. Did you also try to get Lorraine McNeill to represent you?'

'I can't remember. I tried a few. They don't want to publish stuff by guys in jail. Talk about rehabilitation. It's a bloody joke, that's what it is. But I'll be out soon.'

'If the Parole Board let you. I'll ask again. Did you try to get Lorraine McNeill to represent you?'

'I probably did. She was one of the top crime agents.'

'I'll take that as a yes. How did you feel when she rejected you?'

'Any rejection made me feel gutted. But I didn't go and kill these bints. Or anyone. I'm in jail, remember.'

'Oh really? How often do you get out of here? I believe you're training for freedom.'

'I work in a library two days a week. Menial tasks. I've been home a handful of times. I bet you've looked at the records already. You have, haven't you? I don't know when these people were killed, but from your faces, I'd say I've got the perfect alibi for both of them. Am I wrong?' He smirked.

Peters asked, 'Do you know anything about the murders of Lorraine McNeill or Jessica Stanhope?'

'Do you think I'd tell you if I did? But no. Truthfully, no.'

Flick leaned forward and eyeballed him. 'We have information that you have made threats against agents. Do you deny that?'

'Yes. There's a difference between being gutted and doing something about it.'

'Did you speak to anyone about your disappointment?'

'A few friends, maybe.'

'Names, please.'

'I forget.'

'Come on.' Peters put on his sternest face.

'Nah.'

Flick said, 'You don't want a charge of obstructing police inquiries to mess up your parole application, do you, Mr Johnson? Right now, we are going to see the governor, and then we will look very carefully at your prison records again. Is there anything at all you want to tell us today?'

Johnson shook his head. His lips twisted into a cold smile. 'Do either of you come across Noel Osborne? Is he still Sergeant, or is it Inspector No?'

Both officers shook their heads.

'Well, send him my best, will you?' He got up and knocked on the glass door. When it was opened, he did not look back before stepping out.

* * *

'A model prisoner. He did a creative writing course in Wormwood Scrubs, and since he came to us he's hardly put a foot out of line. He'll be out soon.' The governor was a big man with loose flesh. He appeared to be concertinaed into his chair and spoke with a flat, Estuary English voice.

'But he was always in trouble at the start of his sentence,' Flick said. 'Why do you think he changed?'

'The fight just goes out of some people. Age, maybe.'

Flick wondered if that had happened to the governor. Johnson seemed more like a man who had shifted his battleground.

They talked for half an hour, going over the records

that showed Johnson to have been in the jail at the time of the murders. They came away with nothing.

'The boss isn't going to like this,' Peters said as they drove through the village.

'Neither do I,' Flick replied. She hoped Peters would not spread the word about the 'hot tottie' remark.

7

It was Saturday morning. Flick lay on her back, concentrating on the cornice of Tom Marshall's bedroom ceiling and trying to ignore the foul air in the room. Beside her, he emitted snorts, grunts and alcoholic breath. What was he? Their relationship was not settled enough for him to be her partner, and she disliked the term 'boyfriend'. 'Significant other' ticked boxes for her but made most people laugh. 'Lover' was too explicit, 'friend' too bland. 'Lumber' and 'squeeze' were beyond the pale, but not as bad as 'shag-mate', Sharon's phrase. Like most traffic cops, she spent too long sitting in cars doing nothing. Probably 'friend' was best, qualifying it with 'special' when appropriate.

Right now, Tom was not at all special. He blew a waft of stale brandy across her face and she wondered how long their affair would last. A barrister, the previous evening he had taken her to a reception in the Inner Temple. Surrounded by much old wooden panelling and several judges, he had plummeted to depths of sycophancy she would not have believed possible. The worst moment was when he guffawed at a sexist joke told by a recently retired judge, justifying himself by saying the 'dear old codger' was liable to come back and sit part-time.

With other barristers, they had gone on to dinner at an expensive bistro, Tom joining in the fun of ordering wine he could barely afford and certainly not taste. While she had too many espressos, he had too much brandy, Hine VSOP. Once in bed he had pled tiredness, to her relief. Sex was over-rated, she thought, at least recently it had been.

There was one Debut Dagger entry that was full of sex. It was not her sort of book, but she was surprised that it was among the early rejects. The author had invented some imaginatively obscene ways of killing people, so she was probably worth investigating.

As her caffeine-sharpened brain flitted from murder to murder, she felt a stirring beside her. Although he was half asleep, Tom's tiredness had left at least one part of his body. Had she not been thinking about the sexy book, Flick would have pushed him away, but she closed her eyes and fantasised about England's rugby team, going through her personal selection for the imminent Six Nations Championship. Starting with the full back, she was picturing the explosive speed of the right wing when Tom rolled off her, sweating and satisfied. 'Sin bin,' she muttered as she headed for the bathroom.

When she came out of the shower, he was standing in the middle of the bedroom, stark naked and staring at her i-Phone. His body looked puny, white and undesirable.

'Odd fellow, that Osborne,' he said. 'He wants you down at the station. There's been another murder.'

'You answered it?' she shouted.

'Well, yes. He rang twice. You had it on quiet. I didn't want to spoil your shower.'

'What did you say?'

'Just that you were in the shower.'

'What did he say?'

'He sort of made a noise …'

'What did it sound like?'

'Like a gulp, I suppose. I told him we were in Islington. Then he said to tell you to "fit your lovely arse into your knickers and get down the nick pronto". Tom said this in a cockney accent. 'Then he rang off. What's wrong?'

Flick glared at him. She wanted to scream. 'You wouldn't understand,' she said through gritted teeth, and began to dress.

Five minutes later she was in her car. She had brushed aside Tom's offer to make toast or coffee, leaving him hurt and uncomprehending. She drove to her flat. There was no way she was going to work in last night's clothes.

* * *

When Flick arrived at Wimbledon Police Office the desk sergeant told her to go to 32 Kitchener Crescent. She collected the equipment she thought she might need and was heading out when Baggo, panting and dishevelled, burst in the door. He gratefully accepted her offer of a lift.

As she programmed her sat-nav, she smelled a blend

of exotic spices and alcohol on his breath. Her lips pursed, she wound down the window, despite the cold, and concentrated on the comfortable, female, monotone from the dashboard. The disembodied commands steered them west on Worple Road, then right into an area of semi-detached, stone houses. Away from the main roads, the frost had left a thin, skiddy sheet on the carriageway. White rime coated pavements, roofs and front gardens. A watery sun was coming up. It promised to be a good, bracing, winter day.

As Flick turned into Kitchener Crescent, she saw people gathered on the road and pavement half way along. She counted four police cars. As she parked, she saw the large white plastic tent protecting the scene of the crime. Blue and white tape kept the public back. Outside the tape, a middle-aged man and a young woman stood, their shoulders hunched. She wore a flimsy sky blue coat and carried a notebook. In a red, quilted anorak the man looked less cold. He had a camera with a long lens slung round his neck. Ignoring the questions fired by the woman, Flick and Baggo ducked under the tape and, avoiding smeared bloodstains on the pavement, entered the front garden. The tent was to the right of the weed-covered driveway.

'At last,' was all Osborne said when he saw them. 'The body's still where it was found. Have a look when Snapper's finished. Suits on,' he added unnecessarily.

Flick and Baggo pulled on blue sterile overalls and looked round. An untrimmed yew hedge, more than six feet high and dense, shielded the property from the pavement. A wall no higher than eighteen inches, topped by stumps of long-removed iron railings, divided this garden from its neighbour. On the other side of the driveway, an overgrown attempt at topiary looked like a big, headless bird.

'All yours, gentlemen. And lady,' the photographer emerged from the tent. Osborne, Flick, Baggo and Peters ducked their heads as they went in. It reminded Flick of the greenhouse of her aunt's neglected garden. In front of the boundary wall, two mature boxwoods, shaped years ago into balls, formed straggly, untended clumps of greenery. The rest of the ground was covered by patchy grass. Between the boxwoods, the toes of a pair of light brown, buckled shoes pointed upwards. The legs of fawn chinos stuck out from under the foliage. No rime had settled on these items but the chinos were darkened by moisture. A man in a sterile suit rose slowly from a crouched position and moved back to let everyone see.

'An odd one, this,' Dr Dai 'the Death' Williams commented.

'Bloody odd,' Peters muttered as Flick and Baggo pressed forward.

The body was of a man in his forties. His yellow, woollen coat appeared expensive. He lay on his back, arms by his side, brown leather gloves on his hands. His hair was black, plentiful and curly. His staring eyes seemed surprised. But it was his mouth that was remarkable: it lolled open, his tongue sticking out. An ordinary kitchen fork had been driven through his tongue and lay across his right cheek.

Dr Williams squatted down again and rolled the body over. 'Shot in the back twice,' he said, pointing to two red-rimmed holes in the yellow coat.

'Who is he?' Flick whispered.

Osborne replied, 'Denzil Burke. I'll give you two guesses what he did.'

'A literary agent?' Baggo asked.

No one bothered to confirm.

'When did he die?' Flick looked towards Dr Williams, who had already pronounced death and extracted the dead man's wallet from his jacket.

'That's an interesting one.' Williams' eyes lit up. 'He appears healthy and was probably taken by surprise. *Rigor mortis* has only just started. This frost would certainly delay it. He might have died as early as seven last night. It could have been hours later. I'll have to get him on the slab before I can tell you more.'

Osborne said, 'Mrs Burke reported him missing this morning. About the time a passer-by noticed him. She doesn't know yet. I think it's a job for you, Sergeant. Take Baggo.'

'There's no doubt it's him?' Flick asked, her heart sinking.

'None. We've seen his driving licence.'

'So this is not his house?' Flick asked as they left the tent and discarded the suits. It looked as run-down as the front garden. The front door, in particular, needed paint. The outline of a head could be seen behind a dirty net curtain.

'No, Sarge,' Peters said. 'Looks as if it was chosen

because of the cover. He lived at 55 Kitchener Grove. I guess he was walking home when he was surprised and killed then pulled in here. The murderer probably dragged him backwards into the bushes and escaped over that low wall into the next door front garden.' He pointed to where SOCOs were examining impressions in a flower bed. Flick turned back to the house.

'Who lives here?' she asked.

'An old lady, Sarge. Mrs Montgomery. She says she saw nothing.'

'And next door?'

'Unoccupied.' Peters nodded towards a For Sale sign.

Osborne said, 'Right, when you see Mrs Burke, find out as much as you can, but remember to be tactful, Felicity.'

Flick snorted. She and Baggo returned to her car, ignoring the journalist's shrill questions. She drove off quickly and headed back to Worple Road. Once satisfied that she was not being followed, she doubled back to the Grove, avoiding the Crescent.

'White man speak with forked tongue,' Baggo remarked as they drew up outside number 55.

'I was waiting for someone to say that,' Flick muttered as she pulled up the handbrake.

The house was semi-detached yet substantial. Painted white, with large bay windows, it suggested prosperity rather than opulence. Clumps of snowdrops bordered the garden path. In the tiled porch, a muddy rugby ball balanced on a full sports bag. Janis Burke answered the bell, worry etched on her face. She had fine features, with long, brown hair and a centre parting. A thickened waistline was the only sign that she might be over forty. As she sat down in the untidily stylish front room, dominated by a huge fitted bookcase, Flick could see that the widow sensed the worst.

When the first bout of weeping subsided, Flick gave such details as she could, as gently as possible. With prompting, Mrs Burke told the officers that her husband took the train to work, using Raynes Park Station, ten minutes' walk from the house. On Fridays, he went for a drink after work, normally getting home about seven. Sometimes he was later, very occasionally crashing out at a friend's in town. The previous evening he had not phoned to say he would be late, and his i-Phone had been off when she had called him. She had gone to bed, but woken about two. Assuming he was either in town or downstairs in the spare room, she had gone back to sleep. There was no sign of him when she got up and his phone was still off, so she had called the emergency services.

Flick was noting this when the door swung open. A tall boy in his mid-teens with a shock of black, curly hair came in.

'Is there news about Dad?' he asked.

'Oh Philip …' Janis Burke began, then buried her head in her hands.

'I'm afraid your father's dead,' Flick said. The boy swayed and Flick wondered if he was about to faint. He sat beside his mother and put his arm round her. The doorbell rang loudly and insistently.

'God, that's my lift for rugby,' Philip said.

'Do you want me …?' Flick asked.

'Would Dad not want me to play?' the boy asked, his face stricken.

'I think your mother needs you here,' Baggo said quietly. 'I will tell them.' The doorbell rang again.

A minute later, Baggo returned. 'The man is very sorry,' he said. 'He says there is no question of you playing today and he is sorry he rang the bell twice.'

The officers spent a further half hour there. Between cups of tea, they learned that the dead man had not discussed his work very much at home, but that things had been tough in the book business recently. To their knowledge, there had been no particular worries, no trouble with unpublished authors and certainly no threats. After an emotional call to a daughter at university, arrangements were made to formally identify the body early that afternoon.

'You can do this job as long as you like, but that's something you never get used to,' Flick said in the car.

'Inspector No gave it a wide berth,' Baggo agreed.

* * *

The formal identification was one task Osborne felt he could not delegate. Supported by her son, Philip, and Denzil's brother, Janis spoke clearly and firmly. The body was her husband's.

'Why are you not showing us the whole face?' Philip asked as the sheet was pulled up. The mortuary attendant had kept the mouth and the desecrating fork covered.

'No need to distress your mother,' Osborne said roughly.

'What do you mean?' Janis turned on him.

'His mouth was a bit of a mess. You'll be able to see him at peace after the post-mortem.' Flick tried to reassure her.

For a moment it looked as if Janis was going to protest, but she merely shuddered and walked out of the room.

* * *

'The Death says he was killed between six and ten last night,' Osborne told the team late that afternoon. 'Two shots in the back, with an upwards and leftwards trajectory. Bullets were nine by nineteen millimetre Parabellums. Probably fired from a Beretta handgun. The first bounced off a rib and entered a lung. The second stopped his heart. No one seems to have heard anything, and there was less charring than you would expect from point-blank range, so I think the killer used a silencer. The fork was stuck in his tongue after death. It's with the scientists, but Death says it's an ordinary fork you could get anywhere. The SOCOs don't think they can tell us much. Please, someone tell me some good news. Sergeant?'

'Chandavarkar and I both felt Mrs Burke and Philip had nothing to do with it. They alibi each other. He was supposed to play rugby this morning so had a quiet evening in yesterday. They were both really upset, and we thought that was genuine. We went to see Mr Burke's PA at her house before lunch. Again, she was distressed, and we didn't think she was putting it on.'

'She's a great looker, and cried her eyes out,' Baggo interjected. 'I think it's possible she and the late Denzil had the hots for each other.'

'But we have no evidence for that,' Flick said quickly.

'Did you not ask her?' Osborne said.

'That would have been quite inappropriate,' Flick replied.

'Well check it out on Monday. Ask round the office. Anything else?'

Flick said, 'Burke dealt mainly with crime novels. There was the usual number of wannabe authors asking him to represent them. Ms Spence, the PA, will give us a list next week, but she doubts if it will be complete. One interesting thing is that, a few years ago, at the Harrogate Crime Writing Festival, Burke promised to take on six new authors each year. Ms Spence hinted that he had enjoyed too good a lunch when he said it. Anyway, things have been very tight in the publishing business, and he hasn't taken on a single new author since making that promise. One of the tabloids made a fuss about it on a slow news day: "Crime Writers Wronged" was the headline. Mr Ralf Wallace from Bracknell had a bit to say, apparently.'

'That name's come up before,' Osborne said.

'The man with impaired mobility,' Flick agreed.

'Might be worth a visit. Go on Monday.'

'What about Burke's office?'

'Peters and I will go there. You and Baggo are best with the literary types. Have you come up with any suspects after all that reading you've been doing?'

'One or two.'

'Spill.'

'There's a woman who seems obsessed with sex. Her victims die horrible deaths with sex as the theme, and revenge is the motive.'

'How 'orrible? As bad as the shower scene in *Psycho*? Oh, sorry if I spoiled your shower this morning. Were you and your boyfriend scrubbing each other's backs when I phoned?'

Flick wanted to punch the smirk off his face. Aware of blushing, she eyeballed him and said coldly, 'A woman used a wooden spoon to insert a condom into a man's rectum. Then she pumped some water in. Lastly, she added acid to the water. When the condom burst, his screams could be heard half a mile away.'

'I hope she never gets published. Might give my ex some ideas.' Osborne said, aiming a smile at Flick, who continued to look through him. 'Do you think she's worth investigating?' he asked.

'Yes.'

'Well do it next week. Take Baggo. And watch yourself, mate,' he added.

'I shall wear thick trousers and two pairs of underpants, gov. She is not going to get at me so easily.'

8

Osborne gazed across the Thames towards the Tate Modern. It was London, but not the one he had known and loved. His London had been full of Cockney voices, rhyming slang and fish and chips with pickled onions. Results were more important than how you got them, and spades were called bloody shovels. His Londoners knew about the Blitz and respected those who had lived through it, and for all the porky pies that policemen told when giving evidence, life was simpler and truer. He hated all the hypocritical, politically-correct, beating about the bush and arse-licking that was needed to succeed in modern London.

The dead man's office, all picture windows and chrome, belonged to the new London. The place was in shock but not mourning. In the time he had been there, two trendily dressed, busy-looking men, younger than Burke, had stuck their heads round the door as if trying to claim the room. While Peters read Burke's e-mails, Osborne looked sourly at a view more stunning than anything he'd ever been able to see through his office window.

Celine Spence came in carrying a few sheets of paper. Petite, with an hour-glass figure, her olive complexion had not seen the sun for months and this accentuated the effect of her red-rimmed eyes. Only her hair, long, dark and lustrous, had any bounce. Even far from her best, Osborne could see why Baggo thought she was a great looker.

'As I said, we don't keep a file on rejects. If they enclose the postage, we send the stuff back. If not, we put it out. We don't entertain e-mailed submissions. I've asked our in-house readers to list the names they can remember, and I've done the same. Here they are.' She placed the paper in front of Osborne.

'Is that the best you can do?' he asked.

'Yes. I'm afraid so.' She sounded huffy.

'Please sit down,' Osborne said. 'How well did you know the deceased?'

'Very well. I've been his PA for five years.'

'Was he easy to work for?'

'Yes. Very. Unusually easy, as a matter of fact.'

'What do you mean? Didn't mind if you slept in?'

'I don't sleep in. He was … considerate.' Her voice caught.

'Did you see him socially?'

'A bit. Why?'

'We have to build up a picture of his life if we're to learn about his death.' Osborne had learned that line early in his career. Now, he delivered it as if speaking to a stupid child.

Celine's lip quivered. She said nothing.

'So tell us about your socialising with the deceased.'

Celine's head dropped. Tense, her knees clamped

together, she twisted her fingers so it was hard to see what ring belonged on what finger. 'I saw quite a lot of him,' she whispered. 'He loved music, and so do I. We often went to concerts together. Janis isn't musical.'

'Did Mrs Burke know about these concerts?'

'I expect so.'

'Didn't she mind?'

'I don't think so.'

'Did they have what's described as a "modern" marriage?' Osborne leaned forward, not bothering to hide the sneer.

'I have no idea, but I don't think so. They seemed devoted.'

'Despite these concerts?'

Celine raised her head. There were tears in her eyes, which blazed with fury. 'Denz and I were good friends, very good friends, but no more. There was never going to be anything romantic between us, Inspector, because I am a lesbian. L-E-S-B-I-A-N.' Her voice raised with each letter she spelled out. 'Put that in your filthy cigarette and smoke it,' she added, glaring at the unlit fag hanging out of Osborne's mouth.

Peters decided to intervene before things got worse. 'Were you aware of anyone making threats to Mr Burke?' he asked.

'No,' she said quietly.

'Were you aware of anything at all unusual connected to Mr Burke over the last few weeks?'

She shook her head.

'Did he have any enemies you knew of?'

'No.'

Peters glanced at Osborne, who leaned back in his chair, looking steadily at Celine, the fag still unlit. He was smiling.

'That's all,' Osborne said. He got up abruptly, grabbed the papers and strode out of the room.

Peters smiled apologetically at Celine. 'Thank you,' he said quietly.

* * *

'Bracknell is where the lady of the handbag came from,' Baggo remarked as Flick drove confidently through heavy traffic, heading west.

'No. That was Grantham,' Flick corrected.

'I am not thinking of the great Lady Thatcher, Sarge. I am referring to Lady Bracknell, the Oscar Wilde character. "In a handbag?"' He put on a passable imitation of a grand Englishwoman with a deep voice.

'I always thought she was a bit of a caricature,' Flick replied.

'Perhaps, but great fun. I saw *The Importance of Being Earnest* in Mumbai, you know. I was only thirteen, and missed a lot of the jokes, but I laughed myself silly over Lady Bracknell.'

'We can expect Ralf Wallace to be in a wheelchair,' Flick said thoughtfully, a few miles further on.

'In a wheelchair?' Baggo did his Lady Bracknell voice again.

'Grow up, Chandavarkar,' Flick snapped. Instantly,

she regretted it. She turned on the radio to restore normality. Her bad mood had carried on over the weekend and was down to two men: Osborne's unfunny jibes had got to her, and Tom was an idiot to have said what he had on her phone.

Twenty minutes later, speeding along the M3, Flick asked, 'Do you have Wallace's Debut Dagger entry there?'

'Yes, Sarge.'

'Have I seen it?'

Roughly half the entries had been in e-form. While Flick had dealt with those in hard copy, Baggo had read the ones on his computer, printing any worth a second look. He rummaged in his briefcase and produced a sheaf of paper.

'No. I printed it this morning. A decorated hero of the first Iraq War, who is also a lay preacher, is blown up on Armistice Sunday. He was preaching a sermon in the local church. The suspects include a disabled ex-serviceman who gets about using a wheelchair and crutches, and the widow of a soldier. Both soldiers were under the dead man's command. During one incident, they got hit while the dead man, an officer but no gentleman, finished up with a medal. Another soldier was court-martialled, and he appears in the story, too. There are other suspects, of course, but the killer is … guess, Sarge?'

'The soldier's widow?'

'All three. The detective is a nice lady who rumbles them but is quite happy not to be able to prove anything.'

'I'm finding that one story runs into another, but that's memorable.'

'Agatha Christie made a lot out of that basic plot, but Mr Wallace tells you everything at the start. I anticipated the end from reading the first chapter.'

A mile further down the road, Flick said, 'I'm sorry I was short with you earlier ... Baggo.'

'Don't worry, Sarge. I sometimes think it is more difficult for you than it is for me.'

They found Wallace's address without difficulty. 12 Hope Crescent was a drab block of flats in a poor area of town. On the brick wall bounding the car park on three sides, a graffiti artist had described 'the pigs' as 'wankers'. The sexual preferences of someone called Vondo were illustrated by a crude but unmistakable drawing. Flick parked so the car remained in plain view. The smashed windows and missing wheels of a red Fiat showed what might happen if you parked in a corner beside the overflowing bins. Flick was glad they had one of the pool cars.

A peed-in lift took them to the second floor. They exchanged glances then rang the bell of Wallace's flat.

Baggo's finger was poised over the button to ring again. Flick shook her head. 'Remember he's disabled,' she mouthed. A minute later, the letter flap lifted.

'Is that Tesco?' a male voice asked.

'No. Is that Mr Wallace? We are police, Sergeant Fortune and DC Chandavarkar.' Flick replied, bringing out her warrant.

'About time, too,' the voice said. The door opened until a chain stopped it. At letter-box height, a face peered out. The officers heard a snort then the door opened fully. A pale-faced man of about thirty glowered at them from his wheelchair. He wore a thick pullover and smart corduroy trousers. 'Close the door behind you,' he said, executing a deft turn and leading the way into a room to the left of the hallway.

The fresh, antiseptic smell of the flat suggested that it had recently been cleaned. Sunlight streamed through the living room window. The top few inches were grimy but the glass lower down was polished. By the window, a table held a computer, monitor, keypad and paper, two piles of A4, side by side. The typescript on the top sheet was scored by pencil markings. A waist-high bookcase occupied one wall. The books were precisely arranged by height, their spines forming a straight line like guards on parade. One shelf held nothing but carefully arranged items: a blue badge and timecard, a bunch of keys, a box of pens and pencils, an old-fashioned Nokia mobile phone and some notebooks. Two wooden chairs, placed together, occupied the corner diagonally opposite the TV. Everything in that room had its place; nothing that was useful was stored above waist height. There were a number of photographs, framed and hanging on the walls. One showed a football team, Bracknell Town FC; another showed a group of soldiers, posing somewhere hot and dry. Above the computer monitor was a photograph of a group of three. In the centre, a smiling young man in formal military uniform, a sergeant's stripes on his arm, stood proud and strong. He was flanked by his parents, both a head shorter than their son, and not smiling as happily. Ralf Wallace had known better days.

He wheeled himself to the window and turned. The officers stood in the middle of the room, squinting into the sun.

'…and when I tell them off, they give me damned cheek.' Wallace continued the diatribe against local youths he had begun as soon as the detectives entered.

'Mr Wallace, we're not here about that,' Flick said firmly.

'Well, when will you police start doing your job?'

'We are inquiring into a series of murders.'

'Murders?'

'Yes. In the last two months, three literary agents have been killed. They all had a connection with you.'

'Go on.'

'Do you ever go up to London, sir?' As Flick asked the questions, Baggo took notes.

'From time to time. Am I a suspect?' Wallace's voice was cold and matter-of-fact.

'We are at the stage of making general inquiries, sir. And no, you are not a suspect. We are trying to eliminate people from our inquiries. When you do go to London, how do you travel?'

Wallace raised his eyebrows. 'By car. I have a specially adapted one. It's in a garage under the building. If I left it in the car park, it would be gone in five minutes. Do you want to check it for blood or body parts?'

'That won't be necessary, sir. Do you drive it yourself?'

'Yes.'

'How do you get in and out?'

'I use arm crutches.'

'Do you live alone?'

'Yes. I get help.'

'Can you help by telling us where you were last Friday evening?'

'I was here.'

'Can anyone confirm that?'

'No.'

'What about the evening of Monday eighteenth January?'

'I've no idea. Are you sure I'm not a suspect? Why are you asking these questions?' His voice became louder.

'To eliminate you. Did you accuse Lorraine McNeill of discriminating against disabled people during a phone call?'

Wallace's hands twitched on the wheels of his chair. 'So it's blame the spazzy, is it? I give a stuck-up cow a piece of my mind and I become the prime suspect.' Breathing deeply, he rocked his chair in rage. 'What the hell is wrong with this country? We get sent out to Iraq without proper boots or body armour, or even bloody bullets. At Az Zubayr, the Shi'ites ambush me, then yobs who need a good thrashing make life hell for decent people here in Bracknell. I want out of this hovel, so I write a book. I tell it like it is and some posh London cow says it didn't start with enough narrative drive, whatever the fuck that is. When she gets topped, you lot come to me with your questions and don't bother your arses about the yobs. Well, fuck off. Fuck off. Now!' The last word would have carried across a parade ground.

Baggo dropped his notebook. He bent to pick it up, watching out of the corner of his eye in case Wallace should run his chair at him.

Flick tried a counter-attack. 'It was Ms McNeill's receptionist you gave grief to. Like it was Ms Stanhope's assistant you were rude to. Don't speak to us as if we were new recruits you can bully. Sir.' She held her ground in the middle of the floor and tried not to look into the sun. 'So, can you tell us your whereabouts on the evening of Monday seventh December?'

Wallace said nothing. His face was now red. A tic beside his left eye made him appear to be winking.

'And you did not much care for Mr Denzil Burke,' Baggo suggested.

'Not a man of his word. Is he dead too?'

'He is.'

Wallace shrugged. 'I thought I told you to fuck off.' He wheeled himself towards the door, forcing the officers to move. Baggo nearly tripped over his briefcase, which he had set down on the floor beside him. He looked towards Flick, who gave a nod.

'Thank you for your time. We can see ourselves out. Sir.' Flick's tone was icy.

'I do hope your car's all right,' Wallace replied, then watched as they closed the door behind them.

Leaving the block of flats, they noticed four hoodies sitting on a wall, swinging their legs, watching. A Tesco van drove in and parked. The driver and his mate both eyed the youths apprehensively.

On the open road, Baggo said, 'I should feel sorry for him, but I don't.'

'But he's not our murderer,' Flick replied. 'He will probably be strong in his upper body, but he's too weak in his legs to have killed three able-bodied people.'

'He is lethally trained, Sarge. And when I dropped my notebook, I could not help noticing that the soles of his shoes are worn.'

'Oh really?' Flick said. 'Interesting.'

* * *

'When are you going to arrest someone, Osborne?' Everything about Chief Superintendent James Cumberland, known throughout the Met as 'Jumbo', was big. Except his voice, which was high and squeaky.

Osborne shifted in his chair. He and Palfrey had been summoned to Scotland Yard to report on the literary agent murders, and there was little to say.

'It's a challenging inquiry, sir,' Palfrey said.

At least she backed me up here, Osborne thought.

'More challenging for some than for others,' Cumberland snorted. Apart from being physically intimidating, he did not hide his dislike of Osborne.

'It's not an easy case to crack, and that's assuming we have only one killer,' Osborne said. 'But good, old-fashioned police work will get us there in the end.'

'The press have started to give us a hard time.'

'I can't help that.'

'Do you have any leads?'

'We're following up one this afternoon, but it's too early to say how it'll go.'

'There's just this literary agent angle, isn't there?'

'What do you mean?'

'Nothing that could be sensitive, like race or religion?'

Osborne suppressed a groan. Jumbo was the Met's High Priest of political correctness. 'No. If there is, I can't see it.'

'I'm keeping a very close eye on that aspect,' Palfrey interjected.

Cumberland looked thoughtful. 'Who's on your team?'

Osborne said, 'There's Sergeant Fortune …'

'She's very sound. An English graduate,' Palfrey interjected.

Osborne carried on, 'Then there's the DCs, Peters, Bag … Chandakarvup. And uniform, of course.'

The Chief Superintendent's eyebrows shot up his pallid, dome-like forehead.

'You mean Chandavarkar,' Palfrey hissed.

'Oh, sorry, ma'am. He likes everyone to call him Baggo, though.'

Cumberland sighed. 'So you say. At least it sounds like a well-balanced team. But I expect results, Osborne. Before someone else gets killed. And before either of you asks, I don't have the resources to give you any more detectives.'

'Everyone's too busy filling in forms to do proper police work. Sir.' Osborne found himself copying

Fortune's way of insulting a superior.

'Keep me in the loop, Palfrey. And remember, Osborne, I want a good record kept of this investigation. That's all.'

While Palfrey made soothing noises, Osborne simply got up and left. Years ago a bastard like Jumbo would have scared the shit out of him. Now he saw him as an arse-licking barrel of dripping with a squeaky voice. It had been a laugh to get Baggo's name wrong. He had twisted Palfrey's tail and Jumbo's trunk in one go. It was after knocking-off time. Before Palfrey could catch up and give him a bollocking, he headed for his favourite Indian restaurant.

9

'Even if he can walk, he couldn't drag a body.' Flick was definite. After Osborne had told the team that the top brass wanted an arrest, she and Baggo debated whether Wallace was a real suspect.

'I'm not so sure, Sarge. Gov, please may I stage a re-enactment?'

'As long as I'm not the bloody corpse,' Osborne growled.

'Danny, could you play dead, please?' Without waiting for a reply, Baggo took Peters' arm and led him to the far wall. He placed his chair in the middle of the room and sat on it. 'I am Wallace,' he explained. 'My chair has castors, so it is my wheelchair. I am waiting in the driveway of the garden where Burke was found. Danny, Mr Burke, walks by without paying attention to me. Go.'

Obediently, Peters walked by Baggo. As he passed, Baggo raised his right hand and aimed his extended index finger.

'Bang, bang. Note the upward and leftward trajectory of the bullets. Please fall down dead.'

Peters lowered himself to the floor.

'You will win no Oscar for that,' Baggo commented.

'Now lie still and face down, a dead weight.' He got up, turned Peters on to his back and, gripping under his armpits, lifted and dragged him until he was sprawled across the chair, which, using a foot, Flick kept still. Baggo lifted Peters' legs so they were off the ground then wheeled the chair a short distance. With the gothic exuberance of a dentist in a silent movie, he mimed the tongue-forking. Then, with Flick acting again as the handbrake, he pulled Peters off the chair and sat him on the floor, his arms by his side. He gently manipulated him into the position in which the body had been found.

'It could be done,' he said.

'With difficulty, and depending on his disability,' Flick said.

'Well, we can't eliminate him,' Osborne said. 'Danny, you get in touch with the army and find out what happened to him. Did you learn anything yesterday afternoon?'

Peters brushed himself then sat down. 'Just that our killer planned it beautifully. 32 Kitchener Crescent, where the body was found, is owned by Mrs Hazel Montgomery. She's ninety-two, deaf and half blind. She refuses to go into a home. The house is a tip, and it's a real curtains-on-the-window-no-sheets-on-the-bed job. Maybe fur-coat-no-knickers as well, but I didn't go that far.'

Osborne muttered, 'Thank God for that. Jumbo would explode.'

'The bottom line is, she sat at the back of the house all Friday evening, as she usually does. And even if she'd been at the front, she wouldn't have seen much. The next door house is a repossession. It's been empty for three weeks. There were lots of different footprints in the front garden. Our killer knew Burke's route home and selected a great place to ambush him then hide the body. After work, the deceased went for a drink with colleagues. A pub in St James's Street. He left them just after six and would have got to Kitchener Crescent between half past and quarter to seven. Oh, and there's nothing useful from the lab as of this morning.'

'So, Felicity, are you going to see the sexy lady?'

'Today.' She nodded at Baggo. 'She lives in a village near Peterborough, so we'd better get going.'

'We need a break, Sergeant. Let's hope you learn more than how to rid the world of nasty men. How many more suspects have you got from your competition?'

'One or two. The entries closed this weekend, so we'll get the rest of the stuff very soon.'

Osborne shook his head.

* * *

Brankton Hollow was a picture-postcard English village, south-west of Peterborough. The houses were mostly old and substantial, and the gardens had a tidy winter look that promised an explosion of colour in a few months' time. There were two traditional-looking pubs and half a dozen shops. At the north end of the narrow Main Street stood a small, grey Norman church. It had a neat graveyard whose weathered stones reflected the age of the community. Saxon Walk lay behind the church. It comprised a single row of cottages, many of which had been knocked together to make larger properties. The numbering was consequently erratic. Number 11, which had swallowed up number 10, was opposite a black wooden gate leading to the rear of the graveyard.

'Remember that Candy Kissin's real name is Candice Dalton,' Baggo said as Flick parked on the grass verge beside the graveyard wall. 'Shall I lead this time? I expect she reacts better to men than women.'

'Good idea,' Flick said. She imagined a blousy, over-made-up tart who would flirt with men and ignore women.

The front garden caught the sun. It was sprinkled with crocuses and small, blue hyacinths. The wooden outer door was open and through the glass inner door, a cramped hallway could be seen. The bell gave a strong, musical chime.

A small, thin lady with short, wiry hair that made Baggo think of a Brillo pad answered. She peered at them through brown-framed spectacles. 'Yes?' she snapped, her forced smile only marginally more welcoming than her tone of voice.

'Are you Mrs Dalton?' Baggo asked.

'Yes. Of course.'

'Candice Dalton?'

'Yes.'

'Do you sometimes write under another name?'

The effect was immediate and dramatic. 'Who are you? What do you mean coming here?'

'We are police officers, Mrs Dalton. Sergeant Fortune and DC Chandavarkar. We're investigating a series of murders. We'd be grateful if we could come in and ask you some questions. If you are embarrassed to talk here, we could go somewhere else. These are routine enquiries. There's nothing to worry about.' Baggo produced his warrant.

Mrs Dalton inspected it, then glanced past them at the unmarked car and seemed relieved. After a moment of indecision, she opened the glass door fully and let them in. She led the way past a bicycle into the sitting room. It was dusty, cluttered and homely, with brown wood furniture and faded chintz. The mantelpiece alone was devoid of dust. Family photographs, all black and white, were precisely arranged, exactly parallel to the wall and equidistant, those with the largest frames in the middle. The subjects posed formally in an old-fashioned way.

Mrs Dalton sat on the edge of an armchair. 'My husband's out at the moment. I should explain, he has no idea about …'

'Don't worry, Mrs Dalton. We have no wish to embarrass you. We shall use our discretion.' Flick sounded reassuring.

'I don't know how long he'll be. The funeral's on Friday. One of our oldest parishioners, but it's always a shock when they go.'

'Is your husband …' Baggo said.

'The vicar?' Flick finished his question.

'Why, yes. Didn't you know?' Mrs Dalton smiled. 'Obviously not,' she added.

'It is a bit surprising, given what you write about,' Flick said.

'Look, I'll answer your questions, but if my husband comes back, I'm going to pretend you're here about some poor girl that's missing. I do voluntary work at a homeless unit. You won't let me down, will you?' She looked appealingly from one to the other. Taking their silence as affirmation, she added brightly, 'So I'll make a nice pot of tea.'

After Mrs Dalton had left the room, her movements quick and bird-like, Flick inspected the bookcase. The lower shelves contained religious works. Higher up, Stevenson, Bronte, Austin, Dumas and Dickens were arranged, some in better condition than others. *Wuthering Heights* and *The Count of Monte Cristo* were held together by sellotape. The top shelf held faded paperbacks by Conan Doyle, Christie and Sayers as well as newer books by McDermid and Walters.

'My husband and I both love books,' Mrs Dalton said as she returned, carrying a tray of tea and a pile of griddle cakes.

The officers sat on the sofa. Mrs Dalton poured the tea into Old Chelsea cups and handed round the cakes. Flick noticed slight stains on her jumper and trousers, both brown and well-worn. She put her age at about fifty.

Mrs Dalton took a mouthful of cake and a sip of tea. 'Well,' she said, as if they were about to discuss the church flowers.

'Did you ask Jessica Stanhope to represent you?' Flick

asked, before Baggo could say anything.

'Why, yes. I did as a matter of fact. She was murdered, wasn't she?'

'I'm afraid so. Did you resent the way she turned you down?'

'I did. She said she'd seen promise, and asked to see the whole book, but after three months I just got a two-line letter, and she didn't even send it back.'

'Did you try Lorraine McNeill as well?'

'Yes, but she was pretty small-time.'

'Were you upset by the way she rejected you?'

'I don't think she looked at it properly, but that's life, I'm afraid. Do you like the griddle cakes? I made them this morning.'

'Delicious,' Flick said, as Baggo reached for a second.

Mrs Dalton beamed. 'They've won Best Baking in Show at the Harvest Festival for the last three years.'

Baggo said, 'I'm not surprised. Is there much competition?'

'Mrs Cardew, two doors down, thinks hers are better, but she uses a food processor to make the dough. There's nothing like elbow grease, don't you agree?'

'Definitely,' Flick said quickly. 'Did Denzil Burke turn you down too?'

'He turned everyone down,' she spat.

'How did that make you feel?'

'Disappointed, of course. No different from anyone else, I imagine. But we can't always have our prayers answered.'

'We got a warrant to recover the entries for the Debut

Dagger, and I couldn't help noticing that revenge was the motive in your entry.'

'It's a good motive for fictitious murders. You can keep the reader guessing before you reveal it. But you can't think … Oh dear, no. Not in real life. Not for this. It's just not important enough.'

Flick turned to Baggo and nodded. For a moment he looked blank then smiled.

'There is a lot of sex in your book,' he said. 'That is perhaps strange, as you are the vicar's wife.'

Mrs Dalton sat forward and looked earnestly at Baggo. 'We are all born with the desires that God gave us. Some societies function better when that side of life is kept private. This village, for example. But keeping such things suppressed, in day to day living, does not eliminate them. People, most people, like to read racy literature. Look at the best-sellers. I don't think it does any harm. Perverted, abusive practices don't come from sexy books.' She smiled. 'A bishop once told me that human sexual behaviour shows us that God has a sense of humour. I think that's right. It's a mistake to take sex too seriously.'

Trying to appear non-committal, Flick asked, 'How many books have you written?'

'I've completed eight, with several unfinished. I've been writing in my spare time for ten years, until recently all clean and pure. And not short of admirers. But no one wanted to publish my work. Three years ago, I decided to give myself a new name and let it flow, so to speak. I really want to get published, and I've promised

God that I'll give my first advance to Hopeful Homes. It's the charity I work for.'

'Yet your husband does not know about this?'

'He knows I write. Of course he does. But I admit I've kept the nature of the last few books from him. I will tell him. But in my own time. When I get published.'

'Do you have family?'

Mrs Dalton's left shoulder twitched. For a second, Baggo thought she would tell him to mind his own business, but she closed her eyes and said, 'The Lord has not blessed us with children.' There was a note of regret in her voice.

'Do you go up to London often?' Flick asked.

'Once a week, for a couple of days at a time. Helping the homeless.'

'Do you have regular days?'

'Generally Monday and Tuesday, returning Wednesday morning. I wanted to be in London last Friday. There was someone who needed support that day. So I swapped with a friend. I wouldn't normally be here today, as it's a Tuesday.'

'Where do you stay?'

'At the hostel. It's on Mile End Road.' She went to the desk and, after some searching, found a leaflet which she handed to Flick.

'How do you travel?'

'Train from Peterborough. It's an excellent service. Can I ask, are you clutching at straws?'

'Our enquiries are progressing, Mrs Dalton,' Flick said. 'Thank you for your time.'

Mrs Dalton showed them out without fuss. Flick drove to the end of Saxon Way to turn. As they joined the main road, a tall, wiry man wearing a dog collar approached the junction on foot. He aimed a vague, toothy smile at the unmarked pool car as he turned into his street.

'She was in London on the date of each murder,' Baggo said, putting to the back of his mind the thought of the vicar and his wife in bed together. 'Is she a saint who writes about sin or just too good to be true?'

'I don't know. She certainly wasn't what I expected. I think we should visit that hostel. And the sooner the better.'

* * *

'That woman is a saint.' Maggie Locke was definite. She did not hide her surprise that two detectives should be interested in Candy Dalton. 'Monday and Tuesday are her nights here, but yes, she did Thursday and Friday last week, so she's off today.'

The hostel office was cold and uncomfortable. Maggie's ample frame was covered by a variety of shapeless woollen garments. She frequently glanced through the internal window overlooking the dormitory, where two rows of metal-framed beds faced each other across a long hall. Most were unoccupied. A few held shapeless lumps huddled under blankets. An earnest-looking man carrying a clipboard sat on the edge of one bed. Beside him, a skinny youth with a shaved head jabbed his finger to make a point.

'We have three volunteers on each night,' Maggie explained. 'We always have two in the hostel. The other one is either here or out and about. This place is only a stop-gap, but we have positive interaction with other agencies. Our clients have complex needs, and even after we've passed them on, we try to give some of them continuing support. That often involves going out to find them if we know they are in crisis.'

'Do you know what Mrs Dalton did on Friday?' Flick asked.

'She was out most of the day. Patrycja, one of our many Polish clients, needed a lot of support. Candy was with her.'

'Where was she?'

'At court in the afternoon. Patrycja's brother, Pavel, had got into trouble. He's a decent lad, really, but life got difficult for him and he was led astray. He was sentenced on Friday. Eight years. It'll be very damaging.' She shook her head. Both detectives kept quiet. 'Patrycja was shattered, so Candy stayed with her.'

'When did she return here?'

'I'm not sure. I was off. But we keep a log. Here.' She consulted a frayed jotter. 'Yes. She was back by nine. We have a car which we use to pick up clients and she had it.'

'You're a charity for the homeless?' Flick asked.

'Yes. We get them off the streets and steer them towards appropriate longer-term accommodation. With some it's addiction, others poverty. An awful lot have mental health issues.'

'Can you tell us about Patrycja?' Flick asked.

'It's pronounced Pat-rees-ya,' Maggie corrected. 'She and Pavel arrived in Britain over a year ago, and Candy got to know them then. She and Patrycja became quite close. They shared an interest in books. But Patrycja and Pavel were in debt to a gangmaster. He found a poorly-paid job in a warehouse for a short time, but she was so desperate … Well, you can guess. She worked in a high class brothel, but hated it. Pavel's a good-looking boy and could have done the same, but preferred to work for the gangmaster as a heavy. He felt he could watch out for his sister that way. A couple of months ago, he got arrested for an armed robbery. He's been in jail ever since. Patrycja couldn't take prostitution any longer and one night she ran away. Candy found her under a bridge and brought her here. We arranged accommodation for her. But she was in pieces over Pavel. So, on Friday, Candy wanted to support her.'

Baggo asked, 'Where can we find Patrycja?'

Maggie scribbled down an address off Tottenham Court Road 'That's it. Her surname's Kowalski. But I doubt if she'll cooperate with the police after what happened to her brother. She's very damaged.'

'Can you help us regarding Mrs Dalton's movements during the early evening of Monday seventh December last?' Flick asked.

After consulting the same frayed jotter, Maggie shook her head. When asked about eighteenth January, she looked at several pages, tut-tutting and shaking her head. 'Our records aren't always as good as they should be,' she said.

Thanking her, the officers left.

'I bet she could have told us more than she did,' Flick commented as she drove back to the police office. 'Let's just hope that Patrycja is more helpful. We should try to see her tomorrow. Sorry we're so late, by the way.'

* * *

As Baggo left work, putting his head down against a gusty wind that felt as if it came from Siberia, he did not relish a solitary night in his tiny flat. The tube was busy with late workers whose body language shouted 'do not approach'. A few read, but most looked blank and miserable.

'At least spring is in the air,' Baggo said to the casually-dressed young man next to him.

The man ignored him.

'At least you can wrap up against the cold, unlike the heat of the summer.'

The man flinched and moved along the compartment. For the next ten minutes till he got off he pretended to ignore Baggo, while watching him out of the corner of his eye.

Baggo realised his non-friend thought he was on the pull, and decided not to follow him out at Leicester Square. The train went on to Tottenham Court Road. On a whim, he hopped out there. As he battled his way through the bustling, cheerless horde of individuals, along windy tunnels where the only smiles were on advertisements, and up to the cold pavement, he thought of Mumbai, so much warmer in every way, and a sense of longing hit him like a bolt of lightning. Eyes watering, he put his hands in the leather gloves his mother had given him and walked. He soon found he was a few hundred yards from where Patrycja lived. Sheltering in a doorway and puffing one of the small number of cigarettes he allowed himself, he gave himself a pep talk and decided he would do something positive. Thinking hard, he walked slowly but purposefully towards Patrycja's building. On the street outside the block of flats, he told himself he was making a mistake; that the investigation should be done correctly; that he might get into trouble in a number of ways. But by now, his feet had a mind of their own. They carried him to the communal stairs and up to the first floor. Baggo walked along the row of doors, checking names, then tried the second floor. He rang the bell of the only flat without a name.

'Who is there?' The female voice was heavily accented.

'Is that Patrycja? It's Joe, from the hostel. Candy sent me.'

The door opened a fraction and an anxious face peered out. 'I don't know you.'

'Ring Maggie. She will tell you about me.'

Baggo decided to run away if she did phone, but the ruse worked and the chain was released. Taking a deep breath, he stepped inside. Patrycja closed the door quickly and they eyed each other across the hall.

She had a flat, round face. Her eyebrows were painted

darker than her hair, and her lipstick was scarlet. Her small breasts could be seen clearly in outline under a light blue, sleeveless top. Her short skirt was stretched round her hips and she tottered on high stilettos. She smelled of gin and musky perfume. 'What is it?' she said.

'They are worried about you.'

'I'm okay.'

'Can we sit down? They will want a full report.'

'Right.' She led the way into a sparsely-furnished kitchen/sitting room with thin curtains that failed to close. Baggo sat on a hard, wooden chair and loosened his leather jacket. Patrycja sat in the stained and lumpy armchair facing him.

'I am sorry about Pavel,' he said.

She shrugged. 'I am getting my head round it, as they say.'

'Candy was very worried.'

'She has been good to us.'

Baggo saw a fellow-immigrant, struggling in a country often less welcoming than it should be. 'You were not expecting me, but you are expecting a client,' he said gently.

She nodded.

'Did you select some from the brothel and take them with you?'

'What if I did?'

'You will be in danger. But I am not here to judge you.'

'Candy does not judge. I could tell her things.'

'About the pimps?'

'Yes. And about the men. I can say to you, that the English men are very funny. Drink?' She got up and bent to take a bottle from a cupboard beside the sink. Baggo saw the tops of her stockings and suspenders. She did not wear knickers. His mouth dry, he wanted to kiss her, perch her on the edge of the table … She poured a generous quantity of gin and added a splash of water from the tap.

'Yes. Thanks,' he said.

She poured a less potent measure and handed it to him. He sipped it, trying not to be put off by the marks on the tumbler.

Patrycja resumed her seat and took a swallow. 'Do you say to people you are English?'

'I am Indian-English. I was brought up in Mumbai.'

'I am Polish, and I will never be English.'

'You have had a bad time here?'

'Yes. Many English are bastards.' She swallowed a mouthful of gin then looked at Baggo and grinned. 'But many are funny; they like to be tied up and spanked.' She paused and added, her voice soft, 'Some like to hurt women, perhaps a little, perhaps a lot.' She was silent for a moment, then drank again. Suddenly, she smiled. 'An old man liked me to pee on him. A businessman. Important, big man. Another wanted to suck my toes. A lot only talk. What do you like?' She gave him a siren look.

Baggo shifted on his chair. 'Just the usual.'

'I shouldn't have asked. Very un-English to talk about sex.'

Another silence followed. Baggo broke it. 'Have you been to visit Pavel since Friday?'

She nodded.

'How was he?'

'Bad. He expected only six years. My little brother.' Her voice caught.

'It was lucky Candy could be with you on Friday.'

'Yes…' The doorbell sounded. Patrycja sniffed then jumped up, put her glass by the sink and opened a door leading to a walk-in cupboard. 'He's very early. Quick. You go here. I'll take him to the bedroom and change his nappy. Don't worry about slaps. Just go. And close the door.' She poured Baggo's gin down the sink and pushed him into the cupboard.

The space was cramped, dark and smelled of damp. Baggo felt for the door handle, fearful of touching anything that might make a noise. He wished he had gone straight home.

There was a crash. A high-pitched scream was cut off abruptly. There were thumps and the noise of something being dragged. A male voice spoke harshly in a guttural tongue. Just outside the cupboard, a thud was followed by a stifled cry and a second thud. Two men were speaking. Baggo could not understand what they said, but their voices were angry, cruel, insistent. Patrycja's cries were muffled but her panic was unmistakable. A scraping noise was followed by hard slaps on bare skin. Her cries became a low, keening whine. A man grunted and there were more scrapes and slaps.

Baggo tried to picture the furniture in the room.

Then he felt carefully to his right. He had seen bottles there as he entered the cupboard. The noises of violence outside continued. He tried to control the tremor in his fingers as they moved along the shelf. At last, he touched smooth, cool glass. Like a blind alcoholic, he assessed the shape and weight of the bottle then firmly grasped its neck.

Ready for sudden light to hit his eyes, he took two deep breaths. As a sort of prayer, he thought of the God, Shiva, dancing on demons and killing them. Then he turned the handle and burst out of the cupboard.

Patrycja's back was on the table, her legs spread out. She was being attacked by two men, both with shaved heads and leather jackets. One man leaned across the table, his weight holding her down. His back was to Baggo. Without hesitation, Baggo hit him as hard as he could. The man half turned into the blow. The bottle smashed against the side of his head with an explosion of red wine and glass fragments, leaving a jagged bottle neck in Baggo's hand. The first man slumped lifelessly as Patrycja wriggled clear.

The second man had jerked back. He stood between Patrycja's legs, his trousers down, his erect penis continuing to spurt. He bellowed in shock and rage. Baggo dropped the bottle neck and launched himself at the man, who fell to the floor, banging his head on a chair leg. Baggo scrambled until he sat astride him, then began to pummel the ugly, unshaved face. A vivid image from his childhood came back to him; Shilpa, his elder sister coming home late, her face bruised, her clothes torn. He had been sent to bed, only after hearing a new word: rape. Now, a red mist descended. Using both fists, he kept punching, left, right, left, right. He took a visceral pleasure in inflicting punishment till, his face a bloody, spongy mess, the man ceased to react, and the pain in Baggo's knuckles forced him stop.

As he got up, he heard a cry behind him. He threw himself sideways to dodge a knife-thrust and found himself crouched in a corner. The first man, though groggy and unsteady, came at him. He lifted his right hand, ready to deliver a fatal stab, but the fury in his eyes changed to wide-eyed surprise. Making an obscene gurgling noise, he half turned then collapsed like a rag doll, blood spurting from his neck. A trickle of blood seeped from his mouth and his eyes stared. Behind him, Patrycja stood, a large kitchen knife in her hand. Dishevelled, her clothes stained red with blood and wine, her battered face burned with hatred.

'I should have known they would find me one day. Now we must go,' she said.

'The police ...' Baggo panted. He stepped round the spreading red pool, and reached for his i-Phone.

'No police. No police.' She held the blood-smeared knife at his throat, her hand shaking.

Baggo saw the desperation in her eyes. He judged she would not hesitate to use the knife again. He also realised he would not be able to explain what had happened. 'Okay,' he said. He put his i-Phone away.

Quickly, she ran the knife under the tap, wiped it, then put it in a drawer.

Baggo picked up the bottle neck, rinsed it and wiped it on a curtain. 'What about the body?' he asked.

'Wolenski will not allow it to be found here. Too many questions. He'll put it in concrete at bottom of building. We must go before he wakes.' She nodded at the rapist, who lay on his back, his manhood shrunk.

Baggo looked down at the unrecognisable face. He could see he had gone too far, and the breathing was laboured and noisy. There would be blood in the airways. He rolled the man into the recovery position, his trousers still round his ankles. Patrycja scurried round the flat, putting a few things into polythene bags. She searched for a number on her mobile, then spoke severely: 'Nanny's not well. Same time, next week. And if that nappy's dirty, you know what will happen.' She reached into the dead man's pocket and took his mobile. 'I'll text Wolenski once we're clear,' she said. She covered herself with a long, thick coat, wiped her face and put a comb through her hair. While she did that, Baggo used a cloth to wipe surfaces he had touched. For a moment in the hall they paused, then, together, left the flat, pulling the damaged front door behind them.

Outside, Baggo was grateful the blood on his clothes would be less obvious in streetlights, not that any of the passers-by would notice. Trying to sound natural, he said, 'Where are you going to go?'

'I have nowhere,' she replied.

'Come with me,' he said, and jumped into the road to hail a taxi.

Lights and shadows cavorted eerily on the shiny,

black streets. The erratic wind blew umbrellas inside-out and made pedestrians hold their hats. As he sat beside her on the back seat, Baggo felt Patrycja shake. She had been beaten and raped, yet was still in control of herself, knew what she had to do. The brutality of the prostitute's life had desensitised her. After his sister's ordeal, she had been a tearful wreck for months.

For the first five minutes, the taxi driver talked about the weather, then gave up. The rest of the journey passed in nervous silence. Baggo asked the driver to stop round the corner from his flat five minutes from Emirates Stadium. Handing over a twenty pound note, he again wished he had gone straight home after work. What had started as a breach of discipline had escalated into potentially serious jail time.

As soon as she got out of the taxi, Patrycja texted on the dead man's phone, wiped it, then threw it in a wheelie bin. They walked in silence to Baggo's building.

'Only two floors up,' he said.

She did not react.

Outside his flat she hesitated, inspecting the door and the name-plate, then entered cautiously, looking all round. 'Do you live alone?' she asked.

'Yes. Do you want a drink?'

She stood in the middle of the hall, still clutching her bags. 'What do you really do? You are not a hostel worker, and your name is not Joe.'

'What makes you say that?'

'Hostel workers are soft, but you are hard, and your first name starts with B.'

Baggo thought for a moment. 'I am a policeman,' he said.

'You bastard,' she said. 'Don't try to stop me.' She did not shut the door behind her.

Baggo closed it quietly then poured himself a large whisky and a hot bath. He washed his clothes then spent the night worrying about how events might unravel, hoping that the gangmaster, Wolenski, would do a good clear-up job.

10

'Fighting again?' Danny Peters gestured towards Baggo's knuckles.

'No. My computer at home broke down when I wanted to Skype Mumbai. Yesterday was my brother's birthday. I was so furious, I punched the wall.'

'Never thought you had a temper on you.'

'I keep it well hidden. It has let me down in the past. How did you get on with Mr Wallace's medical records?'

'Bloody data protection. They pass you from one official to another till eventually you hit one who has the guts to say yes or no. Unfortunately, it was no.'

'The gov will want to know about Wallace before we can cut through the red tape. Would you like me to see what I can do …?' He nodded towards his computer.

'Thanks, mate. If you find something useful, we can get a warrant and do it officially. The Sarge was talking about you two chasing after some Polish tom, who might give some odd bint an alibi. Do you want me to go with her?'

'Thanks, Danny. This records job might take all morning. Could you explain to her, without mentioning hacking? Best say there's some Debut Dagger entries I want to check.' Baggo had spent half the night agonising as to whether he should go to Patrycja's flat and decided it would be too dangerous. The rapist might still be there and recognise him; he might have been spotted by a neighbour; he might give himself away through anxiety.

After getting Wallace's basic details from Peters, Baggo settled himself behind his screen, his enjoyment of the challenge spoiled by butterflies in his stomach.

Two hours later, he had learned that Ralf Wallace sustained very severe spinal damage in 2004. A man of unusually determined character, he had made more progress than had been expected. Although needing a wheelchair, he could stand and, using arm crutches, walk short distances. Further significant development was unlikely, but the latest report ended with a Delphic comment on the ability of nerves to regenerate. That report was a year old. Ralf Wallace was still a suspect.

Baggo was finishing off covering his traces as best he could when Flick and Peters returned.

'Did you find your tom?' Baggo asked, as casually as he could.

Flick said, 'No. Her flat was a bloodbath, but with no body. A neighbour who peeped out of her door said she left last night with a man. There had been a fight. There was more activity later, but quieter the second time. SOCOs are there now. Patrycja's disappeared. No one at the hostel knew anything. That's what they said, anyway. I'm going to get a warrant for her arrest.'

After trying to look surprised, Baggo hid his face behind his computer screen, breathing deeply.

'What about you? Anything to report from the

dagger entries?' He looked up. Flick stood over him, a quizzical expression on her face.

He kept his hands under his desk. 'Well, Sarge, there's a man who writes about medieval torture. He has a lot of imagination, and his motive is revenge.'

'Doesn't ring a bell. Have I seen that one?'

'No. I'll print it out for you. It was in the latest batch to come in. This one may be short-listed.' Baggo was grateful for the dagger time he had put in the previous Friday. The morning had gone better than expected. But if the police caught up with Patrycja before the gangmaster, what would she tell them?

* * *

'Honest, Noelly, I 'ad no idea you and he 'ad 'istory. It must have happened during my five stretch.' Weasel did his best to look honest as Osborne glared at him.

They sat on rickety chairs upholstered in cracked vinyl at the rear of a spit and sawdust pub in Roman Road, all battered metal grilles and indestructible dark-stained wood. It was Weasel's choice, as he thought a regular in the Mile End Road pub had recognised him. Weasel had arrived first and in the few minutes since Osborne had joined him, three men had swallowed their drinks and left. The barman shot black looks in their direction.

'Bloody sore thumbs, you lot. Aren't you going to buy me a drink?' Weasel asked.

'What have you got for me?'

'Something you need. It's worth a lot.'

Osborne put a five pound note on the table. The movement made his chair creak ominously. 'Get me a coke,' he growled.

Weasel returned and set the drinks down. He raised his double Bells. 'Sludge, or whatever the Sweaties say.'

'Get on with it.'

'All in good time, Noelly. I need this.'

Osborne suspected that Weasel was playing him like a fish, but he had to find out what he knew. He wanted to report some progress to Palfrey and Jumbo, specially if it came from old-fashioned methods.

Weasel rolled the whisky round his mouth then began. 'Willie Johnson, "Johnny" to you, will be getting out on parole very soon, and he's not happy with you. He hasn't been happy with you for years. He heard you're in charge of the agent murders, and thought you might fit him up for them. So he's taken precautions. You with me?'

Osborne nodded.

A big man with a huge belly came in and ordered a drink. Weasel looked carefully at him then relaxed. 'Johnny's got alibis for all three murders.'

Osborne shrugged. He did not know about the third alibi.

'They're crap,' Weasel said.

'The records say he was in the prison.'

'The records are crap.'

'How do you know?'

Weasel banged his empty glass on the table and

looked at it. Osborne slid a second five pound note across to him.

When he returned from the bar, Weasel took a drink then put his face near Osborne's. 'A mate of mine got out of Littlepool recently. He could tell me a lot. I'll have to pay him.'

Osborne winced. 'He's told you already. Fifty.'

'Don't make me laugh, Noelly. A grand. This is serious grassing, and, well, you know Johnny.'

'A hundred.'

'Eight hundred.'

'A hundred today. The rest if you give me evidence I can use.'

'I'm not covering my expenses, Noelly. Three hundred today, then five hundred when you get evidence. Or I walk out.'

Osborne could see he meant it. Concealed by the table, he took six fifty pound notes from his wallet, but held on to them. 'Spill,' he said.

'Johnny bosses that jail. Everyone's scared of him, from the governor down. If prisoners cross him, they get their legs broke. One guy got a big pot of soup poured over him. He was a month in hospital.'

'How does he control the officers?'

'That's the key. Johnny has contacts outside. He used them to threaten an officer's wife and kids. Photos of them on mobiles, that sort of thing. So the officer agrees to bring drugs into the jail. He does it once, but that's not enough. He does it a few times. They film him so they can blackmail him. They make him tell them all the other officers' dirty little secrets. Then they start all over again with another officer's kids. And so on. Johnny's the spider in the middle of all this. He's bright, and he don't take no prisoners, no pun intended. No one dares go against him. He's out of the jail far longer than he's supposed to be, and they write crap in the records. The governor learned all this far too late to do anything about it. If half of this came out, there would be such a bloody fuss. The governor would be out on 'is ear. So he wants Johnny to get parole because then he might get his jail back.'

Osborne was shocked. He stretched the hand holding the cash under the table and Weasel took it. 'Keep in touch,' he said quietly, and left the pub. He had a lot to think about.

* * *

'He's not St Francis of Assisi.' Flick looked up from the A4 pages she had been reading. 'You sense he really enjoys writing this stuff.' Sidney Francis opened his competition entry with a widow dying of the plague. He followed, a few pages later, with a graphic description of an English knight being hung, drawn and quartered. As his story progressed, a knight with a vicious tongue was ducked in a sewer until he drowned. Another had a red-hot poker thrust into his rectum, the same fate as befell Edward II, Flick thought. The final victim had his hands tied to a tree and his feet to a horse, which literally tore him apart. All these things were done by a man to pay back those who had prevented him from leading a religious order of chivalry.

'This Francis lives in Tooting, Sarge,' Baggo said. 'Do you think he's worth a visit?'

'No time like the present. Let's go.' Flick was curious to see what this author was like. Probably short and weedy, with a furtive air, she guessed.

The man who opened the door was tall and thin. He had the premature stoop of the physically lazy academic. Dark eyes were sunk deep behind black-framed glasses. His nose was like a great white beak; and his mouth, narrow and straight, could have been cut by a scalpel.

It had taken time to find the ground floor flat with 'Francis' on a tarnished brass plate, fixed slightly askew on the warped door. The sixties block was typical of the down-at-heel area which, in more prosperous times, would have been ripe for redevelopment.

Francis registered as much irritation as surprise at the detectives' visit. He led them through a nondescript hall into a room where a boy of about ten lay on the floor, doing homework. He scrambled to his feet and stood to attention. Brusquely, his father ordered him to his room. He bent to pick up his books, bowed his head to the visitors, and left. Francis waved towards the scuffed leather sofa and sat on the upright chair beside the window. On the table in front of him, a black laptop was surrounded by a mess of papers and books. Baggo sat down but Flick inspected the bookcase which filled most of one wall. In this investigation, it was becoming second nature. Francis clearly admired Dorothy L

Sayers; he had several Wimsey books. The only modern crime writers were Barbara Cleverly and David Roberts. But history, particularly the medieval period, dominated the shelves. Flick spotted a worn copy of Rosemary Sutcliff's *Dawn Wind*. The adventures of the youth, Owain, had made post-Roman Britain come alive for her as a child. She suspected that, like her, Francis had his copy passed down from a parent. She pulled it from the shelf.

'I loved this when I was a girl.' She beamed at Francis.

'Put it back, please,' he said stiffly, his accent patrician.

Carefully, Flick slid the old book into its space then turned. 'You have written an historical crime novel, I believe?' she said.

'I have.'

'Do you have an agent?'

'What business of yours is that?'

'We are investigating a series of murders, and we have reason to ask questions of a number of people. The sooner these questions are answered, the sooner people can be eliminated from the inquiry. We would be grateful for your assistance.'

'I am a busy man.' He gestured towards the papers in front of him.

'Did you try to get Lorraine McNeill to represent you?'

'I do not need to answer that.'

'What about Jessica Stanhope?'

'The same.'

'Denzil Burke?'

He shook his head.

'Do you realise that we have certain powers? Do you want us to take you down to the police station?'

'You may have powers, but no grounds, I fancy. So, unless you welcome complaints about police harassment, I would advise you to ask any other questions you might have, then leave.'

Flick stared at him, wondering what she should do. She knew she did not have grounds for detaining him.

'Possessing an offensive weapon in a public place is a crime, sir.' Baggo stood by a framed photograph of Francis surrounded by a group of open-mouthed children. He wore chain mail and waved an evil-looking mace. His spectacles added to the absurdity of the scene, which had been pictured in a street.

It was Francis' turn to stare. His lips twitched with indecision.

'Daddy, please say my time's up!' A child's tearful voice called from another room.

Flick moved sharply to see what was happening. Another plea came from behind a closed door at the end of the hall. Ignoring Francis' bluster, Flick threw the door open and, closely followed by Baggo, went in. The room was a bedroom containing a double bed. At the foot of the bed, a boy rather younger than the other one, sat in a Heath Robinson contraption made of wood. Roughly put together, it secured the boy's feet straight in front of him as he sat on the narrow edge of a plank of wood placed vertically on runners. There were notches along the runners, suggesting that the appliance could be adapted for victims of different height. Flick pulled up the plank securing the boy's feet. Gingerly, he set them on the ground then stood, rubbing his bottom.

'Go to your room, Rufus,' Francis commanded. Hanging his head, the boy slunk out.

'Mr Francis, this is no way to treat a child,' Flick said, then was conscious of Baggo's hand on her elbow.

'May I, Sarge?' he asked.

Before she could say no, Baggo addressed Francis. 'Now, Mr Francis, you have put us in a dilemma. If we were to contact Social Services over you putting your son in the stocks, he is your son I take it, there would be a very great deal of embarrassing attention paid to you and your family.'

Francis glared at him.

'It is a most unusual case,' Baggo carried on. 'It may be that we will decide we do not need to use a sledgehammer to crack a nut, but we shall have to be satisfied that you are a cooperative sort of gentleman. So I suggest that we return to the sitting room where you can answer my sergeant's questions, after which we might put the whole situation under review.'

Flick asked, 'How long has he been sitting there?'

Francis blinked. 'Five minutes.'

'I think they might prosecute,' Flick said to Baggo.

Baggo brought out his i-Phone and took photographs of the stocks from different angles.

'This was the boys' idea,' Francis spat. 'All boys need discipline. They know where they stand and are happy with it. They asked me to build this, so I did.'

'Why did you put Rufus in the stocks?' Flick asked.

'He had spilled some tea this morning and hadn't wiped it up, so when he came home from school, he faced the consequences.'

'When did he return from school?' Flick asked.

Francis' eyes blinked again. 'Ten minutes ago, maybe.'

'Or maybe longer, perhaps?' Baggo asked.

Francis looked from one to the other. He focused on Baggo's knuckles and looked thoughtful. 'I fail to see why my writing could be of the slightest interest to you, but I have nothing to hide,' he said.

They returned to the sitting room and took their seats. Baggo prepared to write down what Francis said.

He began, 'Until just under two years ago, I was a lecturer at the University of London, but their short-sighted attitude to the teaching of medieval history forced me to resign. I had always wanted to be an author, to share my enthusiasm for the medieval period as widely as possible. During those centuries, the basics of today's society were hammered out. Human nature took on a purer form, more primitive perhaps, but more honest. Life was cheaper and men acted on their instincts.' He sat forward eagerly, his voice full of excitement. Flick cleared her throat. 'Anyway, I decided to use crime novels as a vehicle for teaching history. My protagonist is a Franciscan friar. Yes, the name attracted me. During the fourteenth century, the friars went round England, living among the poor and helping them. They were decimated by the Black Death, and then, in the fifteenth century, became decadent; they stayed safely in convents, living off rich, gullible men who were desperate for salvation. My hero, Friar Alfred, maintains the Franciscan traditions of poverty and repentance. But he is an educated man. The Wars of the Roses have started, and ...'

'We believe you asked Jessica Stanhope to be your agent,' Flick cut in.

Francis pursed his lips. 'Yes,' he snapped.

'And she rejected you?'

'Yes.'

'Did you approach Lorraine McNeill?'

'The one who wanted a murder on the first page? Yes.'

'And she rejected you?'

'Yes. Someone dying of the plague wasn't good enough for her. There had to be a "proper murder", her assistant said.' He snorted.

'What about Denzil Burke?'

'Yes, yes, and several others. How did you get my name, by the way?'

'I don't need to tell you that,' Flick said.

'I'll find out, and if there has been improper conduct, I'll ...'

'You should do nothing, sir,' Baggo said.

'There has been no improper conduct,' Flick said firmly. 'Do you live alone with the boys?'

Francis shook his head. 'My wife, Matilda, will be back soon. Because the publishing industry has yet to wake up to my worth, she has taken a cleaning job.'

'Do you have access to a car?' Flick asked.

'No.'

'Can you tell me what you were doing last Friday evening?'

'I was doing research.'

'Where?'

'The streets of London. Among the poor. Trying to help them.'

'Like a …?'

'Exactly. Much has changed over the centuries, but the emotions of the suffering poor are the same as they have always been. And no, no one can vouch for me.'

'What about the evening of seventh December? It was a Monday.'

'I have no idea. As a writer, one day merges with another, and I don't keep a diary.'

'What about Monday eighteenth January?'

'I can't help you. I did go off into the hills round the Welsh border about that time, to experience the harshness of winter in the countryside.'

'Alone?'

'Of course. I want to make my readers believe they are looking over Friar Alfred's shoulder, feeling the pain of frostbite as he does.'

Baggo said, 'He sounds quite like Brother Cadfael.'

Francis became animated, bouncing on his chair and clenching his fists. 'But with attitude. He's a good man, not a nice man. Russell Crowe, not Derek Jacobi.'

'How long were you away from home when you went

to the countryside?' Flick brought him back to the inquiry.

'A few days. Three or four. I can't remember.'

'Where did you stay?'

'Stay? In a tent.' He paused. 'One night I cheated and went to a bed and breakfast place, but I can't remember what it was called or even where it was. There was a blizzard that night. I paid cash,' he added, anticipating Flick's next question.

Flick glanced at Baggo, who shrugged. She said, 'Well, thank you, Mr Francis. That will be all, for now. We will be back at some time in the future, and if these stocks are still in the house, we will start a full criminal investigation. They are not to be used ever again, do you understand?'

'How am I supposed to discipline my sons? My sons.' He emphasised the 'my'.

'You are an intelligent man, Mr Francis, so you are well able to explain why the boys should do or not do particular things. You can dock their pocket money, send them to their rooms, ground them.'

'But not smack them?'

'You must never behave cruelly towards them.' She stood. 'Before we go, I think we should check that there is no other inappropriate punishment appliance here.' As Francis spluttered protests, Flick carried on, 'or do you want us to get a warrant and come back with social workers?'

He slumped back in his chair. 'On you go,' he said weakly.

The flat was poorly maintained, with shabby furniture. When they entered the elder boy's bedroom, his face was pressed against the window pane. He turned and Baggo asked him what he was doing.

'Science. I'm trying to work out how water comes from my breath. Mr Runciman doesn't explain very well.'

Baggo joined him at the window, noticing the boy move away slightly. 'I'm Baggo. What's your name?' he asked.

'Harold.' The boy looked at him curiously.

'Well, Harold, water can take three forms: ice, which is solid, water, which is liquid, and gas, which is lighter than air. Your breath is air which contains water in its gas form. Your breath is warm, and the warmer air is, the more water it can hold as gas. When it is cold, your breath cools and the water in it goes from gas to liquid. Do you understand?'

'I think so. Could you repeat it?'

For the next five minutes, Baggo taught Harold about condensation. Flick inspected drawers and cupboards, finding nothing more unusual than a number of plastic swords in the wardrobe. Round all four walls stretched a paper copy of the Bayeux Tapestry. Harold interrupted his physics lesson to gleefully point out the section dealing with his namesake's painful death. At length, the boy smiled and politely thanked Baggo. 'But you're not a teacher, are you?' he asked.

'No. I am a policeman.'

'Dad's not in trouble, is he?'

'What makes you think he might be?'

The boy tensed. 'Nothing.'

'Harold, how often does he put you or your brother in the stocks?'

Harold looked away. 'Not often,' he said, his voice low.

'Every week?'

Harold shrugged.

'For how long?'

'Quarter or half an hour. But we both prefer that to being smacked.'

'What does he smack you with?' Flick asked.

'The flat of his wooden sword, usually.'

Flick put her hands on the boy's shoulders. 'Well, Harold, your dad will be in trouble if he puts you or your brother in the stocks again, or smacks you with a sword.' She handed him her card. 'Please phone me if anything like that happens. You must.'

Harold welled up. 'We don't want to be taken away,' he said, shaking all over.

Flick said, 'We're going to warn your dad, but this can't continue, and you must tell me if he does it again.'

Harold said nothing, but, dropping the card, turned to the wall and examined a section of the Bayeux Tapestry.

As they left, Baggo wished him luck with his science. The boy ignored him.

In the bedroom across the hall, Rufus seemed to have recovered from his recent punishment and showed the detectives his collection of plastic medieval soldiers. He told them that most nights he and his brother were allowed to have a sword fight before bed.

'This is intolerable,' Flick lectured Francis in the sitting room, the door firmly closed. Looking detached, Francis listened. He did not say anything, but when she finished, his lips twisted into a sneer.

When the officers left, they saw Francis watching from a window as they climbed into their car. Flick drove a short way down the road then stopped.

She said, 'I want to speak to the mother, and I bet he phoned her on a mobile, telling her to stay out of the way till we were gone.'

Five minutes later, as the street lights were coming on, a thin woman, bent with supermarket bags, made her way along the street. A minute after she had entered the flat, Flick rang the doorbell. Francis answered and, seeing who was there, tried to shut the door. Flick had her foot in the way, and Baggo put his weight to the door till it compressed Francis against the wall.

Matilda Francis was fair-skinned and wore no make-up. Her long skirt and woollen jumper were worn and stained. 'What is it? What's wrong?' she asked, her fluted, girly voice and Oxbridge accent uncomfortably out of place.

'It's about your boys. I need to talk to you,' Flick said firmly.

Matilda looked at her husband, as if seeking guidance, but his expression remained sullen and angry.

'Let me put these away first,' she said, carrying her bags into the kitchen. She returned, wiping her nose, and went into the sitting room with Flick.

'We stay here,' Baggo said to Francis.

The two men stood in the hall, alternately ignoring and glaring at each other. From the sitting room, Flick's voice could be heard, strong and insistent. After five minutes she came out, her face flushed. Behind her, Matilda sat weeping on the sofa.

'Did she admit anything, Sarge?' Baggo asked once they were back in the car.

'No. I think it's the usual story. Her helpless little girl act makes me mad. He's a creepy control freak, but I told her to stand up to him. I hope she got the message,' Flick said.

'A strange man,' Baggo commented. 'I half expected to find a scold's bridle hanging behind the bathroom door instead of a bathcap.'

'A bit of me thinks we should report him to Social Services anyway. We didn't say we definitely wouldn't.'

'He has been warned, Sarge. And he is scared of us. He knows we will be back. And it would do those boys no good to be taken into care. You know, in Mumbai, just along the street from us, there was this family; the father was a soldier, and he disciplined his two sons with great harshness. If they put a foot out of line, they would get a beating. But they were happy boys, excellent sportsmen. The last I heard, one is a doctor, the other an accountant, very nice young men, my uncle tells me.'

'But what are they like in their own homes?'

'That I cannot tell you.' He smiled. 'You English are quite namby-pamby towards children and animals.'

'Times have changed, Baggo. A father like that can

leave a child with mental scars that last a lifetime, long after the bruises have faded. We'll definitely do a spot check in a couple of weeks, however the inquiry's going. By the way, how did you get your knuckles into that state?'

11

Giving way to no one, Linda Swanson meant business as she strode along Knightsbridge, the click of her stilettos drowned by traffic. Ignoring the muttered apology of a well-dressed man who had brushed against her in passing, she contemplated a rather special week. If things worked out as she planned, she would sell *The Whole Pravda* to a major publisher, making Nikolai Chapayev a household name and herself a wealthy woman. Dirt-dishing memoirs of someone high up in Russian security during Putin's rule were as rare as hens' teeth, and this book would tarnish the former KGB head's reputation for ever. Truthfully, Linda had warmed to Putin as she read the manuscript; he stood no nonsense and did what he had to do. She had gone to sleep the previous night imagining him with her, but, as usual, had woken alone. She was proud of her nickname, Cruella De Ville, and did not acknowledge that to most men she fancied it was a turn-off.

Neither could she admit to herself that she was lonely; it was just that she liked her own company and didn't suffer fools at all. Callum Richardson was a fool, and she had spent a satisfying weekend in the country applying red ink to his latest crime novel. She was fed up with crime, with its hackneyed plots, preposterous characters and predictable outcomes. Its redeeming feature was that it had helped establish her at the top of her profession. Maybe Richardson would go elsewhere when he received her comments, but she didn't care; the moron couldn't tell a split infinitive from a gerund.

At twelve thirty exactly, she sashayed through the glass doors of Harvey Nichols and, cutting through the Monday lunchtime shoppers, took her reserved seat at the Nail Bar. She could not understand women who had their nails done on a Friday; it was during the working week that she wanted her talons to be beautiful, and deadly.

'Good afternoon, Ms Swanson. What colour do we want today?' Honey put on a smile. Her week always improved after Monday lunch time, the moment her most awkward client left without tipping.

'I want red.' She stressed the I. 'Show me what you've got.'

Honey put a selection of bottles on the bar. 'We have either St James, Tate, Shoreditch, or Victoria.'

'Either means a choice between two alternatives. There are four bottles here. You didn't learn much at school, did you?'

'Sorry, Ms Swanson.'

Linda noted the blush spreading up the girl's neck. Cutting her down to size was no challenge. She inspected the bottles and put a finger on Tate, the one most resembling fresh arterial blood.

Honey knew better than to chatter to Ms Swanson,

and the manicure passed in silence. Once every long, sharp fingernail had been trimmed and painted, Linda nodded and placed her hands on the bar in front of her. Honey poured a glass of champagne, which Linda sipped as her nails dried. This was one of her favourite moments of the week; she felt powerful, renewed, ready for the battles ahead. She assessed the weaknesses of the people with whom she would negotiate, and how she might exploit them.

She felt a sharp pain at the right side of her lower back, and yelped in surprise. Within seconds, her torso became numb and her skin tingled. She could not focus properly. There was a terrible burning then a tightness in her chest. With a strangled croak, her head fell forward. A spasm sent her crashing to the floor.

As she lay twitching and struggling for breath, passing shoppers, gaping and curious, formed a semi-circle round her. A couple of women screamed, then panic spread round the store. Before an ambulance could arrive, Linda Swanson was dead. She had remained conscious to the end.

* * *

'Ms Swanson was murdered, poisoned by fatal injection, just like Markov. It is Russian Secret Service, I tell you. They have vowed to silence me, stop my book. But I will not be silenced. I will not.' His ragged, black beard shook as Nikolai Chapayev ranted at the television reporter.

In his office, Chief Superintendent Jumbo Cumberland turned down the volume and scratched his dome. He was glad that Detective Inspector Simon Marsden was in charge of this investigation. He was a man who got results. He wondered if he should phone him to make sure he would follow up Chapayev's allegations.

Before he could decide, the phone on his desk rang. It was Sir Alfred Carr, a senior Home Office mandarin. If Jumbo was ever to become Commissioner, Sir Alfred's support would be vital.

'Yes, Sir Alfred, I've got Marsden on the case. He's one of my best men,' Jumbo gabbled.

'Yes.' It was a long, slow yes, carrying a lot of meaning, none of it clear. 'That was what I wanted to speak about.'

At home, Jumbo secretly enjoyed repeats of *Yes, Minister*. He sensed that Sir Alfred was in Sir Humphrey mode, and hoped he would understand any vaguely-expressed message.

'Chief Superintendent, this is a delicate matter. I have had a number of approaches from the Foreign Office. Our Russian friends have been very exercised in relation to Mr Chapayev's book for some time now. They say he is most unreliable, with many unresolved issues. They do not want his book to be published. Now, that's a long way from saying that they might try to warn off our publishing industry, a very long way, but should official suspicion for the Harvey Nicks murder, as it has already been called, fall on someone from the Russian Embassy, or someone connected to it, relations between our two countries would be damaged.'

'Damaged. Yes.'

'Energy is vitally important. You understand?'

'Of course. Gas, petrol and so on.'

'We could expel some of their people, but they would just expel the same number of ours. Very messy and unsatisfactory.'

'Indeed.'

'And a thorough investigation can take so long. My contacts in the Foreign Office do not like uncertainty.'

'Uncertainty, quite.'

'"I'd rather rely on George Smiley than George Dixon", someone said to me. I don't agree, of course. But I see his point. And the national interest.'

'Absolutely.' Where was this leading?

'This man Marsden has a reputation for being incorruptible?' Sir Alfred asked smoothly.

'Correct.'

'And effective in getting to the truth?'

'Very much so.'

'However long it took, and wherever his inquiries led?'

'As I say, one of my best men.'

'That could lead to problems.'

'Problems?' Jumbo did not like the way the conversation was going.

'Yes. The sort of problems I've been talking about.'

Jumbo said nothing.

'I believe that a number of literary agents have been

murdered recently.' Sir Alfred's tone became matter-of-fact. 'Perhaps it would be better if the Harvey Nicks murder got lumped in with those cases.'

'With Marsden in charge ...'

'Good heavens, no. And no is the word, isn't it? Inspector No, coming up to retirement, wanting a full pension and having a file bursting with reasons for not giving it to him. Someone you can steer away from the Russians, should that become necessary.'

'I could steer him?' Jumbo's voice became a squeak.

'You have a reputation for having a safe pair of hands, James. That's what we look for when we're talking about the top jobs.'

'Oh yes. I see.'

'I thought you would. Well, good evening, James. I suspect it may be a busy one.'

As he ended the call, Jumbo cursed under his breath. He did not know how he was going to break the news to Marsden, who had already appeared on television, requesting assistance from anyone who had been near the Nail Bar at the time of the killing.

12

'Would you Adam and Eve it, four hundred quid for a bleeding handbag!' Osborne stood open-mouthed at the counter next to the Nail Bar.

'For a handbag!' Baggo said, then sniggered.

Flick shot him a glare. Osborne's slobbishness was bad enough without Baggo being silly. Phoned after leaving work the previous day, and in unusually early, Osborne had brought his team with him to inspect the crime scene. Flick occasionally shopped in Harvey Nicks, and she felt embarrassed to be seen with Osborne. His clothes were stained, the top button of his yellow shirt was missing and his colours clashed. His habitual aromas of curry and nicotine seemed particularly pungent, and his derision at the style Harvey Nicks stood for could not have been more obvious.

As Osborne turned his scorn to the sunglasses counter, Flick applied her mind to the case. The killer had been among the members of the public circulating on the ground floor. People walked to and fro directly behind those sitting on the Nail Bar stools. The killer had done this, using a syringe to inject poison into Linda Swanson as they passed. They had done their homework, taking advantage of the fact that the victim came to the same seat at the same time every Monday, a seat which the CCTV cameras did not cover. Early word from the lab was that the poison was probably aconite. This came from Monkshood, a plant found in herbaceous borders round the country. The killing had been audacious, with all the hallmarks of a professional hit. The dead woman had been a literary agent, but the killer had left no message on the body, and the news was full of quotes from Chapayev, blaming the Russians. Georgi Markov had been murdered in London in a similar way some years earlier, and KGB involvement had been suspected then.

Flick could not understand why Simon Marsden had been taken off the case. She had met him at Police College and he had won her respect. It was almost as if the Harvey Nicks murder had been down-graded.

It was clear from his face that the store manager thought the same when he asked Osborne to remove the police tapes from round the Nail Bar. The previous day, Marsden had ensured that photographs had been taken, all items of interest had been bagged and the area dusted for fingerprints. Riled by the manager's presumptuous and condescending manner, and scratching his crotch ostentatiously, Osborne insisted that the tape should remain in place until his initial inquiries were complete. The immaculately neat man turned on his well-polished heel with an exasperated sigh.

'Bloody tailor's dummy. Keep the tape up till this afternoon,' Osborne muttered to Baggo, who had been about to supervise its removal.

Danny Peters had been talking to the girls who worked at the Nail Bar. He came up to Flick and quietly suggested that she might be the best person to speak to Honey Jack, who had done the victim's nails.

In a quiet room, Flick tried to calm a tearful Honey.

'I didn't see nothing, I swear. Them Russians won't come after me, will they?'

'We don't know it was the Russians, and no, I'm sure they won't worry about you.'

'Well I'm dead worried about them.'

'Did Ms Swanson say anything that was at all unusual yesterday?'

'She weren't a one to natter to the likes of me.'

'Did you hear anything at all that she said after she'd been attacked?'

'Well, I went round the bar as fast as I could. She lay there, twitching, her eyes staring. I'll never forget it, as long as I live. Her mouth moved and she seemed to whisper something.'

'What?'

'Dunno. Sounded like "Olpra". Is that Russian?'

'I don't speak Russian. Was she finding it difficult to speak?'

'I think so. I was in pieces. One minute she was there, sipping champagne. The next …' Honey dissolved into tears again.

Flick thanked her and told her not to worry. Handing her a card, she told her to get in touch if ever she wanted to, or if she remembered anything that might help.

'You don't look like top dog. Where is Marsden?'
Osborne's first meeting with Nikolai Chapayev in his
hotel room was not going well.

'He's off the case and I'm on it. And in my time I've
banged up more villains than Marsden's had hot dinners.'
He looked to Danny Peters for support, and got it.

'The boss practically cleaned up the East End a few
years back,' Peters said loyally.

'East End, East End. What do I care for your East
End? My agent is dead, because she was my agent. And
she was only one with the balls to take on my book.
Putin has a reach that goes round the world, and he's
proved it. I demand her murder is investigated by a
policeman with half the balls of my, my … heroine.'

Osborne put his face so close to the Russian that he
almost touched his beard. 'Listen, matey, people say a lot
of things about me, but they don't say I've no balls. If
some Russky's killed this woman right here in London,
I'll nail the bastard if I can, and I'll do everything in my
power to get round human rights and bleeding
diplomatic immunity. Now, are you just a bloody noisy
tosspot, or are you going to help me?'

The beard twitched and the Russian's dark eyes
narrowed. His head moved forward. Osborne saw he was
a real fighter and braced himself for a blow. But after a
tense moment, Chapayev stepped back and began to
laugh.

'You tell me I am tosspot, so you have balls. I think I

like you. Only I will know once you have done your work. We sit down, and I will tell you about my book.'

Half an hour later, Osborne and Peters understood why the Russian authorities would want to suppress *The Whole Pravda*. Chapayev had a remarkable memory, with specific recall of names, dates and places. He also had an acute analytical mind, and he could draw inferences from apparently unconnected events. When, at last, he paused, both policemen were convinced that Putin was guilty of atrocious abuse even Osborne could see breached human rights. He wished more English prosecuting counsel were as persuasive.

Before Chapayev could begin another monologue, Osborne said, 'Okay, so Putin's a villain. How do you know that the Russians killed Ms Swanson? There is someone around London who's murdered three other literary agents in the last couple of months. They might have killed her.'

'They screen with smoke. They kill other agents to throw you off scent.' Chapayev's eyes blazed. 'They have done that often. In many countries.'

'Have you seen anyone from the Embassy, or anyone connected with the Embassy, doing anything you could describe in evidence?'

'Dogs, underlings, from Embassy have watched me.'

'That proves nothing.'

'And Linda was watched, not by Embassy, and I know who.'

'Tell us.' Osborne was losing patience.

'South Ossetians. "My enemy's enemy is my friend."'

'South Ossetians?'

'In 2008 the Russians helped them against Georgia. There is a price for everything. In London, South Ossetians meet at Pyotr's Place, a Russian restaurant in Delaney Street. Camden, you know.'

'How can we prove that they watched her?'

'Sam, from Book Village, her agency. He will tell you of his time as James Bond.' Chapayev smiled at the puzzled expressions. 'One day I was at agency, with Linda. She like my book, but not my English, so she gave me editor, Tanya. Tanya often mince my words. "Kill your darlings," she keep saying. We had many arguments. One day, Tanya, Linda and I were in Linda's room and I saw in the street a man I thought was watching for me. Linda sent for Sam, a clever boy who work for her, and I told him to follow the man as long as he could. Then I told him how to do this without being seen. I left after we finish work, but the man did not tail me. When Linda left later, he followed her home. After watching half an hour, he went to restaurant. Sam learn quick from me, and he took photos on his mobile. He look inside and saw man pouring tea then going through to back room. Restaurant is Pyotr's Place. South Ossetians have it.'

Peters said, 'They wouldn't have diplomatic immunity.'

Chapayev snorted. 'But they help the Embassy. Their faces are not known. It is more difficult to spot them.'

Peters shook his head. 'Do you really think a South Ossetian killed Ms Swanson?'

'I cannot tell for sure, but they might have. They helped by following her.'

Osborne pointed his finger at the Russian. 'If they did, we could get them as accessories, even if we were not able to touch people at the Embassy.'

Chapayev beamed. 'And their trial would be Russia on trial, as sure as if Putin was in the dock.' He got up, towering over Osborne. Suddenly, he lunged down and planted a slobbery kiss on each cheek.

'Cut that out, will you?' Osborne spluttered. Peters stifled a laugh.

Osborne wiped his sleeve across his face. 'Is there anything else you know? Did Ms Swanson ever say she was scared, or tell you about threats? Anything at all?'

'No, and she was scared of nothing. I tell her that with her claws she was literary lioness, and she purred, like a great kitten.'

There was nothing more to be learned from Chapayev. As they left, Osborne phoned Baggo, who was at the agency, to make sure he spoke to Sam.

* * *

"Olpra" could have been her trying to say *The Whole Pravda*,' Flick suggested. 'The members of the team had gathered in the CID room and were trying to collate what they had learned.

'That's another pointer to the Russkies or their mates,' Osborne said. 'Did you find anything interesting at her house, Felicity?'

Flick scowled. 'No. Sir. She lived alone. The family come from Yorkshire, but they don't seem close. She had a few female friends, mostly from her student days, not so many male friends. A neighbour told me she had odd one-night stands, always with younger guys. She had a country home in Gloucestershire where she went most weekends. The local police didn't know anything about her.'

'And her street, Mornington Place, isn't far from that restaurant. Easy to see why the Russkies got their South Ossetian gofers to tail her. Did you learn anything from her office, Baggo?'

'They all lived in terror of her, gov. She was one very scary lady. She was called Cruella de Ville, and liked it. She reduced more than one published author to tears. She seems to have been a creature of habit. Almost every weekend she spent in the country, usually with one or two manuscripts. Her Monday routine was sacrosanct: she arrived in the office at Pont Street after the rush hour, worked for a couple of hours, then went round the corner for her twelve thirty appointment at the Nail Bar. Very predictable. I took her computer and will see what I can find on it. She's not on Facebook or Twitter.'

'Did you see Sam?'

'Yes, what you would call a likely lad. He followed a man he described as a "dark-haired, scrawny little runt" from the Book Village Agency to Mornington Place, ending up at Pyotr's Place. He took photos on his mobile and stored them on his computer. He has promised to send them to me. I got the impression the scrawny runt was not experienced in espionage, as he concentrated only on the person he was tailing, and did not spot Sam.'

'This time there's no desecration of the body, or a message,' Peters said. 'Do you think this is really a political killing, gov?'

'Everything points that way,' Osborne agreed, then was interrupted by the phone. 'Sir,' he said, his tone patient but world-weary.

Osborne did not believe in telling his superiors too much, particularly someone like Jumbo, but he was forced to acknowledge that he was working on the Russian angle. The others watched as he listened to Jumbo, his face registering boredom, then irritation, then puzzlement.

'Anything wrong, gov?' Peters asked once the call was over.

'Nah. But I need thinking time.' Osborne pulled his coat from its peg and left.

The phone rang again. Cautiously, in case it was Jumbo again, Flick picked it up. When she put it down she grinned broadly.

'They've arrested Patrycja Kowalski trying to leave the country. We'll go to Dover and see her tomorrow morning, Baggo.'

* * *

Pyotr's Place smelled of fried food and spices, with a musky background. It was warm and dimly lit by wall brackets with burnt lampshades that had seen better days. From a gilt frame on the wall opposite, a Russian Orthodox priest stared at Osborne. Facial hair made it impossible to tell if he was smiling or frowning. A dog-eared card beneath the photograph proclaimed: 'This Restaurant Blessed by Archpriest Valentin Sergeyevich Egerov 4 May 1996'. Some lines in Cyrillic script appeared to say more. Apart from the shiny plastic table-cloths, little about the restaurant seemed to have changed since the blessing.

Osborne was the only diner: either the restaurant struggled or its customers came in late. He knew that in his roundabout way, Jumbo was warning him off the Russians, which he didn't like, so that evening he had decided to try Russian food. His starter, Grenki, a spicy combination of cheese, egg and garlic, served with tomatoes, was surprisingly tasty.

'Are you Russian?' Osborne spoke slowly and unnecessarily loudly to the waiter, a short, furtive man, badly shaved, with thinning black hair.

'Niet. I am South Ossetian.'

'So is this a South Ossetian restaurant then?'

The man shrugged. 'Perhaps.'

'Do many Russians come here?'

Another, more expressive shrug. 'Sometimes they come. Not always.' He carried away the empty dish.

When he returned, Osborne tried again: 'I saw a Russian on the telly. He had a big beard. Talking about some murder. Do you know anything about him?'

The waiter shook his head and roughly set down a plate on which a mixture of beef, fried onions and rice sat on a big cabbage leaf. 'Golubtsy,' he said, turning away before Osborne could ask any more.

It was a trencherman's portion, and Osborne wished this restaurant was nearer his flat. As he was finishing, a tall man, tidier and better dressed than the waiter, came through the swing door leading to the kitchen and approached his table.

'Welcome, sir. I am Mihail Pyotrovich Serov, the owner of this restaurant. Pyotr was my father, unhappily now dead, but I kept the name. It is good to follow tradition, no?'

'I agree,' Osborne said. He saw the man look expectantly then added, 'I'm Smith. Noel Smith.'

'Well Mr Smith, as this is your first visit here, will you join me in a drink? Vodka?'

'I don't drink, but I could murder a cup of your Russian tea.' A large brass samovar sat on a table in a corner, making intermittent bubbling noises.

'My pleasure.' Serov went to the kitchen and returned carrying a cup which he filled up from the samovar. He brought it to the table and set it down before Osborne. 'May I join you?' he asked.

This was exactly what Osborne wanted. Serov fetched a glass containing a clear liquid and sat down. The tea was hot and very strong. Osborne prided himself on his asbestos throat. He downed it in two gulps.

'Vanya tells me you have questions,' Serov said.

'Yes. I was wondering what sort of a Russian community there is in London, just out of curiosity.'

'There is a large Russian community. Some escaped

when things were different. Some are here for business, taking over your football teams, maybe.'

Osborne did not react. 'Do those who disagreed with the government mix with, well, Embassy people?'

Serov did not blink. 'No. We see some Embassy people here, but they stick together.'

'Do you get much ill-feeling over the 2008 war with Georgia?'

'Georgians do not come here. They are not Russians.' Serov's mouth twitched. 'Come, have more tea.' He got up and refilled Osborne's cup. 'Do you like it?'

'Yes. Very strong. I like that.' He drank deeply. 'Did you see that Russian writer on the telly last night, blaming the official Russians for killing that woman in that poncy store?'

'Yes, I did. People tell me he is mad, but some will believe anything of our country, so he gets away with it.'

Osborne sat back. He felt a muzziness spreading through his head. He had not felt it for years. He closed his eyes and tried to concentrate. But he had already been gripped by that old, familiar sensation; he knew that he wanted, needed, more of it.

'Would you like to try something else?' Serov asked. 'I know you'll love it.'

'Yes. I'll love it,' Osborne muttered. His will had been broken, and he was going to wrap himself in a comfortable blanket of intoxication.

13

'In, out, in, out,

You shake it all about.

You do the Hokey Cokey and you turn around.

That's what it's all about –hey!'

The large, black woman behind the reception desk of the Dover Detention Centre swivelled her chair through three hundred and sixty degrees, lifted her arms and grinned broadly. 'That's what it's like here, darlin'. And it's damn hard to keep track of who's in and who's out. I can't see a Kowalski here.' She ran her finger down a type-written list of names.

Flick pursed her lips and tapped her foot in impatience. She had detested the Hokey Cokey since, as a ten-year-old, she had been compelled to participate, and the woman's impromptu performance made a bad morning worse. The journey to the South coast had been a nightmare due to tailbacks from an accident in the Channel Tunnel. Now, despite arrangements made by phone the previous evening, their visit had come as a surprise to the receptionist, whose manner remained cheerfully unconcerned.

'Tell you this, darlin',' the woman said in a broad Cockney accent. 'Working here, you gotta either laugh or cry, and I laugh. Ha, ha.' She pulled a file from a drawer, licked a meaty index finger, and carried on with her search.

Standing beside Flick, Baggo allowed his hopes to rise. If he was going to be found out, it would be much better if he confessed before he had the whistle blown on him. Twice during the interminable drive he had started to speak, then lost his nerve and said something banal. He respected Sergeant Fortune, but she was a bit of a stickler. In many ways, he would be better coming clean to Osborne, who had survived enough pickles to wreck half a dozen police careers. Some miles short of Dover, he decided to tough it out: he would give Patrycja a pleading look and hope she did not implicate him. After all, had he not intervened, she would have suffered a good deal more at the hands of Wolenski's thugs. But as he watched the receptionist scan her lists, he knew that if Patrycja had got permanently lost in the system, one of his nine lives would have been used up, for sure.

'Ah, 'ere she is!' The receptionist dashed Baggo's hopes. 'Go along the corridor to your left once you go through security. I'll give you interview room five. I'll have her sent down. Mind, as it's lunch time, you'll have a good half hour to wait.'

On their way to the interview room, Flick got coffees from a machine. They found room five, which was drab, grey and dismal. They sat on shabby, uncomfortable chairs and drank the warm, beige liquid that tasted of cardboard.

After a long silence, Flick asked, 'Are you all right, Baggo?'

'Fine, Sarge. Just fine.' He forced a smile.

'Nothing's bothering you? You seem a bit quiet today.'

'I find myself thinking of home, Sarge.'

'I hope you feel England's your home.'

'Oh, I do, Sarge. But one person can have more than one home, and today I think of Mumbai.'

The silence that followed was broken by footsteps in the corridor. As Flick sat up straight behind the small table, Baggo eased his chair back so that she would not see his expression. An escort pushed a sullen-looking girl of about twenty into the room. She had a round face and wore a very short skirt.

'Patrycja Kowalski?' Flick asked.

The girl nodded. Baggo felt a weight lift from his shoulders. This girl was not the Patrycja Kowalski that he knew.

* * *

Osborne wrapped his bath towel round himself and cleared some of the steam from the mirror. Both eyes were bloodshot, but the right one was puffy and sore as well. His lower lip was swollen and blood seeped from a cut that hurt when he licked it. His head ached and his stomach churned. Despite lying in a hot bath for twenty minutes, he still felt chilled to the marrow.

Every time he tried to remember the previous night's events, more ghastly details came back to him. A young cop had found him, cold and very confused, in the back seat of his own car, which had been parked on a yellow line in Camden. The engine had been running, and that had saved him from a bitterly cold night, but the cop had wanted to charge him with being drunk in charge of the car. It had taken his badge and a more experienced colleague in a patrol car to make the youngster back off. The older man had persuaded the rookie that it would be best for the Inspector to be driven home, and the young man had done this, seeing Osborne to his door and helping him with his keys. Osborne had half-undressed and collapsed on top of his bed. Now it was broad daylight. He should be at work.

His days as a drunk had taught him that turning up while completely unfit was a very bad idea. He pulled on pyjamas and picked up the phone. 'Food poisoning', 'up all night being sick', 'just a twenty-four hour thing, I hope', tripped off his tongue as glibly as ever. Luckily, it was Peters he spoke to. Fortune and Baggo were chasing after some Polish bint who might give someone an alibi. He swore as he ended the call; he had definitely had enough of Eastern Europeans.

He settled himself back in bed, the covers over his head, when his mobile sounded. A text. It could wait. Then another. And another. And another. Maybe he should check. He lumbered over to where his jacket lay on the floor, found the phone and called up his messages.

The first had two words: 'STAY AWAY'. Next came a photograph. Osborne groaned when he saw himself, lying on his back on a bed, his trousers round his ankles. There was someone else in the picture, a blond-haired, well-muscled man, completely naked. He was lying beside Osborne, and each had a hand on the other's crotch.

The second written message was worse: 'THERES MORE'. The photograph that followed showed Osborne in the same position, smiling stupidly, but the blond man's open mouth was now beside his erect penis.

Gingerly, Osborne felt himself, wondering what had been done to him. Everything seemed normal, but that was only half of it; if these photos got round the nick, he wouldn't be able to show face again. He checked his pockets. Nothing had been taken, but he could tell from where his credit cards were that someone had gone through his wallet. He had been nobbled, good and proper.

Sitting on the edge of his bed, he forced himself to think back in an organised way. He remembered the long, sweet drink Serov had brought to his table; he pictured the back room he was taken to, the rough-looking men round the table, and a handsome, mature woman. Veronika, that was her name. She had sat next to him and filled his glass. He remembered the men talking about the evil Georgians, then they started on Chapayev; Veronika hated him as a traitor. He had joined in; the men had laughed at his jokes, and Veronika's hand had crept up his thigh. She had guided him upstairs. There had been a fight: he remembered being hit, but no pain. He checked his knuckles; they were tender. He was glad he had put up some resistance. He stared at the blond man's face; he had no memory of it, but if he met him again … He clenched his right fist.

As he tried to go back to sleep, he realised he was between a rock and a very hard place. If he treated Linda Swanson's murder as another literary agent killing, Chapayev would rant about him to the press and make a nuisance of himself. If he concentrated on the South Ossetians and Russians, he would be the laughing-stock of the Met within days. And Jumbo would not be happy.

Worst of all, he craved a drink.

* * *

'I find it hard to believe any of our suspects is guilty.' Flick sounded as depressed as she felt. The morning had been a complete waste of time. At first she had thought the girl was pretending, but after quarter of an hour's questioning, became convinced that she had never heard of Candy Dalton, and had no brother called Pavel, in or out of prison. Now, with Osborne off sick, she had called a meeting with Baggo and Peters to assess progress.

'But whoever is doing this is clever and will not stick out like a sore thumb,' Baggo said.

'Johnson is a real villain, the only one with a record, so I make him favourite,' Peters said.

'Wallace is a trained killer, and he can do more than he pretends, I'm sure,' Baggo said.

Flick said, 'Candice Dalton is a mass of

contradictions, and she feels very deeply about things, I think.'

'That medieval freak sounds pretty scary,' Peters said.

Flick pointed to the pile of A4 sheets on the table in front of them. 'Well, I think we should go through what's left of our long list, entry by entry, and see if we can find any more who are worth interviewing.'

The others murmured agreement.

Flick took the first one off the top of the pile and scanned the synopsis. 'Cilla Pargiter has written *Buried Alive*. An archaeological dig in Egypt goes badly wrong when the spirit of a murdered priest seeks revenge for his premature burial.'

'I hope they left lots of nice things for him in his tomb, or did they just do that for Pharaohs?' Baggo muttered.

Flick glanced at him. For no apparent reason, he had brightened up as the day had gone on.

* * *

'My office, Scotland Yard. Now. I don't care what you're doing.' Jumbo's voice squeaked down the line. It was hardly the greeting Osborne had wanted on his return to work. The previous day had been his first day's illness since he became sober, and he had wanted a quiet, easy morning.

There was nothing for it but to obey. Osborne cursed as he drove across town. Jumbo was an ass, but a dangerous one. Palfrey had not been included in the summons, so he would not be able to hide behind her immaculately-pleated trousers. He would have to be careful.

He found the Chief Superintendent pacing up and down. His eyes blazed and there was sweat on his dome. He threw down a red-top newspaper. 'Well?' he shouted.

Osborne had not seen it. On the front page was a picture of Chapayev, mouth open and pointing a finger. The headline read: **RUSSIANS KILLED MY AGENT**.

'Oh,' Osborne said.

'The Russians are furious, the Foreign Office is furious. So is the Home Office. And I am incandescent.' The last word came out as a cross between a bellow and a squeak, but from someone of Jumbo's size and rank, it scared Osborne.

'Relations between us and the Russians are very delicate, and they are important to us. I warned you the other day. Yet here's this man saying you'll hunt down the killer regardless of diplomatic immunity or human rights. Why, Osborne? Why?'

'Well, sir, I saw Chapayev before you spoke to me.'

'But you've no business saying that. And don't deny it. Chapayev recorded your conversation.'

Osborne's heart sank. 'Oh. Sorry, sir. I never meant that to reach the public.'

'Of course you didn't, you fool. But it did.'

'If you want me off the case, sir ...'

'No, I do not.' Jumbo put his face in Osborne's. 'In case I have failed to make myself clear to you, I want you to find someone we can charge with the other literary agent killings. And Ms Swanson's murder will be among the charges that accused faces. Do you understand me?'

'Yes sir. Will that be all, sir?'

'Try to cover up that black eye, will you? And I don't want to know where you got it.' As Osborne reached the door he added, 'This may well be one of your last cases. You'll no doubt be looking forward to a comfortable retirement. I hope nothing happens to put that in jeopardy.'

Seething, and tortured by his newly-awakened craving, Osborne drove slowly towards Wimbledon Police Station. As he digested Jumbo's ill-disguised threat, it occurred to him that Chapayev's press briefing might, in the end, protect him from scandal. He parked in a quiet street where he sat for a while, chain-smoking and thinking. His eye drifted across the road. There was a row of shops, one of which pulled him like a magnet. He got out of his car and crossed the street.

* * *

'How are you getting on with your crap crime writers, Felicity?' Osborne's mood was bullish when he got back to the nick.

Flick looked at him with contempt. More dishevelled than usual, he sat with his feet on his desk, munching his third doughnut and scratching his crotch. Baggo and Peters exchanged sly grins.

'We have four main suspects, so far, and it has been difficult to eliminate any of them.' Flick described their findings, noting that, for the first time, Osborne paid close attention.

'Is there anyone else worth a look?' he asked.

'There's someone from Dogmersfield we were thinking of visiting.'

'Dogmersfield? Where's that?'

'Hampshire. A country village.'

'Why?' He threw the paper bag at the bin, missed, but left a trail of sugar across the floor.

Flick leaned forward. 'It's a revenge-based story: a man is found in his bath, electrocuted by a heater that has fallen or been dropped in. And the bathroom door is locked. His wife is suspected, but her lawyer, Phyl Sloane, a woman by the way, investigates. She discovers the handyman who worked on the house is the son of a man who was ruined by the victim years ago, and committed suicide by drowning himself. The handyman fitted one of those safety locks you can unpick from outside, crept into the house, drugged the wife, got into the bathroom and killed the husband, then locked the bathroom door from the outside again. So the murder sort of fits with the grievance.'

'Who's the writer?'

'R. L. Lawson. I don't know more than the name and address.'

'I think we should pay a visit this afternoon.'

Flick was astonished. 'We?'

'Yes, Felicity. We. 'Cos WE need to quell public anxiety by getting off our arses and making a bleeding arrest. We're supposed to be policemen, not some middle-class book group.'

Peters cleared his throat before either Osborne or Flick could make their relationship even worse. 'There's a lot of stuff in from the lab for the Harvey Nicks murder,' he said.

'Give it here.' Osborne stood and reached out an arm, nearly touching the front of Flick's jacket.

Peters handed over a thick sheaf of paper.

Osborne groaned. 'Give us the short version, will you?'

'Well, gov, the poison was aconite, from Monkshood. They must have squeezed the juice out of a lot of plants, because what was injected was a very strong dose. That's the main thing. The syringe was common-or-garden, there were no fingerprints on anything. Pretty professional, I'd say. Are we going to have a look at that South Ossetian restaurant? Chapayev was on the phone earlier, looking for you.'

Osborne said quickly, 'Not today, Danny. We're all off to Dogfield.'

'Dogmersfield,' Flick corrected, her voice icy.

* * *

'Nice place,' Baggo said to Peters as they drove through the village, homely and attractive, even on a gloomy, damp afternoon. In front of them, Flick, grim-faced, drove while Osborne snored. The M3 had been unusually quiet and Flick had ignored the speed limit. She and her two backseat passengers wanted the awkward journey to end as soon as possible.

The sat-nav proved helpful, and Flick located Lawson's address without difficulty. She parked on the verge, got out and slammed her door.

'Do you think he's been drinking? Look at that eye,' she muttered to Baggo as Osborne shook himself and slowly clambered out of the car.

Baggo shrugged. He suspected the boss had been drinking and fighting, but he didn't want to say so.

Osborne pushed open a squeaky gate and headed up a sloping path to the front door. It was a solid door, weathered, slightly warped, and pitted with metal studs; a door to repel enemies. The house was detached, with a mature wisteria covering much of the stone frontage. The pitched roof dipped in the middle. One slate had detached itself and sat perilously on the gutter above a sash window.

The bell sounded loudly with two rings. A full minute passed before the door was opened and a man peered out. He had a full head of white hair and a pale, lined face.

'Mr Lawson?' Osborne demanded.

'Yes.' The voice was mellifluous, upper middle class.

'Mr R. Lawson?'

'Yes. Who are you?'

Osborne thrust his warrant under Lawson's nose. 'We are police officers, and we have some questions for you. We'd like to come in.'

'Of course, of course.' Lawson opened the door and shuffled across a dusty, cluttered hall, dominated by a huge, dark Welsh dresser. The officers followed him to a small, cosy room where a TV crime series was blaring from an old-fashioned television. 'Sit down,' he said, although Osborne had already occupied the most comfortable armchair.

It took a few moments to turn off the TV and for everyone to find seats. Lawson, a small, neat man, perched on a hard chair which Peters placed in front of the television, facing Osborne.

'I believe you write?' Osborne asked.

'Why, yes.'

'About crime?'

'Sometimes.'

'What else do you write about?'

Lawson looked puzzled. 'All sorts of things, but you must be here about crime.' He smiled and touched his right eye.

Osborne smiled back. 'We just need to have the full picture, Mr Lawson. Have you tried to get your writing published?'

'Oh yes. But you must know that.'

'Do you have an agent?'

'No.'

'What do you think of literary agents?'

'From the little I know of them, I do not like them one little bit.' His voice shook as if he was unused to expressing himself as forcefully.

'Why not?' Osborne leaned forward and gestured to Baggo to take notes.

'I am sure that there are some very nice, honourable ones, but some are just stinkers.' He pursed his lips and his eyes blazed.

'And what have you done about it?' Osborne asked quietly.

'Nothing. They don't even have a professional body worth complaining to. Toothless. I think it's deplorable.'

Osborne looked triumphantly at Flick.

Afraid of what he might say next, she shook her head.

He was not going to be put off. 'Before we go any further, Mr Lawson, I should tell you that you are not obliged to say anything, but anything you do say will be taken down, and used in evidence. If you fail to answer a question, that failure may be founded on in court. I ask you again, what have you done about literary agents? Four have been murdered recently, as I'm sure you know.'

What little colour there was drained from Lawson's face. 'I … I haven't, wouldn't …' he stammered, then fell forward and sideways, striking his head on the brass fender.

Flick produced a clean handkerchief, which she used to staunch the gash on Lawson's temple. Meanwhile Baggo rushed to the kitchen to fetch a glass of water. By the time he returned, Lawson was sitting on the floor, groaning. A minute later, the door burst open and a large woman, several years his junior, with a bust that would have graced the figurehead of a galleon, screamed then retreated to the hall.

Peters needed to hold her wrist to stop her dialling 999. 'We are the police,' he repeated as Baggo waved his warrant card in front of her.

Twenty minutes later, Lawson was resting in another room and the woman, Mrs Lawson, was listening, stony-faced, as Osborne tried to explain what had happened.

'How on earth did you make Inspector?' she asked when he finished. 'He is R for Robert Lawson. I am R for Rachel, L for Laura Lawson. I am a retired solicitor, and I have tried my hand at writing crime fiction. My husband is older than I am, and he is not as sharp, mentally, as he used to be. In his prime, he had more brains than the lot of you put together,' she spat out angrily. 'He has taken to writing to the local paper about all sorts of things, but mostly about crime, burglary in particular. He had a letter published yesterday, and no doubt thought you were here to talk to him about his theories. So of course it came as a shock when you practically accused him of being a serial killer. I go out to enjoy an afternoon's bridge and come back - to this!' She put her face close up to Osborne's, wrinkled her nose and drew back. 'Now listen very carefully, Mr Osborne, I want you and your lackeys out of my house within one minute. I don't want to see any of you ever again, and I shall be complaining to your superiors. I shall take my husband to hospital now, and when he is feeling better, I shall strongly encourage him to sue the pants off you. Now GET OUT!'

Heads down, the officers left.

'I'm very, very sorry,' Flick said before Mrs Lawson slammed the front door.

'Well, she could be a killer,' Osborne said after they had driven several miles in silence. 'You'd better be the one to question her, Felicity, but maybe leave it till next week.'

14

Richard Noble's breathing was laboured as he passed the bottom gate of Hardcliffe's field. He looked at his watch and cursed; he was still off the pace. This was the third half-marathon he had run in the last two months, and unless he improved he would be lucky to beat four and a half hours. The London Marathon was nine weeks away. Parker was evasive about how his training was going. Typical. He had always played his cards close to his chest. Years after they had first met, how well did he really know Lionel Parker? The stake in their personal race, £500 to Marie Curie, would not bother Noble, but his partner would milk the bragging rights, and that would be insufferable. Why, oh why had he risen to the challenge? Drink, pride and braggadocio. That was a good word; one of his authors had used it recently, a woman with a feel for the richness of the English language.

He tried to keep his stride rhythmical as his route took him along Hardcliffe's farm road, and into the tulgy wood – that was what he called it. As the dark-trunked, skeletal trees dimmed the late afternoon light, and the pot-holed road rose steeply ahead, he recited *Jabberwocky* to himself, and wished he might whiffle through the tulgy wood as the Jabberwock had done.

Uphill, he slowed almost to a walk, but kept going. On the brow, he resisted the temptation to stop and recover his puff. Downhill, his stride lengthened. Just round the bend at the bottom, he would turn down the footpath leading past his garden gate. He had less than half a mile to go – for today.

To his right, a deep trench ran along the verge. Hardcliffe was putting in new drainage pipes, but the men were slow. The trench had crept up the side of the road over several months, leaving an untidy, raised trail of infill like the slime left by a snail.

Something caught his right ankle, then his left. As he fell forward, his outstretched hands took the impact with the ground. Suddenly, a shock went through him. He felt excruciating pain and he could not move. Something pushed him to his right. He scraped across the road until he fell and landed on the damp, cold earth at the foot of the trench. The charge of electricity stopped and he tried to move, but a second burst hit him and a boulder landed on his back. Then heavy lumps of clay soil began to fall on top of him. Remorselessly, they covered his head and body, weighing him down. He could do nothing to save himself. Face down in crushing darkness, he tried to scream, but knew that all his killer would hear would be a muffled, agonised animal noise. He realised that he was about to die and thought desperately of Vanessa, and Gill and Jenny. Then he repeated to himself The Lord's Prayer. He automatically asked for his daily bread, sincerely begged forgiveness and grudgingly forgave those who had trespassed against him. Then he blacked out. After a lifetime of fine dining, the last thing Richard Noble tasted was earth.

* * *

'Wallace is one hell of a man,' Danny Peters told the rest of the team, meeting on Monday morning to discuss progress, or the lack of it. Peters had spent Friday in Bracknell, observing Ralf Wallace's block of flats in the hope of assessing his incapacity. Unobtrusively parked on the road, he had a good view of the flats. It had been early afternoon before he had glimpsed Wallace, who had emerged in his wheelchair and started to propel himself up and down the car park as fast as he could. But he was not the only observer; three hoodies sat on a wall, swinging their legs and nudging each other.

'Hey, Spazzy!' one called.

'You need a fucking motor for that thing,' shouted another.

Wallace ignored them and continued his exercise. The hoodie who had called out first jumped down and came behind Wallace. He got hold of the handles at the back of the chair and pushed down, lifting the front wheels and taking control. For some minutes, he steered the chair about the car park in a crazy, zig-zag manner, Wallace shouting at him to stop. Peters was on the point of intervening, but did not want to destroy his cover. As it looked as if the hoodie was going to ram the chair into a corner, Wallace reached down and pulled on his left brake. The chair flew round, causing the hoodie to lose his balance and his grip. Having regained control of his chair, Wallace backed into the corner.

'You bloody little coward,' he yelled.

The hoodie reached into his pocket, produced a flick knife and advanced towards Wallace. Peters was half way out of the car when Wallace grabbed the hoodie's right wrist, pulling and twisting it. Off balance, the hoodie dropped the knife and yelped, but Wallace was not finished with him. He continued to twist the arm until the hoodie's back was half lying on him. He pushed the arm up while holding the boy's left shoulder down then another twist had the arm up his back. The boy was now face down. Holding the arm up his back with the right hand, Wallace used his left hand to grasp the back of the hood and smash the boy's face into the arm of the chair. He did this a second time then paused. Using his left hand to keep the arm twisted, he pulled on the boy's low-slung jeans until he was bent over his left knee. Then he tugged down, lowering both jeans and pants easily.

Peters finished his account: 'So he laid into the little scrote for a bit then tipped him off his knee. The scrote shuffled back to his mates, who were laughing at him, his face as red as his arse, blubbing and holding his wrist. Best entertainment I've had in months.'

Osborne and Baggo grinned. Flick asked, 'What happened to the knife?'

'Wallace picked it up and put it in the bag at the back of his wheelchair.'

Flick asked, 'Did he get up?'

'Yes. He stood up, all stiff-legged, and started to walk up and down the car park as if nothing had happened, pushing his chair in front of him.'

Baggo asked, 'A bit like a zimmer?'

'Right. He didn't go too fast, but he seemed quite stable. He went up and down a few times then walked back into the building. He's got some nerve, I'll tell you, and his upper body must be very strong. Once he had a hold of the little scrote, he did exactly what he wanted to him.'

'Which is what a lot of people will have itched to do,' Osborne said. 'Well done for not intervening, Danny. I hope he doesn't turn out to be our man. He's a bloke after my own heart.'

'But he's just moved up the suspects' ladder,' Flick said.

'Well what have you got to report, Felicity? Do you have anything to show for your film-watching? Apart from empty bags of pop-corn.'

Flick and Baggo had spent several hours trawling through CCTV footage from Harvey Nicks and the surrounding area in the hope of spotting one of the suspects.

'One or two possibles, but the quality's awful.'

'Who are the possibles?'

'Candice Dalton and Sidney Francis, but we couldn't be sure, and a half competent defence counsel would make mincemeat of us if we were more definite.'

Osborne snorted. He had spent Friday lunchtime having an unproductive talk with Weasel, who had found no one willing to speak on the record about Johnson's hold over Littlepool Prison.

Baggo said, 'Sam, the boy from Ms Swanson's agency, sent some photos he took of the man who followed her. I have them on my computer. Do you want to see them, gov?'

Osborne tried to hide his wince. 'Might as well have a gander,' he said.

If the number of photos was anything to go by, Sam had enjoyed his unconventional assignment. Half of them showed nothing except people's backs, but in one a man with thinning, dark hair looked over his shoulder, a cigarette in his hand.

'That's a good enough view to trace him,' Baggo said.

'There's a lot of men that look like that,' Osborne said. It was the waiter from Pyotr's Place. Another photo showed him entering the restaurant.

'Have we not got enough for a warrant to search this Pyotr's Place?' Baggo asked, pointing to the photograph. 'There is something very fishy about that establishment, apart from their food.'

'Don't try to tell me what to do, Chandakarvup,' Osborne blustered. 'We'll shake up the crap crime writers and make an arrest. I don't want any more of these agents killed on my watch.'

Wondering who to shake up, and how to do it, Osborne scratched his crotch. The telephone rang and he answered it. When he ended the call, he said, 'Another bloody agent's got themselves murdered. This one's been buried alive.'

Hardcliffe's wood was just outside Headley, to the east of Hampshire. On Sunday evening, a desperately worried Vanessa Noble had gone looking for her husband when he was late in returning from his run. She had warned him that, carrying too much weight, running a marathon would be the death of him. After driving about in the dark with their two teenage daughters, she had phoned the police. The three of them had gone out again on a stumbling, fruitless search before passing a miserable night.

The call had come as they picked at breakfast. Drainage workers had noticed the disruption of their excavations and the bravest of them had jumped into the trench and scraped the soil until the body had been revealed. The breakfast call had not told them this, merely that a body had been found, the caller non-committal concerning the details. These details became clear when Vanessa had gone to identify the body, and she had returned home in a state of shock. To lose her husband due to a heart attack was one thing, to imagine him murdered, fully conscious as soil was heaped on top of him, was more than she could cope with.

Telling the girls had been awful. She had phoned their school, Roedean, to explain why she was keeping them at home, maintaining her composure with an effort. Then she phoned their solicitor, Marcus Ramsay. When the doorbell sounded, she had expected it to be Marcus, but it was Lionel Parker who stood awkwardly on the doorstep before wrapping his arms round her. This physical contact destroyed her reserve, and she spent the next half hour weeping.

* * *

Flick had dropped Osborne and Peters at the murder scene before going on with Baggo to visit the widow. The Noble family home was a mock Tudor manor house with fields at one side and at the back. Two ponies watched their arrival, wearing winter blankets but chewing grass with unconcerned contentment.

A lean man in his early forties answered the door. He introduced himself as Lionel Parker, a family friend. As he led the way to the drawing room, where Vanessa was, he explained that he had known Richard at Cambridge and they had formed their own literary agency, Noble Parker, based in Guildford. He lived nearby in Fleet and had come round as soon as the solicitor had rung.

Vanessa, fair and thin, did not stand when the detectives came into the room. She lifted a pale, tear-stained face and held out a limp hand. Her other hand lay in her lap, clutching a sodden handkerchief. Parker sat on the sofa beside her, a solicitous expression on his face.

Hesitantly, she described the events of the previous twenty-four hours. She could think of no one who might want to murder Richard, there had been no threats she was aware of, and his recent behaviour had been quite normal. For the last few weeks he had gone for a run every Sunday afternoon. While his route had varied, he had always finished by going through Hardcliffe's wood. He had been training for the London Marathon, she added bitterly, looking daggers at Parker.

Turning to him, Baggo asked, 'How does your agency deal with submissions from new authors?'

Parker frowned. 'What does that have to do with this dreadful business?' he snapped.

'Possibly quite a lot, sir. I would be most grateful if you would tell me.'

'Frankly, we ignore most of them. We have a quick look at some, but the publishing business is highly competitive, and new talent has to be exceptional before we consider representation.'

'Do you reply to aspiring authors who contact you?'

'No. We let silence speak for itself.'

'Like the silence of the grave, perhaps?'

Parker sat forward, his eyes boring into Baggo's. Speaking slowly, he said, 'That must rank as one of the most tasteless, insensitive remarks I have ever heard. Clearly, the Metropolitan Police is nothing like what it was. No doubt they will find some excuse for you, but I trust that your sergeant will educate you about how we behave here as you leave. Mrs Noble has had quite enough.'

Flick coughed. 'I have one question. Did Mr Noble handle crime novels?'

Parker nodded curtly. 'Yes.'

Baggo also coughed. 'And I have one more, if this does not upset English etiquette. Do you have any record at all of aspiring authors who have submitted to you?'

Parker curled his lip. 'I would have thought it was obvious from what I have already said that the answer to that particularly stupid question is "no".'

Flick stood up, nodding to Baggo with one eyebrow raised. She spoke words of condolence, conscious of their futility and turned to go.

Baggo said to Vanessa, 'I know you have had a most terrible shock. I am very sorry if I offended you, but there was a point to all of my questions. You know, I really want to catch your husband's killer.'

There was a ray of warmth in Vanessa's answering smile that only Baggo saw. Flick and Parker turned as a teenage girl entered the room. She was well-built, with a ruddy complexion she had not inherited from her mother. Her eyes were red from crying.

'Mum, do you need the phone? Like I really need to speak to Louise?' the girl said.

Before Vanessa answered, Parker said, 'Can't it wait till later, Gill? You're still quite traumatised.' He put his arm round her shoulder, but she shrugged it away and moved across the room to her mother.

'Mum?' she said.

'All right, darling. What's Jenny doing?'

'i-Pod,' Gill replied. She looked at Flick and Baggo. 'Police?' she asked then, without waiting for a reply but shooting a glare at Parker, left.

'She's very upset,' Parker said quickly.

As they drove out of the gate, which boasted a statue of a white lion on either side, Flick said, 'I wonder …'

'I wonder, too,' Baggo agreed.

'So what do we know?' Osborne asked as Flick drove up the M3 towards London.

Peters, who had just come off the phone to the pathologist, said, 'It's another clever killing. The doc reckons Noble was running downhill when he was tripped. The palms of both hands were grazed. Then he was tasered twice. They found two sets of electrodes in his back. He was pushed into the open drainage ditch and landed face down. Two ribs were cracked at the back, and that fits with the boulder that was right on top of him. Then the soil was piled on. Horrid way to go.'

Flick said, 'He went out running every Sunday afternoon and always took the same route home. I don't suppose the killer left a footprint at the scene, or anything helpful like that?'

'Correct, Sarge,' Peters said. 'We're against someone meticulous, that's for sure. There were tyre tracks, but not necessarily anything to do with the murder, and pretty common anyway.'

Baggo said, 'Noble didn't acknowledge submissions from aspiring authors. You can imagine him being buried alive, screaming blue murder for help and getting no answer.'

Osborne asked, 'What's the widow like?'

Flick said, 'As upset as you might expect. Noble had a business partner, Lionel Parker. He was at the house, and we wondered if there might be something between him and Vanessa Noble. One of the Nobles' girls reacted very badly to him.'

'He did not take to me,' Baggo said.

'Probably got some taste, then.' Osborne laughed. 'Damn. Damn. Damn. We're playing catch-up all the time, with nothing to go on. We need to start putting pressure on the crap crime writers.'

Flick said, 'There's one we didn't put down as a suspect because she lives in Newcastle. Her victim was buried alive. Her name is ...'

'Cilla Pargiter,' Baggo said.

'Well you two know where you are heading tomorrow,' Osborne said.

15

The train north was nearly half an hour late. It gave Flick and Baggo time to see that the papers had now decided that one person, 'Crimewriter', was responsible for killing the agents. The police did not look good, particularly as Inspector Osborne had been unavailable for comment. Palfrey had also ducked under the parapet, and it had been left to Cumberland to reassure the public that the investigation was making progress. The fact that such a senior officer had come forward to say so little merely emphasised the problem.

Eventually, the train pulled into Newcastle Station. At the entrance of the great, soot-blackened, Victorian building, Flick and Baggo easily found a taxi to take them to the Jesmond area of the 'toon', where Cilla Pargiter lived. They were unable to understand most of what the driver said, and conversation petered out, though he cheerfully gave them his company's card for their return to the station.

The red brick terrace suggested neither affluence nor poverty. The front garden of number twenty-four comprised a square of straggly grass bisected by badly-laid paving stones that bore traces of having been painted many years previously. It seemed that no one was in, but as Flick's finger was poised to press the bell a second time, the door was flung open and a fat, middle-aged woman greeted them with a smile that quickly faded.

'Not today, my loves,' she said, making to close the door.

Just in time, Flick got her foot in the way. 'We're police,' she said. 'Are you Ms Pargiter?'

The woman tensed then peered suspiciously at them. 'You'll have your warrant cards?' she asked. Her hands shook as she took a pair of spectacles from the pocket of her thick, paint-stained, woolly cardigan and examined them.

'You'd best come in, I guess,' she said, and led the way to a sitting-room that resembled an art gallery. Paintings covered every wall. Most were still life or animals, but there were landscapes and some portraits as well.

Above the fireplace was one larger than the rest, showing the heads and shoulders of two young women. Scarcely more than girls, they appeared identical with oval, grey eyes and ski-jump noses framed by long, straight, blonde hair. Both had strong chins. Their lips were pulled down on the right, making their expressions difficult to read. The girl on the left, more in profile, was half-turned towards a sandy beach and a black rock jutting from an azure sea. The girl on the right looked away from her sister, her head slightly bowed.

'Is this about Penny?' the woman blurted out before Flick said anything.

'Penny?' Flick asked.

The woman sat down heavily. 'My daughter,' she said, looking up at the picture.

'I'm sorry. I don't follow,' Flick said quietly.

Frowning, the woman sighed. 'She was drowned. Nearly four years ago.' Her voice catching, she added, 'Her body was never recovered. Swept out to sea. I keep hoping …'

'I'm sorry,' Flick repeated. 'Are you Cilla Pargiter?' she asked.

She shook her head. 'That's my other daughter, Penny's twin. Cilla will be back soon,' she explained. 'What do you want with her, anyway?'

'Her name cropped up in an inquiry, that's all. We have a few questions we'd like to ask her. Nothing to worry about.' Flick tried to sound reassuring.

The woman shifted in her seat and looked from one to the other. 'Right. That's a mercy. I'm Margaret Pargiter, by the way. I suppose you won't say no to a cuppa tea.'

'You could have warned me. I thought you looked her up on Facebook,' Flick snapped as soon as Margaret had left.

'I tried to catch your eye. But there was nothing about her sister. As I said in the train, it was a very dull profile.'

Unimpressed, Flick stood to have a closer look at the painting, comparing mother and daughters. The oval eyes and the nose were similar. Years younger and stones lighter, Margaret could nearly have been either of these girls. Her chin was less prominent and her mouth, full-lipped but unremarkable, lacked the distinctive downward twist. From the kitchen came the sound of nose-blowing. When she returned, forcing a smile, Margaret carried a tea-tray with a plate of cakes.

'Does Cilla live here?' Flick asked, trying not to wince at the industrial-strength brew placed in front of her.

'Yes. Her and Penny.'

'Penny?' Baggo asked.

Margaret smiled. 'Her child,' she said. 'She'll soon be three.' She turned to Flick, woman to woman. 'I'd thought Alan Trelawney, the father, favoured Penny, but it was Cilla who was pregnant. I was quite surprised when she called the baby after her sister. Though they were very close,' she added quickly.

Flick asked, 'What does Cilla do?'

'She cleans. Offices, you know, and a couple of houses. She'll be back soon. She picks up Penny from nursery on her way home.'

'Does she write?' Flick asked.

'Why, yes. She does. Once Penny's off to bed. She's clever, you know. Would have had an Honours Degree from St Andrews University if she hadn't got pregnant.'

'What does she write about?' Baggo asked.

'Detective novels set in ancient Egypt. That was her subject at university. How did you know about her writing? Is this something to do with these literary agents getting murdered?' Margaret sounded alarmed.

It was useless to deny it. 'We're asking a lot of questions of a lot of aspiring authors,' Flick said. 'Does Cilla have an agent?'

Margaret folded her arms. 'I'd rather not answer any

more, if you don't mind. You can speak to Cilla when ...'
She was interrupted by a shrill 'Hellooo!' As the front
door clicked shut, a small, blonde girl ran into the room,
waving a sheet of paper with twigs glued to it.

'Peg, Peg, I done this!' Penny thrust her work of art
onto her grandmother's knee.

Margaret put on her specs and gave it her full
attention. 'Very good, Penny, but what is it, love?'

'It's a tree! A winter tree. It hasn't any leaves, see?'

'Of course it is. Silly me.'

There was a moment of silence before Penny looked
at Flick and Baggo, who were sitting on the sofa. She
bowed her head away from them. 'Who your friends,
Peg?' she whispered.

'These are ...' At this point, Cilla came in and smiled
vaguely at the officers. 'Police,' Margaret said with
emphasis. She got up, took Penny's hand and led her out.
'Let's get some juice, love,' she said.

'Bye, Penny. I liked your winter tree,' Baggo said
before Margaret closed the door behind her.

'Do you want to see me?' Cilla asked, searching the
officers' faces. Taller than her mother, she held herself well.
Her light blue blouse and jeans were clean and neat and her
darting eyes suggested both personality and intelligence.
The picture did not do her justice, Baggo thought.

Flick soon got to the point. When she mentioned the
agent murders, Cilla began to play with her hair, pushing
it back from her face then twisting it. She said she had
submitted material to all of the dead agents, and
admitted she did not like the high-handed way they dealt

with new writers. She had not yet persuaded an agent to represent her, but was cautiously optimistic about a female agent based in Manchester.

'Do you go to London often?' Baggo asked.

'Do you suspect me?' She pulled the right side of her mouth down, exaggerating the mannerism her mother had painted.

He replied, 'We are questioning a lot of aspiring authors with a view to eliminating as many as possible.'

'So the answer is yes, though there are "a lot" of others. What is "a lot"?'

Flick intervened. 'You can't expect us to tell you that, Ms Pargiter. The better you cooperate, the sooner we'll leave you in peace.'

'I hope you do. But I have to tell you, I've half-expected a visit. You see, I've been in London at the times of all the murders.'

Flick and Baggo exchanged glances. 'You have?' Baggo asked. 'Why?'

'Because I have friends in London. Mates who kept up with me after I dropped out of uni. And I take Penny to see her father. It so happens that the murders have all taken place on days I've been in town. Being a mystery writer, I notice that sort of thing.'

'We'll need a list of the places you've stayed at, please,' Flick said.

'I almost always stay with Lesley Mortimer. She has a flat in Islington.'

'We'll need Penny's father's name and address, too,' Baggo said.

'Alan Trelawney, Five Mosshill Court, St John's Wood. He's a Cornishman. And I've never stayed with him. He's living with a nice Cockney girl who's expecting any day soon, so please don't trample there in your size fourteens.'

'Personally, I have only size nines, so I trample with the utmost delicacy and discretion,' Baggo said.

Cilla looked hard at him. He raised his eyebrows and she started to giggle. He held up his feet for her to inspect and that made her worse.

Flick drummed her fingers on her notebook. 'Could we have the names and addresses of the friends you've seen in London, please?'

'I'll need my diary. Do I have your permission to leave the room?'

'You don't need my permission,' Flick said coldly.

When the door closed, Flick turned on Baggo. 'Just because she's behaving in a childish way doesn't give you an excuse, Chandavarkar,' she hissed. 'This is a murder inquiry.'

'She giggled out of nerves. I'm only trying to get as much as possible out of her,' Baggo muttered.

They sat in silence for nearly ten minutes. Both were wondering if Cilla had escaped by the back door when she re-entered and, with mock formality, handed a sheet of A4 to Flick. 'Names, addresses, phone numbers and dates, as far as I can remember. But please don't embarrass my friends. Some of them have landed pretty good jobs.'

'We don't upset people if we can help it,' Flick said.

'Thank you.' For the next half hour they went through Cilla's movements around the time of each murder. She did not have an alibi for any of them.

'Lesley Mortimer seems happy to put you up. You've spent several nights with her, including a lot of Mondays,' Flick commented.

'She's no housewife. I do a bit of cooking and cleaning for her, and I stay in for deliveries. Alan's a chef. His hours are pretty anti-social, so usually he sees Penny on Sundays and Mondays, and I head north on Tuesdays.'

'I liked the first chapter of your book,' Baggo said, when they finished. 'The priest is an intriguing character, and Hatshepsut was an amazing woman. One day I would like to read the rest.'

'Thanks for that.' Her eyes sparkled as she gave a broad, lop-sided smile. 'Are you interested in ancient Egypt?'

'Yes. The next time I go home to Mumbai, I hope to see the Valley of the Kings and the Valley of the Queens on the way.'

'Well make sure you visit the Cairo Museum. It's fantastic.'

Flick looked at her watch then phoned the taxi number. It arrived quickly and Cilla showed them out, giving Flick a brusque nod and Baggo another crooked smile.

'Don't chat up suspects,' Flick said as the taxi drove off. The rest of their long journey was spent in silence, each of them thankful for the murder mysteries they had bought that morning at King's Cross.

* * *

The next morning, Baggo was glad the sergeant was out of the office. She had irritated him with her cast-iron knickers act. He could tell her love life, if there was one, was not wonderful. Round the nick, she had a reputation for primness, and there was no hint of any lapse into ladetteishness. A few times he had heard her speak on the phone to someone called Tom, but her voice had been cold, their conversations matter-of-fact. There had been no whispered endearments, and she had ended one call looking as if she had just sucked a lemon. Her face was quite plain, he thought, but there was something attractive, and perhaps lively, underneath. She was interested in the extraordinary game called rugby, which looked to him like a legalised fight. A make-over, a few drinks and a shag would do her the world of good. He wished she would relax a bit more. She spent too much time in sergeant mode.

He had not consciously flirted with Cilla Pargiter, just made her relax. That was good police work, in his book. Why was life so difficult, particularly where women were concerned? His father, a consultant urologist at the Bedford Hospital, was determined that he should marry a girl from the Indian community, and a Brahmin at that. Two years earlier his sister, Shilpa, had put up no resistance to the marriage he had arranged for her with the son of a successful restauranteur. Baggo wondered if the boy was gay, but two years on they seemed settled together. Now his father was as desperate for a first grandchild as he was to find a bride for Bagawath. The previous weekend, he had paid one of his rare visits home to find a businessman, originally from Chenai, his wife and daughter there as well. The girl, Rani, had been pleasant, but equally resentful of the match-making attempt. Once they realised they both felt the same way, they got on like a house on fire. He wondered if her parents had been as disappointed as his when told exactly why they had hit it off so well. The truth of the matter was, Baggo found European girls, preferably blondes with fair complexions, fantastically attractive. He could not help it, and Cilla Pargiter ticked all his boxes. It was just a pity she was a suspect in a murder inquiry.

He consulted the list of her friends. Lesley Mortimer was clearly the one with whom to start. He phoned her mobile and they arranged to meet at a café near Covent Garden at one o' clock.

* * *

Flick was apprehensive as she drove into Dogmersfield. Rachel Lawson had been very angry, with cause, and she was not someone to mess with. She parked the car, took a deep breath, and approached the front door. Rachel Lawson answered the bell without delay.

'Please give me five minutes of your time, Mrs Lawson,' Flick said quickly. 'There are questions that have to be asked, and this is the easiest way, I assure you.'

'Is that dreadful inspector with you?'

'No. I'm alone.'

For a moment, Flick wondered if the door was going to be slammed in her face, but it opened wide and she stepped in.

'Come into the kitchen, please. I don't want my husband upset again,' Mrs Lawson said, her tone peremptory.

It was clearly the hub of the house. An Aga occupied one wall, a pan of meat that had been browning sitting off the heat. Potatoes and carrots lay peeled beside the sink. On a busy work surface, dusty with flour, a casserole dish was ready to receive its contents. In the middle of the room, a well-used wooden table held assorted papers, a laptop and a phone.

Mrs Lawson cut through Flick's apology for the previous visit. 'Water under the bridge, but that inspector is an idiot and I will be lodging a complaint in due course. My husband is fine now, but the whole thing shook him up badly. Now, I thought you, or someone else, would be back, and as the dates of the murders have been well-publicised in the press, I have compiled a table showing our movements at the times in question. You will see that I can give you only my word for all except Ms Swanson's murder, but for that morning I have a water-tight alibi. My husband underwent a minor surgical procedure, and I was at Fleet House Nursing Home with him all day. I have written down some of the people who will support me. If you decide to speak to them, I would be obliged if you were as discreet as possible.'

Taken aback, but also relieved, Flick stammered her thanks.

'Not at all, officer,' Mrs Lawson cut across her again. 'I assume that is all. If so, please go.'

Flick could not remember being given so much information in such a short time, with such a lack of respect. She read the paper she had been handed then set the sat-nav for Fleet.

* * *

'We called them the Geordie Girls,' Lesley Mortimer said, speaking through a mouthful of bruschetta. 'They went around together all the time and loved to party. They had loads of friends. Poor Cilla came back in third year, pregnant, with no Penny. It was so horrible. We couldn't bear it. And she dropped out after a couple of weeks. I tried to talk her out of it, but she was so down. Actually, I was scared, if she stayed at uni, she might, you know. A lot of students do, like.'

'I know,' Baggo said. He saw that Lesley could talk for Britain. It would just be a question of keeping her on the right topic.

'We kept in touch, of course. She even came up to St Andrews a couple of times in fourth year. She said it was to research her book, but we all knew she wanted some fun. I can't imagine having a baby to think about all the time. She's a great mum, of course. We all knew she would be. But you wanted to know about her coming up to London. Usually it's a couple of times a month, depending on Alan's shifts. He's a chef, you know, at The Ritz. He was at some Jamie Oliver place in Cornwall when he met Cill. I keep looking for him on TV, but he hasn't managed that yet. I couldn't bear to try to cook with the nation watching. Actually, I can't boil an egg, but you don't need to when you're an investment banker. You just need to be hard-boiled yourself.' She gave a brief, horsey laugh.

'Cilla's mum's great,' she continued, 'but I think Cill needs to get away from her. I don't know, but I think there was a time when she blamed Cill for Penny's death. Don't know how she could. They were so close. It was a drowning accident, and the body wasn't found. Cill doesn't talk about it, and clams up when she's asked. Don't blame her, I suppose.'

Baggo nodded sympathetically.

'I know these murders are terrible, but literary agents can be horrible. Cill has this really, really good novel. I've read it, and it's miles better than half the stuff you see on the shelves. Yet she can't even get an agent to show it to publishers. Of course she is hurt and angry. I know I'm in a dog-eat-dog world, but it's not as bad as the literary world. I keep reminding her about all the great writers who've been rejected umpteen times, but it doesn't cheer her up much.'

'What does she do during her time here?' Baggo asked.

'Oh, sorry. Yes. Well, we go to the pub, meet friends. There's the odd party, but as she doesn't usually arrive till Sunday, not so many of these. Little Penny's with Alan most of the time. Actually, Cilla comes and goes from my flat. She has a key, and I let her drive my car. She's even got a child seat for it. I like the company, and it's useful as she's often here on Mondays, so I get deliveries and tradesmen to call when she's going to be around. She's a terrific cook, too.'

'Has she ever done or said anything that looks suspicious now that you know we're investigating murders?'

Lesley screwed up her face. Slowly, she said, 'I know she's cut bits out of the paper. I think they may have related to the murders, but as they'd been cut out, I couldn't be sure.'

'How often?'

'A few times, but I didn't pay attention. I just thought it was a bit odd. I remember coming home on some Tuesday nights, including yesterday, and the week before, to find the paper cut up.'

'Did she say why she did that?'

'No, but she would be away when I got back, and I never thought to ask her.'

'What about last Sunday? Can you remember when she arrived?'

'No. I spent the day with a friend and got in about, yes, eight it was. She was there, watching TV. We had a glass of wine then bed.'

'If I give you a list of particular days, could you give me as much detail as you can about what Ms Pargiter did on them?'

'No chance without my Blackberry, which is at the

office. What dates are you interested in?'

Baggo told her and she made a note. Then they exchanged e-mail addresses. He took down details of her car then thanked her.

'I'll look all this up when I get home and e-mail you.' She looked at him, frowning. 'She's my friend, but I'm not going to lie for her. I can tell you, though, she did not kill these people.'

* * *

Whoever had plunged the lethal syringe into Linda Swanson was neither R. Lawson nor R. L. Lawson, both of whom were in the process of making a lasting impression on the staff of the Fleet House Nursing Home. He had been convinced that the man in the next room had stolen his newest flannelette pyjamas, while his wife oversaw every detail of his care with a protective zeal as touching as it was irritating. With time to spare, Flick decided to return to the Noble household.

She recognised Gill's dumpy figure with the ponies beside the house and decided to talk to her away from her mother and Parker.

'They'll be glad to get their blankets off today,' was her opening remark.

Gill shrugged. 'Suppose.'

'What are their names?'

'This is Buttercup.' She stroked the white flash on the nose of the light brown one she was feeding. 'And that's

Daisy.' She indicated the smaller, pure black pony grazing nearby.

'Nice names. Do you ride much?'

'Yes. Like, I love all horses and ponies.'

'I used to ride a bit, but I didn't have a horse, and it became difficult.'

Gill showed no interest, but whispered something into Buttercup's ear.

Flick tried again. 'Does your sister ride?'

'Yes, but she's so more interested in other things.'

'Such as?'

'Music and stuff. Twittering.'

'I hear the funeral's tomorrow.'

Gill nodded and whispered again to Buttercup.

'Lionel Parker's doing the eulogy.'

Gill pretended she hadn't heard.

'You don't like him, do you?'

'So what?'

'Gill, your father was murdered, and I know you're really upset, but I'm trying to find out who killed him. If I'm to do that, I need to know what was going on in your family.'

'Why? Everyone says it was, like, Crimewriter who killed him.' Her voice caught as she said 'killed'.

'Who's everyone?'

Gill shook her head. 'Everyone on Twitter. Blogs.'

Flick sighed. If the traditional press did not apply enough pressure to an investigation, the new media, virtually uncontrolled, could make things very difficult.

'It may be Crimewriter or it may not. We wouldn't be

doing our job if we made an assumption like that. Why don't you like Lionel Parker?'

Gill wiped the back of her hand across her eyes then pressed her forehead against Buttercup's nose. 'It's him and Mum.'

'I'm listening,' Flick said softly.

'I've seen them kissing. Like once. He's always around the house. He pretends, pretended, he wanted to speak to Dad, but I saw through him. So did Jenny. She hates him, too.'

'Did you see him on Sunday evening, when your dad went missing?'

She shook her head then turned violently to Flick. 'Even if Lionel did kill Dad, Mum had, like, nothing to do with it, I promise. She's cried her eyes out, and she's been so not cool with Lionel.'

'How do you mean?'

As Gill screwed up her face, a shout came from the house. Parker rushed over and addressed Flick angrily.

'You have no right to harass this girl, officer. She is very distressed.'

'I have no intention of harassing anyone, Mr Parker. We were talking about horses. May I have a word with you, please?'

Parker looked from Flick to an equally stony-faced Gill and back again. 'Come to the house.' He turned on his heel and marched towards the front door.

'Thank you,' Flick said to Gill. 'If ever you want to talk to me, here's my card.'

Gill hesitated before taking the card, but she put it in

a pocket of her gilet and turned back to Buttercup.

Parker held the front door open as he waited for Flick.

'In here,' he said, showing her into a room lined with bookcases and filing cabinets, dominated by a large, mahogany table used as a desk. It was obviously the dead man's study.

'I don't want Vanessa upset further,' he said, occupying the leather swivel chair behind the table. He crossed his legs and sat back. 'Well, what is it?' he barked.

Flick was not going to be intimidated. Without waiting for an invitation, she sat in the balloon-back chair facing him. 'What were you doing between three and six on Sunday afternoon?'

He sat forward and glared. 'I can't believe you asked that question.'

'Well I did. What were you doing?'

'I was at home.'

'Can anyone vouch for you?'

'No. I live alone, and no one was visiting. Does that satisfy you?'

'Have you ever been married?'

Parker was silent for a moment. 'That's none of your business, but I suppose you'll be able to find out anyway. I was divorced some years ago.'

'How would you describe your relationship with Richard Noble?'

'Best friends. Had been since university.'

'Never a cross word?'

'That's a fatuous question.' He sat back again. 'Of course

we had disagreements, but nothing serious, nothing that lasted. We ran a very successful business together.'

'Do you have any idea about the terms of Mr Noble's will?'

He answered quickly and his eyes flashed to the right. 'None whatsoever.'

'Lastly, how would you describe your relationship with Mrs Noble?'

Parker's face had been getting redder with each question. He stood up, his fists clenched. Flick could see that he wanted to attack her and prepared to move quickly.

Speaking very quietly, he said, 'Of all the impertinent questions you have asked, that is the most abominable. I refuse to dignify it with a reply.'

Flick smiled at him as she rose. 'Thank you, Mr Parker. This interview has been most informative. I shall see myself out.'

Instead of getting into her car, she walked over to Gill. 'Who's the family solicitor?' she asked.

'Marcus Ramsay. He's in Guildford,' Gill replied without hesitation.

Pleased that her stock with Gill had risen, Flick walked slowly to her car, aware of Parker's highly-coloured face framed by the study window.

* * *

'I fail to see the point of this, Sergeant, but if you tell me it is relevant to your inquiry I shall, of course, give you all the assistance I properly can.' Marcus Ramsay was not the stereotype family solicitor. He was tall, with a round, fresh face and panda eyes. His golden tan ended abruptly at polo-neck level. Flick noted his athletic movement as he resumed his seat after shaking her hand. Tie-less and jacket-less, he sat back and looked inquiringly at her across an uncluttered desk.

This lawyer is a lot more fanciable than the one I have at home, she thought. 'It is relevant,' she said, poker faced, noting the absence of a ring on his left hand.

'I thought someone they're calling Crimewriter was responsible.' He spoke with an unforced public school confidence.

'That's just the press and Twitter. It may be one person, but we have to look at each crime individually. If we didn't, Crimewriter's brief would take us to the cleaners.'

'I'm jolly glad I don't do crime. A good friend has gone into that game. He defends all sorts of ghastly people. I couldn't do it, I don't think.' He flashed a brilliant white smile. 'If a client ends up in court, for any reason, I reckon it's a defeat.'

A likeable lawyer, Flick thought, if a bit posh. She said, 'Could you tell me about Richard Noble's will?'

'Not much to tell. Apart from a few legacies that are not particularly big, everything goes to Vanessa.'

'How old is the will?'

'Just over ten years.'

'Had he been thinking of changing anything?'

'Spot on, Sergeant.' He gave her another view of his

gleaming teeth. 'He had been consulting me regarding Inheritance Tax planning. I believe Vanessa was against him running that marathon, and, frankly, I saw her point. Richard liked his food. He kept a very fine cellar, too. I mean, he wasn't a drunk, or anything like it, but he carried a pound or two more than he should have. Anyway, it having dawned on him that he was not immortal, he came to see me and we discussed the options. After some humming and hawing, he went for a trust tied up with a bond. His two daughters were to be the only beneficiaries. That involved an immediate payment of £300,000 to set up the trust. He had to realise some investments and was doing that when he died. The paper-work was in draft form, and the process could have been completed within a fortnight.'

'Do you know if he discussed this with Lionel Parker?'

'I have to be careful here, but Richard told me that setting up the trust now meant putting on hold plans the agency had to expand. In New York, I believe. He did say Lionel was cross with him.'

'Have you any knowledge of a relationship between Mr Parker and Mrs Noble?'

Unsmiling, Marcus said, 'I hope you don't expect me to gossip, Sergeant.'

Flick pushed on. 'Did Richard Noble have any suspicions that he shared with you, Mr Ramsay?'

'No. If that's all …'

Noting the polite but icy tone, Flick decided not to outstay her welcome. In the car, she reflected that it might be necessary to re-visit the handsome Mr Ramsay later in the inquiry.

* * *

Baggo sat in a coffee shop round the corner from The Ritz, trying to spot Alan Trelawney as he arrived after lunch service. All the likely candidates had company or joined a table. At length, a tall, sharp-featured young man came in. His jet-black hair was unfashionably long, and he brushed it back as he looked round. His black leather jacket hung loosely, revealing an open-necked check shirt and jeans with a white belt. To Baggo, he seemed like a sort of urban Heathcliffe, a man with pulling power. He went over to him, introduced himself, showed Trelawney to a table apart from other customers then went to buy two coffees.

'Cilla's a good mother,' Trelawney said defensively, once Baggo had explained the purpose of their meeting.

'No doubt, but we need to know a bit more about her.'

'Try asking her.' The Cornish burr came across strongly.

'We have spoken to her and her mother. Hopefully, we will be able to eliminate her from our inquiries once we have learned some more. I gather you were working in Cornwall when you met her and her sister?'

'That's right. Fifteen Cornwall. A great training. Got me to The Ritz.'

'And they were on holiday?'

'Yes.'

'Did you not date Penny, the sister who died?'

He raised his eyebrows. 'Yes.'

'Yet, Cilla got pregnant?'

'Stuff happens.' Nonchalantly, he sipped his coffee.

'Are you sure the little girl is yours?'

'Yes.'

'Have you had a DNA test?'

'No. But I'm sure. What does that have to do with these murders?'

'We have to know the full picture, Mr Trelawney. Does Cilla bring Penny down quite often to see you?'

'Yes. Roughly twice or three times a month, depending on my shifts. Usually she drops Penny off on Sunday afternoon and picks her up on Tuesday morning. I don't know what she does between times.'

'Last Sunday, do you remember when she dropped Penny with you?'

Trelawney's hooded eyes narrowed to a slit. 'It was quite late in the afternoon, I believe.'

'Can you be more precise?'

He scratched the stubble in front of his left ear. 'It was definitely after four. Perhaps nearer five.'

'Is there anything that helps you pinpoint the time?'

'I remember it was time for Penny to be fed. I'd made fish fingers for her.' He gave an earthy chuckle. 'Not as good as packet stuff, naturally.'

Baggo sat back and shook his head. 'Chivalry could land you in very hot water, Mr Trelawney,' he said.

Trelawney screwed up his face. 'What do you mean?'

'What I say. Ms Pargiter has already told us when she dropped Penny with you.'

'Oh.' He drained his cup. Avoiding Baggo's stare, he said, 'All right. The fish fingers must have been for lunch. Sorry, I forgot.'

'Mr Trelawney, if you mess me about you could find yourself behind bars, and this does Cilla no good. No good at all. Now, I'm going to give you a list of dates and I want you to tell me as much as you can about each of them. Do you have your diary here?'

He nodded. They spent the next twenty minutes going through the dates when agents had been murdered. Penny had been looked after by her father at the time of each killing. Trelawney repeatedly stressed that he had seen nothing suspicious and that Cilla was an excellent mother. He promised to contact Baggo if he remembered anything relevant, but they both knew his memory would not extend beyond details that were exculpatory.

* * *

The hour between five and six was officially Cocktail Hour in the Roman Road pub, but the last time a customer had asked the barman for a screwdriver, he had wanted to stab someone. Osborne sat at the back, waiting for Weasel. A few shifty-eyed regulars occupied the other end of the pub, glancing in his direction as if he carried the plague.

'I just tell 'im a load of rubbish,' Weasel hissed at

them as he limped past. 'The drinks'll be on me when the fat bastard slings 'is 'ook.'

He sat beside Osborne, and said quietly, 'This you 'ave to 'ear, Noelly, but it'll cost you. The word's out that I'm helping you. I tell everyone I just give you rubbish, but I still got a slap.' He rubbed his left leg. 'Wot's this?' He looked with derision at the forty pounds Osborne had slipped under a beermat.

After that sum had been doubled, and Weasel had taken another twenty to buy a large whisky and a coke, he got down to business.

'Fifth of March. That's Johnny's release date. On licence, of course, but that's not going to stop him coming after you.'

'Really?' Osborne's bowels loosened. He wished he had something stronger than coke in his glass.

'Yeh. And he reckons you're itching to expose his crap alibis and fit him up as Crimewriter, who's been killing them agents. He's certain there's a prison officer who's ready to squeal. I don't know who that is. Now, you've got to know just one important thing, but it'll cost you.'

Another eighty pounds found its way to Weasel's pocket, with another twenty to buy, this time, two double whiskies.

'I thought you were off this stuff, Noelly.' Weasel placed the glasses reverently on the table. 'It'll be the stress, I reckon. I'd be blinking stressed if I had Johnny after my guts in a couple of weeks.'

The standard blend barely touched the sides of his

throat as Osborne drained his glass. As the heat radiated from his stomach, he breathed deeply and scratched his crotch. 'What is it, damn you?' he hissed.

'All in good time, Noelly. All in good time.' Weasel swirled round his tongue the Speyside malt he had ordered for himself. Seeing Osborne was fit to burst, he leaned towards him. 'You ain't never going to pin Crimewriter on him, because the 'Arvey Nicks murder took place about lunchtime on fifteenth February, which just 'appened to be the date of his final Parole Board hearing. I think that was in the afternoon. He's told his mates in Littlepool, that whether you fit him up as Crimewriter or not, you'll be dead meat by Easter. He's serious about you, Noelly. I'd watch out if I was you. Either that or put my affairs in order.'

'Could you get a message to him, from me, saying I promise he won't be accused of being Crimewriter?'

'That'll be a ton. And it won't work. 'E's mad because you fitted him up for the stretch he's finishing.'

'Tell him anyway. And I only have sixty. You've cleaned me out.'

Weasel shook his head. 'Seeing as it's you, Noelly. But remember to bring plenty the next time.'

It was time for a change of tactics. Speaking quietly and slowly, in the way that had encouraged many to confess in the days before interviews were recorded, Osborne said: 'Remember who it is you're dealing with, you poisonous little scrote. Still collecting other people's credit cards, are you? When were you last in the Scrubs? Now, I don't give a barmaid's tits about the truth. I want evidence that'll sink Johnson. Once he's out, the rest of the cons'll be at each other like ferrets in a bag, trying to become the jail's top bloody ferret. Now, I want to know who's going to win that battle, and I want them on my side, getting me the evidence I need. I can help them, Weasel, arrange for stuff to be found on particular persons. You know the score. And you are going to help me to help them. Right?'

His face twitching, Weasel nodded feverishly. 'Right, Noelly, right. No offence meant, big man.'

'None taken. Yet. Be in touch.' Osborne stood and walked out slowly, conscious that every eye in the pub followed him.

As soon as he had gone, Weasel scurried over to the regulars.

'Who wants a drink on Inspector No? Probably your last chance to get one. Dead man walking, 'im.'

16

'Mrs Smith for you, Sarge,' Danny Peters called.

'Who?'

'Says she's from Sandwich. Something to do with the Debut Dagger.'

'Oh, that Mrs Smith. Could you transfer the call?'

Half an hour later, Flick was heading for lunch at Sandwich with 'that charming young Indian officer' in the passenger seat. Not in the mood for Chandavarkar's chatter, she turned on Radio 2 then mentally switched off.

The weekend had left her unsettled. Tom, who had drunk a lot of good claret at Sunday lunch, had complimented her on her parking ('You are clever. You know, you park like a man,') and had taken umbrage when she complained about him being pompous, sexist and patronising. Half an hour later, they had ended their relationship with a blazing row. She didn't mind him dismissing her political correctness, as he sometimes expressed himself with scant regard for others' feelings, but the accusation that she had no sense of humour hurt.

'You only laugh if someone else puts up a big sign with "joke" written on it,' he said. Of course she took life more seriously than most, but did it go further? Did she laugh at all if other people didn't? When had she last laughed on her own? Why did she find Chandavarkar vaguely irritating, when everyone else smiled at his way of speaking? Why did she prefer not to call him Baggo? In short, did Tom have a point?

He wasn't so bad, she told herself. Just over-influenced by his arrogant fellow barristers. He was no more sexist than most men, and much more considerate than many. He talked intelligently, read widely, remembered her birthday. His politics, like her own, were Liberal, and his basic instincts were sound. His personal habits were not coarse. She had been comfortable with him, most of the time anyway. He had proposed to her once, but she had turned him down so emphatically that he hadn't raised the subject again. A few months ago, she had wondered if, after all ... But he persistently spoiled himself with silly, unfunny remarks.

Beside her, Chandavarkar, no, Baggo, chuckled at something Ken Bruce said on the radio. She forced herself to smile. She had nearly gone alone to see Mrs Smith, but she had clearly wanted to see Baggo. She had also wanted to meet the Inspector, but Flick had drawn the line at bringing him. Quite apart from having to put up with him in the car, he was likely to antagonise their host so she would give them no more help. She was sure he was drinking again, and she couldn't understand his approach to the inquiry. In fact, she couldn't understand why he was still in charge of it. He vetoed any inquiry into Pyotr's Place or the Russians, despite the leads Chapayev had given them, and he was impatient for someone to pinpoint a writer so that he could throw the proverbial book at them. Perhaps, if he made a complete mess of things, he would be forced to retire. Would that blight her career too? Certainly, it would do her no end of good to be seen as a driving force behind a high-profile success, but that was a distant prospect.

Flick gasped at the mass of brilliant red blossom on the camellia in front of which they parked. The few weeks since their first visit had seen many changes in Mrs Smith's garden. Yellow and blue crocuses blanketed the grass beside the driveway and a forest of green spears promised an abundance of daffodils.

'Spring is in the air, Sarge. It is good to be alive,' Baggo said, stretching and inhaling the fresh, seaside air.

Flick looked across the car roof. Baggo was smiling and swinging his arms. He has a point, she thought. 'You're right, er, Baggo,' she said. 'I bet we'll get a good lunch at least.'

The Smiths, Jane and Arthur, as they insisted on being called, gave them a warm welcome.

'Guess what little extra I put in it?' Jane beamed as appreciative noises greeted her chilli con carne. 'Dark chocolate,' she carried on. 'It's amazing how it goes with strong meats. It can lift venison. I think I might use it as a way of inserting poison into a dish. In my next novel, of course.'

'She threatens to practise on me,' Arthur said, dead-pan.

Flick caught herself smiling after Baggo had chuckled.

The inquiry was not mentioned during the meal. Jane asked various questions about how police procedure had changed over the last seventy years, then Arthur and Flick had a lively discussion about rugby. 'I'm Scottish, actually,' he explained. 'I was named after a wonderful rugger player. I was a fly-half, you know. Just missed out on a place in the Varsity Match.' They both reckoned England and Scotland had a way to go, and that France would probably win the Six Nations.

After lunch had been cleared, Arthur left for his office. On his way out he passed an imaginary ball to Flick, something neither officer could imagine when they had first met him.

Jane brought more coffee to the sitting room. 'May I ask how your inquiry is going?' she said. 'These murders are causing great concern in the publishing world.'

'We haven't found it easy,' Flick said slowly.

'Are you really conducting two inquiries, the so-called Crimewriter one, and one involving the Russians and Linda Swanson?'

Flick said, 'We're keeping an open mind, but could we talk, in confidence, about one or two suspects we've got among the Debut Dagger entrants?'

Jane sat forward. 'I hoped you'd say that.'

Baggo pulled four files from his briefcase. 'It would be very helpful to know what these entries tell you about each author. They may not tell you anything, of course.'

Jane opened the top file. 'Let's see the opening line. "It had been a typical day in the desert, hot, dry and tense. Bob Tomkins shuffled the grimy cards and dealt another hand." Not the best, I'm afraid.'

She leafed through the remaining pages then opened the next file. '"Friar Alfred gently pulled the widow's eyelids over sightless eyes. His elegant Latin prayer was drowned by the bestial howls of four new orphans." Better. Let's see the next one.' She continued reading. 'Oh dear,' she said after a minute. 'I think you'd call this top-shelf stuff.' She wrinkled her nose. 'I hope no one gives this one a contract, but you never know these days.'

Turning to the last file, she said, 'I remember this one. It's actually shortlisted. "Timeless sand ended the priest's time on earth. As scorched grains snuffed out his life, one thought prepared him for his voyage on the boat of the dead: revenge."' She put it with the rest. 'Being buried alive is a ghastly death. Poor Richard Noble. Is that all you want me to look at?'

Flick said, 'There are two more, but they have alibis for one of the murders. Any thoughts you have would be welcome.' She nodded to Baggo, who handed the Johnson and Lawson files to Jane. 'Once you've had a chance to think about them, we'd be most grateful if you were to get in touch. And thank you for the splendid lunch.' She got up.

'Before you go,' Jane said, 'I have an idea.'

* * *

On the way home, they decided to check up on the Francis family. The exterior of the flat was no more inviting than it had been the last time they had called. A solitary light burned in the sitting room. Out of the corner of his eye, Baggo saw a curtain twitch as they approached the door. He rang the bell twice without anyone answering, then put his mouth to the letter-box. 'I know you are in. This is the police. If you do not open the door in thirty seconds, I will break it.'

'No warrant,' Flick mouthed, but forced entry was not required.

'I'm sorry. I didn't hear the bell over the radio,' Matilda Francis looked flustered as she opened the door a fraction. Baggo pushed gently and stepped into the dark hall. Flick followed, closing the door behind her. Matilda put her hand up to her forehead and stammered that her husband was out. Baggo led the way past her into the sitting room. Shaking, Matilda tried to brush hair across her face, but failed to conceal a purple lump above her left eye.

'Where are the boys?' Flick asked.

'In their rooms.'

'We want to see them. First, though, how did your forehead come to be bruised?'

'I walked into a door,' she whispered.

'I just know that's not true,' Baggo said quietly. 'The more often you lie for him, the worse it's going to get. Believe me.'

'We'll come back to that,' Flick said. 'Where is your husband?'

'I don't know.' She wiped her face with her sleeve.

'When did he leave?'

'Some time today, and I don't know when he'll be

back. He has research to do. Lots of research.'

Flick stood close in front of her. 'Was he here on Sunday twenty-first February? That's Sunday before last.'

'Oh yes. He was here.'

'What did you do?'

'I cooked lunch and we all watched television.'

'What was on?'

Her face fell and she shook her head. 'I'm not sure. I … I can't remember.'

'What about Monday fifteenth February, a fortnight ago today, about lunch time?'

'He was here.'

'Is there anything that makes you remember that?'

'Apart from his fist,' Baggo cut in.

'Nothing in particular.' Matilda stared at Baggo, almost flinching, as she answered Flick's question.

'When did you walk into that door?' Baggo asked.

'The Wednesday before last, I think it was. I'm not sure.'

'Where are the boys?' Flick repeated.

'In their rooms, doing homework,' she whispered.

Without saying more, Flick went to Harold's door. She rapped once then entered. The boy lay on his bed, books open in front of him. He wore a cast on his right forearm.

'Hello, Harold. How did you get that?' Flick asked.

Harold's eyes darted about. 'Fell on my way back from school.'

'Was your dad there when you fell?' Baggo asked.

The boy's mouth opened and he looked at the floor. 'No.'

Flick carried on. 'Are you sure?'

He nodded.

'Was your brother there?'

'No.'

'Don't you walk to and from school together?'

'Not that day.'

'Which day was it?'

'The Wednesday before last.'

'Have you or your brother been smacked or put in the stocks since we last saw you?'

Close to tears, Harold shook his head.

Feeling increasingly uncomfortable, Flick asked about the days of the Swanson and Noble murders. Monosyllabically, Harold confirmed that his father had been at home on both dates. The television programme his mother had forgotten was a film about Robin Hood.

When Flick finished, Baggo was last to leave the room. He turned and said, 'Bad luck your mum's head being injured. On the same day as you fell, too.' The brief flash of anger he saw on the boy's face confirmed what he thought.

Rufus started when they entered his room. He said little, spoke quietly and avoided eye contact, but appeared less troubled by the questions. He gave the same answers as his brother, except he said he was there when Harold had fallen on an icy pavement. He had to think briefly before saying his dad had not been present.

'We'll be back,' Flick promised as Matilda showed them out.

In the car, they discussed what to do.

'We should really inform Social Services,' Flick said.

'I'll bet my bottom dollar he is abusing the lot of them, but it will never prove, and they will all firm up on their lies. Besides, it might mess up Jane's plan if Francis feels he has to concentrate on fighting the social workers.'

'What if he really hurts one of them?'

'We need only a couple of weeks, and if he is Crimewriter, we'll stop him killing people, and abusing his family. For good, I hope,' Baggo added, grinning.

There was nothing funny about that, Flick thought, but she grinned anyway. 'All right. We'll do it your way,' she said.

* * *

As Flick reversed into a space in the pool car park, her i-Phone sounded. Baggo answered for her. He listened for a minute then turned to her.

'Osborne will be with us in a jiffy. Another agent's been murdered. We're to go to the scene. A car park.'

Flick cursed under her breath and turned off the engine. 'Pit stop,' she muttered and got out.

'Good idea,' Baggo said to himself. Following her into the building, he nearly collided with Osborne and Peters.

'Wrong way, Baggo. You're coming too,' Osborne barked.

'I'm sure you don't want my weak bladder to compromise your crime scene, gov.' He ran to the toilets, and was out of earshot before Osborne could think up a suitably obscene reply.

Her pit stop over, Flick was not going to hurry for Osborne. She saw him look at his watch as he waited in the front passenger seat, so walked slowly and stretched before getting back into the car.

'Everyone got their pink lipstick on? Got to look our best if we're meeting a dead body. He's got plenty of time, even if I bloody haven't.'

She ignored him.

Their destination was a public, multi-storey car park off Bayswater Road. It had been closed to all but police. A crowd had gathered outside. Some were curious bystanders and others, more agitated, wanted to drive away in their parked cars. Flick eased her way through the melee and found a space on the ground floor. The flash of a camera told them that the press knew of the latest killing. They used the stairs to go up to the fourth. An area had been taped off, and sterile-suited SOCOs were already busy dusting for fingerprints. Horns and raised voices from below could be heard through the open walls. Near the lift, a white canopy shielded the body. Osborne went straight there.

The body was of a casually-dressed male who looked about fifty. He lay on his back. A red puddle had formed under his waist. On his forehead there was an irregular area of red from which trickles of blood had oozed.

Dr Dai Williams was shining a pencil torch into the wound, his face almost touching the dead man's. 'It looks as if this chap's been shot or stabbed in the back. This injury to the forehead is probably some form of desecration after death. The killer may even have tried to write something, but I can't see what.'

'Bastard,' Osborne muttered.

'Exactly so. But a clever one, I think.'

Osborne snorted. 'We both know the score, Doc. We need you to tell us as much as possible ASAP, and you can only do that once you've got him back to your morgue. What do we know about him?'

A uniformed sergeant stepped forward. 'He's Laurence Robertson, age fifty-one, sir, a literary agent. He works near here and lives in Notting Hill. I got that from his wallet and papers he carried in his briefcase. He was found by a motorist just after six pm, already dead. The man phoned us by mobile and stayed here. He's giving a statement now. The body has not been moved as far as I am aware.'

'Is anyone checking to see if any of these people downstairs saw anything? I don't want the bloody newspapers telling me the names of witnesses.'

'There's something under this car.' The shout came from a constable lying beside a four-by-four. Carefully, he pulled something metal from beneath the vehicle and held it up. It was a nail gun. A nail protruded from the barrel. 'There's blood on it,' he said.

As everyone else craned to see what they assumed was the murder weapon, Baggo turned to Flick.

'I wonder ...'

'Where certain people are right now.' She finished the sentence for him. 'We should ...' She nodded towards Osborne.

'Best not, I think. Tell him, I mean. Sarge?'

She nudged Peters. 'Baggo and I are off to check some alibis. You tell the Inspector in five minutes.'

As Peters protested and Osborne gleefully proclaimed that the killer had just made his first big mistake, Flick and Baggo slipped away.

A camera flashed as they sped out of the narrow exit from the car park.

Flick said, 'This should be one of Candice Dalton's nights at the Mile End Road hostel. We'll try there first.'

Baggo got out his i-Phone and his notebook. 'I'll arrange for some other people to receive visits.' He reached up to put a blue light, in silent mode, on the car roof, then phoned a succession of police stations, starting with Bracknell.

He ended the last call as they drew up outside the hostel. By then he had invoked the name of Chief Superintendent Cumberland himself in an attempt to persuade one over-burdened duty sergeant to send someone out to Dogmersfield in double-quick time.

Inside the hallway, Candice Dalton sat at a table, sipping a cup of tea and talking earnestly to a young man with darting, frightened eyes and filthy, ill-fitting clothes.

'Could we have a word, Mrs Dalton?' Flick asked.

'In a minute, once I've finished with Derek,' she replied firmly.

'This is urgent,' Flick snapped.

'So are Derek's housing needs. This won't take long.' She made a note in the ledger. 'Date of birth?' she asked the youth.

Without a warrant, Flick decided to give in, but as soon as the young man had shuffled off through the door leading deeper inside the building, she leaned over the table and asked Mrs Dalton to account for her movements over the last three hours.

'Oh. Do I need an alibi?' she asked, then brought her hand to her mouth. 'Not another agent? Oh no.' She shook her head.

Flick said, 'I'm afraid that's right, but please tell us what we need to know. Time is precious.'

'I think I'm entitled to know if I'm suspected of killing someone.'

'We're trying to eliminate as many people as we can. That's why time is important.'

'Well, I've nothing to hide. I looked round various places where people who need our help might be.'

'Did you have a car?' Baggo asked.

'Yes. I took the hostel car. Oh, and I went to a bookbinder in Highgate to pick up a present for my husband. He'll be fifty on Wednesday.'

'Can you give us evidence of this?' Flick asked.

Mrs Dalton sighed. 'I've a lot to do this evening, but I suppose you're only doing your job. I think I've got something here that might help.' She picked a large, shabby handbag off the floor and rummaged in it. Eventually, from her purse, she drew a credit card slip and handed it to Flick.

Flick examined it carefully. It was a Mastercard slip. The payer was Candice Dalton, the payee Horace McElhinney, Bookbinder, Highgate. The payment was

£89.40, verified by PIN, and the transaction had taken place that day at 17.44.

'If you must see the book, I warn you it's rather special, so please be careful,' Mrs Dalton said, getting to her feet and heading for the door. She led the way round the back, passing from a dark lane to a small courtyard, suddenly lit by a movement-sensitive lamp, where two cars had been abandoned rather than parked. One was a Vauxhall Nova, the other a Fiat Punto, and both needed a wash. Skidding slightly on the film of ice that had formed on the uneven paving stones, Mrs Dalton approached the Punto and unlocked the passenger door, which boasted a dent the grime could not conceal. From under the passenger seat she brought a parcel wrapped in brown paper. '*The King's Book of Sports* by Govett. It's about the games you could play on Sundays under the Stuarts. It's very rare. This copy was in terrible condition, but it's lovely now. Do you want me to unwrap it?'

'That won't be necessary, Mrs Dalton. Thank you for your time.' Flick said.

'Yes, please,' Baggo said simultaneously.

Mrs Dalton looked from one to the other.

'If it wouldn't be too much trouble,' Flick said, shrugging.

Mrs Dalton placed the parcel on the car roof and slowly began to unwrap it, trying not to tear the paper. She exposed a small, calfskin-bound volume, the title printed in gold on the front. Baggo ran his fingers over it.

'Beautiful,' he murmured.

Flick thanked Mrs Dalton tersely, turned on her heel and strode towards the police car. As Mrs Dalton re-wrapped the book, Baggo thanked her more profusely, his hand feeling the frost that was forming on the Fiat's bonnet.

'Cool as a cucumber,' he said, once in the passenger seat of the police car.

'An excellent alibi,' Flick conceded. 'Her engine was cold, too. I felt it while she was fiddling with her parcel.'

Baggo grinned. 'I was talking about my feet. It's a cold night, Sarge.'

'Where to now?' Flick asked.

Before Baggo could answer, his phone vibrated. 'The Inspector,' he said before answering.

'What the hell are you and Fortune playing at? Get you arses back to the station double-quick. You'd better have something good, or you're both dead meat.'

17

The whiteboard had been almost entirely taken over by the Crimewriter inquiry, as everyone now called it. Other cases had been either shifted to other officers or put on the back burner. They occupied a small area bounded by a thick line of red marker ink. Baggo busied himself writing up the latest developments in green; a visit from Chief Superintendent Cumberland was expected at noon, and he would demand to see progress.

Osborne, in earlier than usual, swept a pile of unfiled papers into a drawer of his desk and drew his sleeve over the surface. His feet crunching the sugar he had sprayed over the vinyl floor, he crossed the room and stood behind Baggo.

'So, six victims now,' he said. 'What about the suspects? We can lose the kinky journo. The twisted bastard only came into Stanhope's case. And for Christ's sake scrub that stuff about Chapayev and the Russkies. Bloody Jumbo'll have a fit if he sees that. We're looking for one killer for all these cases.'

'Have you heard much from Chapayev recently, gov?' Baggo asked. There was something odd about Osborne's attitude to the Russian angle, and Baggo could not put his finger on it.

'He hasn't phoned for a bit, thank God. I spoke to him last week and told him in no uncertain terms that his press rantings weren't in the least bloody helpful. I said our inquiries are proceeding quietly but well.'

'How did he take that?'

'Lots of bluster and shouting, as you'd expect. I told him I was going to solve the case and I was more interested in catching the bleeding criminal than starting World War bloody Three.'

'Ooh, gov. He would love that.'

'Too right he didn't. But I haven't heard from him since. Bloody Eastern Europeans come here and think they can bring their bloody wars with them. Same as ...' He cast his eye over the board. 'Why don't we have photos of all the crap crime writers?'

'Because Dalton, Francis and Lawson are not on Facebook, gov, and they do not have records. The pictures of Wallace and Cilla Pargiter are not very good, but we are spoilt for choice with Johnson.'

Osborne grimaced and lit a cigarette. 'Well, make sure you put up all the stuff about alibis. The more we get on the board, the more Jumbo will like it.'

'It is a pity about Johnson's parole hearing. It gets him neatly out of the Swanson murder.'

'Ah, there you're wrong, Baggo. Danny found out yesterday that the hearing was at half past three. Ms Swanson was skewered just before one o' clock and Johnny could have got from that ponsy store to a tube, then to Victoria. There's a station five minutes' walk from the jail. He could have been tucked up in his little cell, ready to see the do-gooders, by two thirty.'

'That would take nerve, gov. If the trains let him down …'

'Johnny's got plenty of that. More's the pity. He's our number one suspect. You do realise that, Baggo?' He snatched the pen and scrawled 'COULD KILL L. S. AND STILL MAKE HEARING' under Johnson's name.

'Yes, gov. Do I keep Candice Dalton and R. L. Lawson on the board?'

'You bet. I want to let Jumbo see how busy we've been. Have you double-checked that credit card alibi?'

'I was going to do that this morning, gov.'

'It'll keep for a bit. As soon as Fortune brings her pretty backside into work, I want the pair of you to visit Robertson's office.' He studied the board, sucking nicotine deep into his lungs and holding it there before grudgingly allowing thin wafts of smoke to drift from his lips. 'So the long and the short of it is, we can't eliminate anyone after last night?'

'Francis was definitely out at the time of the murder, and he couldn't say exactly where he was when questioned later; Dalton you know about; Johnson was definitely in his cell three hours after the killing, but …'

'Like Swanson's murder. Pity they didn't send someone round sooner. He sets up these situations, Baggo. You mark my words.'

'Lawson was checked too late to be helpful, though her alibi for the Swanson murder is rock-solid. Wallace was out on his own. He says he went for a drive to admire the Berkshire countryside and watched the sunset from a hill while the rush hour was on. We haven't traced Cilla Pargiter yet, but she wasn't at her friend Lesley Mortimer's.'

'It's Johnny, Baggo. He's our man as sure as whelks are whelks. But how the hell do we prove it?' He scratched his crotch then spoke in a low voice. 'That man is evil, Baggo. Plain evil. Forget what he went down for, it was what he didn't go down for that sickened me. What these bloody fools with their rose-coloured spectacles thought they were doing letting him out, I don't know. Tigers don't go changing their stripes, do they, Baggo?'

'No, gov, they do not. The Parole Board sits in an ivory tower and the members do not realise how difficult it is for us to keep the elephants from knocking it down.' He paused, instinctively uneasy about discussing anything Indian, except curry, with Osborne. 'In Mumbai we were privileged and protected, but it was impossible to ignore the unpleasant realities of life. We understood that if we wanted clean streets, we had to get our hands dirty sometimes.'

Osborne smiled. He placed a hand on Baggo's shoulder. 'You're all right, Baggo,' he said. 'A real copper.' He pinched the butt of his cigarette, put it in his jacket pocket and immediately lit another.

'I didn't get a chance to tell you last night, gov, but Mrs Smith, Lavinia …'

'Thank you, Sergeant, for gracing us with your presence,' Osborne bellowed as Flick arrived for work. 'If your make-up is properly on, please take Detective Constable Chandavarkar to Mr Robertson's office and make appropriate inquiries. Today would be good.'

Flick went straight up to Osborne, her face reddening. 'This is the first time you've been in before me this year, you fat slob,' she said through gritted teeth. 'And if you report me for calling you a fat slob, sir, I'll report you, again, for sexist and inappropriate language and behaviour. Including smoking.' Nodding to Baggo, she had a quick look at her tidy desk before striding out of the room. Baggo smiled and shrugged at Osborne before following her.

Glancing sideways in the car, Baggo saw a tear in Flick's eye. She scowled at the road ahead, her knuckles white on the steering wheel. He thought of a number of things he might say, but realised none of them would improve matters.

By the time they reached the elegant white buildings of Inverness Terrace, she had recovered her composure. 'Let's go,' she said, forcing a smile.

There were two pristine, white pillars on the front step of Laurence Robertson's office. The portico they supported and the solid, white door oozed style, tradition and wealth. Flick took a deep breath then rang the bell. A girl with a cut-glass accent answered. Almost imperceptibly, she curled her lip when Flick introduced herself, but led the officers upstairs to a spacious office in which every available surface was piled with books, mostly hardbacks. Above what looked like the original fireplace was a picture of a man holding a plaque. They could barely recognise the person they had seen on the car park floor; the photographer had captured eyes that twinkled and a twisted, quirky smile.

'He was a good man,' said a quiet voice behind them.

Amelia Renwick had been Robertson's PA. Her skirt was short, her hair styled, but smudged make-up and false eyelashes springing loose from their moorings suggested that her concern for her employer had been more than skin deep. In a controlled way, she answered the officers' questions; Robertson had dealt with fiction, including crime; he liked submissions by e-mail; he had at least a look at each one, sending a rejection to almost all of them; a few were invited to send their work in hard copy, but most of them were rejected also. She said she could provide a list of those who had sent manuscripts, but not those rejected at the e-mail stage.

'There is one thing you should know,' she added hesitantly. 'Last year at the Harrogate Festival he said something about needing a new crime author like a hole in the head. Unfortunately, a journalist was listening and it got reported. I don't know if that helps,' she added, twisting her fingers in her lap.

She had no problem about the officers searching for information, and gave Flick the keys of the desk and Baggo the passwords for the laptop. While she was away for the list of manuscripts, they got to work.

At first there was nothing that surprised Baggo about the dead man's computer. There were files containing business letters and files containing novels. He had e-mailed authors and publishers. There were a few to or from friends, arranging lunch or golf. His inbox contained one e-mail from 'PP@btinternet.com'. It had been sent the previous year, on fifteenth November. Its title was 'Here it is', and it took up 693 KB. The paper clip beside it indicated there was an attachment. Baggo opened it. There was nothing in the e-mail but the attachment, marked 'Buried'. He clicked on it, Norton Security passed it and he opened it. A page of script came up on the screen. As the rest of the book was loaded, Baggo read the opening: 'Timeless sand ended the priest's time on earth. As scorched grains snuffed out his life, one thought prepared him for his voyage on the boat of the dead: revenge.'

Baggo closed the window and returned to the inbox. For a moment he sat, deep in thought. As his eye scanned the room, he saw the photograph above the mantelpiece in a new light and the penny dropped. He glanced at Flick, who was examining papers she had taken from the filing cabinet. As Osborne gunned for Johnson, Flick suspected Cilla Pargiter; she had thought the cuttings about the murders very suspicious. But Baggo could not stop himself from dreaming about Cilla, from imagining himself with her after the inquiry was over. Thinking hard, he read some other, inconsequential, e-mails then said: 'There's a lot here, Sarge. I'll need to take this laptop back to the station.'

'Nothing here, though,' she replied. 'Once she comes back with the list, let's go. Have you found anything interesting?'

'No, Sarge,' he said, too quickly, as the door opened and Amelia Renwick returned. She handed Flick three sheets of A4. Baggo noticed that both false eyelashes were now properly moored and grouting had been applied to the mascara. As he made out receipts for the list and the laptop, he asked, as casually as he could, if Robertson had been thinking of taking on any new authors at all.

'I don't think so, but I can't be sure. "There's talent out there, but it's a lousy time for it," was something I heard him say a lot,' she replied.

The officers thanked her for her time and left, reaching their car in time to stop a traffic warden summoning the removal truck.

It was just before midday when they got back to the CID room, but the meeting Osborne had been dreading was already underway. Cumberland glared at them as if they were late and Flick muttered 'sorry' without meaning it. In front of the whiteboard, Dr Dai Williams continued to describe the corpse he had just finished dissecting. Cumberland and Palfrey sat together on the scruffy chairs normally used by Flick and Baggo. Neither looked happy. Suddenly feeling guilty, Baggo put Robertson's laptop in a drawer of his desk then perched on the surface as he paid attention to what Dai 'the Death' had to say.

'… like Denzil Burke, shot twice from behind, this time with a nail gun. Now, to fire a nail gun, there has to be pressure on the tip of the barrel, because normally nails are driven innocently into wood. So the killer has sneaked up behind poor Mr Robertson, pressed the tip of the nail gun hard against the lower part of his back,' he turned and used his right hand to indicate the spot, 'and fired upward and leftward. Then another, just the same.' He faced his audience and paused to let this sink in. 'Fifty millimetre nails,' he added.

'The second nail passed through the lower right ventricle, stopping the heart, and causing death within a few seconds. Now it gets interesting. The killer has turned Mr Robertson on his back and desecrated the body.' The Welsh lilt in the pathologist's voice made this deed sound specially repellent. 'He has fired the nail gun into the dead man's forehead. But he doesn't know, or he's forgotten, his anatomy. The bone at the front of the skull is particularly dense and strong. It is one of the body's most effective weapons. Glaswegians know this from their kissing. The nail goes part of the way in, but jams half in, half out of the barrel.'

'A hole in the head,' Baggo exclaimed. 'Sorry, Doc.'

'What's that?' Cumberland's squeaky voice cut across Williams.

'The dead man recently said that he needed a new crime author like a hole in the head, and was reported saying it, sir. We've just learned that from his PA.'

'Interesting, Chu...' He bent his head as Palfrey leaned over and whispered. 'Chandavarkar. Well done. Carry on, Doctor.'

Pointing to a picture of the gun and the jammed nail, Williams continued: 'Our killer pulls the jammed nail out of the skull then uses it to cut two letters on the skin of the forehead. The letters are N and U.' He indicated the most revolting of the pictures he had added to the whiteboard.

'New!' Osborne exclaimed. 'It has to be linked to that quote.'

'That's obvious, Inspector,' Cumberland snapped. 'This is clearly one of a series of murders, and again the killer has left no clue about his or her identity. I take it the killer could have been a woman, Doctor?'

'Absolutely, Chief Superintendent.' Williams nodded.

'Well, what do we know about the latest one, Inspector?'

Williams moved to one side as Osborne stood in front of the board. His tie was straight and his clothes didn't look as if he had slept in them. His left hand drifted towards his crotch, but he pulled it back and lodged it safely in his trouser pocket.

'It seems he always parked in that multi-storey, and generally left his office at about five thirty. He lived in Notting Hill and Peters and I went there this morning to see the widow. She's Isabel Robertson, aged thirty-six and pregnant with their first child. He'd not been previously married and had no children. She's due in six weeks, is it?'

'Yes, gov,' Peters confirmed. 'She was very upset. Very,' he added.

'What is she like?' Cumberland asked.

Osborne opened his mouth then thought better of it. He shouldn't use the word 'bimbo' in this company, but couldn't think of any other way to describe her. 'What would you say?' he asked Peters.

Danny Peters would have used the same word. 'Er, well-dressed, careful with her appearance …'

'That could be my Aunt Agatha,' Palfrey snapped. 'Is she attractive?'

A red tide crept up from Peters' neck. 'Well, ma'am, you could say so, if you liked that type.'

'Is "bimbo" the word you're skating round, by any chance, Detective Constable?'

Cumberland let out a squeak.

'Sorry, ma'am, sir, but yes.'

'How long had they been married?' Palfrey continued.

'Two years, she said. She'd worked in his office, but I don't know what she did.'

'Did he have any enemies you know of?'

'No, ma'am.'

Cumberland coughed. 'What inquiries have you made, Inspector?'

Osborne had been leaning against the wall. He wanted a smoke, a drink and something to eat, but could have none of them. Knowing he needed to sound organised and in control, he stepped forward once more.

'I reached the crime scene rapidly. It was already sealed off and I instructed the search which uncovered the murder weapon. This was the first time I had known about one of these crimes soon after it was committed and I instructed Fortune and Chandavarkar to check the whereabouts of the suspects we had previously identified. The results are less helpful than I had hoped, but it appears that one of the suspects, Candice Dalton, was at a bookbinder's in Highgate at the time of the killing.' Using the whiteboard as a prompt, he talked about each suspect. He thought he was doing quite well when Cumberland interrupted him.

'You say each of these people is a would-be crime writer, rejected by all the victims. They show imagination in how they kill people in their books and their motive is revenge. They either live in London or visit regularly. But how do they learn so much about their victims' routines? Particularly that man killed when he was out running?'

'Our killer is very meticulous, sir.'

'I know that, but how did they find out Noble's route?'

Baggo cleared his throat. 'May I say something, sir? Richard Noble was a twitterer.'

'A what?' Cumberland scratched his dome.

'He was on Twitter, sir. It's a social networking site ...'

'I know that.'

'Sorry, sir. Anyway, he moaned like hell about the training he had to do for the marathon, describing his runs, step by painful step. Anyone could follow his tweets, not necessarily revealing their true identity when logging in.'

'Can you link anyone who followed Noble's twitters with our suspects?'

Baggo shook his head. 'I have tried and failed, sir.'

'Chandavarkar's our IT man, sir,' Osborne explained.

Cumberland sucked in his breath. 'Well I trust you've impressed on him the necessity of keeping within the privacy laws. We don't want evidence that's been tainted by being "fruit of the poisoned tree" as lawyers call it. I was at a conference just last week at which the Justice Secretary impressed on us the importance of respect for privacy. We are not a police state.' He made the last sentence sound like an article of faith. 'So.' He looked round the room, mentally descending from the moral high ground. He frowned at Osborne. 'How do you propose to catch this killer before they strike again?'

'Old-fashioned police methods are still the best, sir. But until we come up with a result, it might be better if these agents took more care of themselves, went round accompanied, varied their routines, didn't advertise their movements in advance, that sort of thing.'

Cumberland's mouth fell open. 'Aaargh,' he said, sounding like someone having their throat examined. 'We have to be careful not to cause panic. And we can't afford to give round the clock protection, or anything like that. There's sure to be someone who'll demand that, and threaten to sue if they don't get it. Best leave it to their own common sense, I think.'

Flick had been listening thoughtfully and knew she had to get her tactics right. 'But sir, none of these murders would have taken place if the victims had done what Inspector Osborne has just suggested. Some people simply don't have common sense,' she added, hoping it didn't sound cheeky.

Palfrey nodded. 'I think Fortune has a point, sir.'

Cumberland took from his pocket a well-ironed linen handkerchief and wiped the film of perspiration that had appeared on his brow. 'Very well, Superintendent. But please don't scare people unnecessarily. That's what crime books are for.' His mouth creased into a supercilious smile which died when he realised no one else appreciated his attempt at humour. 'The long and the short of it is, you have no strategy for catching this killer apart from what you call old-fashioned methods?'

There was an embarrassed silence. Then, as Osborne muttered 'We'll get him', Flick coughed. Tentatively, she said, 'Yesterday, Chandavarkar and I visited Lavinia Lenehan, the crime writer, who organises the Debut Dagger competition for the Crime Writers' Association. The crime writing community has become very worried by these killings, and they want to help us if they can. Our list of suspects actually came from material Ms Lenehan provided. She has a plan, and is prepared to help execute it.' She looked round. Everyone was attentive; only Osborne scowled.

'She believes that our killer has personality traits that would be bound to surface at a writer's retreat, where their work would be criticised and they would have to interact with other writers. She is convinced the murderer would make some crucial mistake.

'Now, the shortlist for the Debut Dagger is due to be announced at the end of March or beginning of April, and those concerned are not told till then. But before the real shortlist comes out, Ms Lenehan is prepared to contact our six suspects and tell them they have been shortlisted and that the judges want an extra opportunity to assess them. She and some others in the publishing trade would hold a retreat within the next couple of weeks. It would be residential and last for a few days. I think it might work.'

'I've never heard of anything like that in my life,' Cumberland squeaked.

'This is no ordinary inquiry, sir.' Palfrey said firmly.

'We would have to pay for it,' Flick added. 'But it can probably be done for less than ten thousand.'

'Ten thousand!' Cumberland looked appalled.

'Ms Lenehan, Jane Smith in real life, has sounded out Cameron McCrone, the author, and Tara Fisher, an editor with a big publishing house, and they're willing to attend the retreat full-time with her. She's tried to get an agent as well, but hasn't had any luck so far.'

'And where would this retreat take place?' Cumberland asked.

'Ms Lenehan knows an hotel in Pitlochry. In Scotland.'

'Scotland! But would we not have to involve the Scottish police?'

'It might set a good example of cross-border cooperation, sir,' Palfrey said.

Flick added, 'And the suspects would be more likely to take things at face value. If we held it in Kent, let's say, they would be more likely to suspect that we were behind it.'

'But, but, wouldn't this be one of these, these entrapment, *agent provocateur* situations?' Everyone could see Cumberland was clutching at straws.

'No, sir. We wouldn't be encouraging the criminal to do anything illegal,' Flick said.

'The defence will see this as a sort of trickery, won't they? "Fruit of the poisoned tree" and all that.'

Palfrey snorted. 'Even if some head-in-the-clouds lawyer were to say we couldn't use something the killer said on the retreat, at least we'd know who we were after.'

'And we'd get them with old-fashioned methods,' Flick interjected, nodding towards Osborne, whose eyes widened with surprise.

'I'd like to think about it,' Cumberland said.

Flick grimaced. 'Time is very tight, sir. Ms Lenehan is ready to push the button as soon as she hears from me.'

Palfrey said thoughtfully: 'I think we have to move quickly, sir. We've had four murders in the last month. If this works, I can see it being hailed as a huge success for innovative policing, involving partnership with members of a threatened community and close working with Scottish colleagues. And it won't be that expensive, compared with conferences, for example.'

Eyes closed, Cumberland rested his chins on his chest. 'Very well, but I don't want this to cost a penny more than necessary,' he said at length, then turned angrily to Osborne. 'Why didn't you tell me about this, Inspector? You're supposed to be in charge of this inquiry.'

As Osborne opened his mouth, Flick cut in: 'The Inspector generously allowed me to put the idea forward as I had liased with Ms Lenehan, sir.'

'Oh. Good, good. And Inspector, report to Superintendent Palfrey in connection with this retreat. She will give me a full account once it's over.'

Cumberland looked at his watch, rose slowly to his feet and sailed majestically out of the room. Flick rolled her eyes at his back.

After Palfrey had also left, Osborne and Flick faced each other.

'Thanks for that, Sergeant,' Osborne muttered.

Flick shook her head. 'How did that man get where he is? He's a penny-pinching, petrified behemoth of correctness,' she spluttered.

Osborne grinned. 'Did you have a dictionary for breakfast this morning? To me he's just a fat wanker.'

18

Baggo made himself comfortable as the train rattled north out of London. He had slept for only a couple of hours, having spent the night reading *Buried Alive*. The previous afternoon he had phoned the bookbinder who had confirmed that Mrs Dalton had indeed collected the book for her husband's birthday at the time shown on the credit card slip. The man sounded elderly, and he would have talked happily about books all afternoon, but Baggo had stopped him. He had Laurence Robertson's computer and phone to deal with. These contained no more surprises. Unobtrusively, he had put the file marked 'Buried' on to a memory stick and taken it home. Now, on his first day off for weeks, he was heading to Newcastle to learn more about the girl who had kept him from sleeping.

The train was hot, and he nodded off, but woke with a start as the train pulled away from a busy platform. The man beside him reassured him that it had been York, and he was fully alert by the time he descended from the train at Newcastle.

The taxi ride to Jesmond was quick. On the Pargiters' doorstep, Baggo asked himself what on earth he was doing. His previous off-*piste* adventure had nearly ended in disaster, for him if not for Patrycja. If he mishandled the conversation he was about to have, the whole inquiry might be compromised. As for his career ...

Margaret Pargiter raised her eyebrows when she opened the door, but let him in and showed him into the sitting room. She did not offer tea, but sat opposite him on the edge of an armchair. Her hands were smeared with different colours of paint, and a streak of light blue above her left eye continued into the unruly hair above it.

'I am sorry to disturb you, but is Cilla in?' he asked.

'No. She's at work and Penny's at nursery.'

'Is Cilla short for Priscilla?'

Margaret frowned. 'Why, yes. Have you come all this way to ask that?'

'Are you sometimes known as Peg or Peggy?'

'As are most Margarets, yes.' Her eyes half-closed, she looked at him carefully.

'You knew Laurence Robertson, didn't you?'

'No.' Sitting up straight, she stared at him, defying him to contradict her.

'Does Cilla know him?'

'No,' she said vehemently. 'Where is all this leading?'

'I found her book,' he said quietly.

'What book? Where?' Her voice, full of indignation, rose in both tone and volume.

'The book that someone e-mailed him. It was still attached to the e-mail. Who is PP@btinternet.com?'

Her head drooped and she twisted a lock of hair round a paint-stained finger. 'Mostly me. Cilla occasionally uses it. I heard about Laurence's death on the radio this morning. There was a policeman with a high voice talking.' She looked at Baggo. 'Laurence had a deep voice, you know. Would you like tea?' She asked, her voice weary, resigned.

'I'd like the truth.'

She pushed herself up. Standing over Baggo, she said, 'Well I need a cup of tea before I tell you that.'

During the five minutes she was out of the room, Baggo stood in front of the painting of the twins. Framing Cilla's face with his hands, he could see, in the mouth particularly, a younger version of Robertson. Margaret was a skilful artist; she had captured the essence of a particular, opaque look that defined her daughter's face as it had made the dead man distinctive. Was he Cilla's father, or some other relation? He wondered how much of the truth he was about to be told.

'I made some fairy cakes yesterday,' Margaret said as she returned. She set the tray on the table, sat down and carefully poured tea into hand-painted china cups. 'This is a bit of an occasion,' she explained.

Baggo sensed that it would be a mistake to hurry her. He ate two cakes and drank his tea in silence, waiting. At last, Margaret set down her cup and spoke.

'Please don't tell Cilla this unless you have to,' she said.

'I cannot promise anything like that, but I will keep your secrets if I can.'

She shook her head. 'I suppose that will have to do.'

She clasped her hands in her lap and took a deep breath. 'Cilla believes I do not know who her father is. Or was. I have always told the twins I was in a commune in which we believed in free love. In fact, well, you must have guessed, Laurence and I were lovers. We actually lived quite conventional lives, in Bristol actually, and were going to get married. But he met someone else, and … I was devastated and just wanted him out of my life. Completely. I came up here then discovered I was pregnant. My parents were dead and I had no one. That's when I joined the commune. The twins arrived, I registered the birth, giving "unknown" as the father. For their first three and a half years, the twins lived in the commune. And they were loved by everyone. All the men acted as dads. They competed for the twins' affection.'

For a moment she paused, a sad smile on her face. 'But it wouldn't have worked in the long term, and I decided to come up here, back to my roots, and bring the twins up "properly". One thing I never deviated from was that Laurence Robertson should never know about them, and they should never know about him. Well, Penny died, then Cilla was struggling to get her book published. I realised that Laurence had become a successful agent. I hated doing it, but I wrote to him, explaining everything. Did you find that letter? No? I bet he destroyed it. He wrote back, asking me to e-mail the book to him. I had a copy on my computer, so that was no problem. That was last November, and I haven't heard a cheep from him, and I'm sure Cilla would have told me if she had. Cilla knows nothing about any of this, and I begged Laurence not to tell her. That's the truth, like it or not.' Her voice caught, she wiped her eyes with her sleeve, and looked imploringly at Baggo. 'Please keep it all secret. Particularly as Cilla can't know her father now, even if she wanted to.'

'I'll try,' he said.

'Thank you,' she said, her shoulders relaxing. 'Now, please go. I don't want to have to answer awkward questions about what you wanted.'

'I have to ask, was Cilla in London on Monday?'

'Yes,' she said, her voice and face drained of emotion.

'Forgive me, but I would like to know your whereabouts early on Monday evening.'

Margaret started then smiled. 'You want to eliminate me from your inquiries, I suppose? I had a migraine and went to bed. No one can vouch for me, and, as I turned all the lights off, the house will have appeared unoccupied.'

As Baggo got up, she put a hand on his arm. 'I'm not heartless. I know I should feel something, Laurence being murdered like that, but I can't feel anything for him. It's been a long twenty-five years. Very long. And I am scared, for Cilla, that she'll get the blame. Can you see that?'

He tried to read her expression. Was there guilt there, as well as fear and pleading? 'I do see,' he said.

Baggo was still stunned when his train was half way back to London. And he didn't know if he could or should keep Margaret's secret.

'Yes!' Flick said to herself as she put down the phone.

'Anything I should know about, Sergeant?' Osborne stood beside her desk. He had a smile on his face.

'Er, yes. I was about to tell you.'

'Well come with me and tell me in the car.'

'In the car? It's nearly lunchtime and Palfrey will be here at two.'

'I know, Sergeant, but I think you're going to like this.'

Flick got up and followed Osborne to the car pool. To her surprise, he already had keys and climbed into the driver's seat. Once she had her seatbelt on and he had started the engine, he said, 'We're going for lunch. Together and on me. We need to talk.'

'But, I …'

'Please, Sergeant.'

Flick was aghast, but there was no way out without appearing hopelessly petty. 'Right,' she said.

They drove in silence to a street leading from Worple Road, rich in old-fashioned food shops. A greengrocer, a butcher, a fishmonger and a general store, all had Asian names above windows cluttered with fresh produce and bargain notices. Osborne slowed and bumped down a narrow, pot-holed lane. At the end was a patch of waste ground where he parked. As Flick got out, Osborne smiled at her. 'I can see what you're thinking, but my ex liked this place and she hated most curries.' He set off back down the lane, towards the street.

Some years earlier, Flick had sworn she would never

again set foot in an Indian restaurant, but when Osborne led her to the garish red door of a restaurant called Abdul's and opened the door for her, she set her face and went in.

'Ah, Mr Osborne! How are you today, sir? Your usual table?' The beaming waiter, dressed in western shirt and slacks, showed them to a table in an alcove deep within the restaurant. Flick shuffled away from Osborne along a bench upholstered in worn draylon and found herself facing a blown-up picture of an Indian couple, presumably Abdul and his wife, holding hands on the white bench in front of the Taj Mahal where Princess Diana had once posed in solitude.

Only two other tables were occupied, both by Caucasian men casually dressed. The menus, like the table covers, were plastic, and Flick noted that everything seemed clean.

'Cobra or water?' Osborne asked. 'Cobra's Indian beer, like lager,' he added, fidgeting with the menu.

Flick sensed that he was as nervous as she was. 'Water's fine, thanks,' she said.

He asked for two bottles of mineral water.

'Popadums,' he said, as a plate of bread-like wafers arrived. 'You'd be best with mango on it.' He selected one of the sauce dishes accompanying the popadums and pushed it across the table. 'The lime's good too.' He helped himself and put it down beside Flick. 'You're not a veggie, are you?' Crunching a popadum, she shook her head. 'Then I'd advise Kashmir chicken, if you like chicken. It's got spice in it, but it's not hot. My ex had a fancy for Malayan chicken, too. It's mild.'

The waiter took their order, Osborne requesting his 'usual', then they finished the popadums. Flick was determined not to break the increasingly awkward silence that followed.

'Why did you help me out yesterday?' he asked eventually.

'Because I want you to actively support Lavinia Lenehan's plan.'

'What did you mean by saying that we could get the criminal using old-fashioned methods?'

'I wanted to annoy Cumberland.' She saw his grin and grinned back.

'But why did you go off to check alibis without telling me?'

'In case you said no. I was sure it had to be done immediately.'

'We've got to get the right person, you know, and there's one that stands out.'

'Do you think so? Francis gives me the creeps; Wallace is seriously angry with life; Dalton is a mass of contradictions. Pargiter's strange. She cuts out reports of the murders, and her sister drowned in odd circumstances. I think they were competing against each other for the man who's her daughter's father. So … well, it's hard to say.'

'You haven't mentioned Johnson.'

'You know him better than I do, but why should a man about to be paroled from a life sentence risk killing a lot of literary agents? It doesn't make sense.'

'Believe me, he's our man, Flick.' He paused, letting

the significance of her preferred name sink in. 'He's evil through and through, with a helluva lot of nerve.'

'What about the Harvey Nicks murder? Do you think he could have done the rest, and the Russians ordered the hit on Swanson?'

'He did the lot, Flick. Mark my words. And I'm going to prove it.'

'Well, he's a likelier suspect than Mrs Lawson, though she cossets her husband like a mother hen. She'd kill for him, I reckon, but I see her as our least likely suspect. And she has a good alibi for Harvey Nicks, so if she did the rest, that would put the Russians in the frame for Swanson.'

'Forget the Russkies, Flick. That man Chapayev is off his rocker. He's just playing politics. Trust me.'

Flick opened her mouth to respond, but the food came and by the time the plates had been arranged, she had decided to stay silent. To her surprise, she found the Malayan chicken tasty and good. Trying to ignore the aroma wafting from Osborne's prawn vindaloo, she finished all but some rice and sauce.

Osborne ordered coffee and the bill, which he paid in cash. He told her about how he had come to love Indian food, without wanting ever to go to India. A loud belch as they left the table reminded Flick that their alliance would only be temporary. But it was an alliance, and in the car she updated him on her morning's work. When they returned to the station, she thanked him politely, pleased that she had managed to avoid calling him either sir or, worse, Noel.

* * *

'This weekend? How on earth have you managed that?' Palfrey was taken aback. After a disasterous press conference the previous afternoon, she expected that, mauled by journalists, Cumberland would distance himself from the inquiry, leaving her as the senior fall-guy. She was determined that would not happen. She had no illusions about making Commissioner, but she felt she had at least one more promotion in her. She had demanded an up-date every day at two.

Flick said, 'Not me, ma'am. Lavinia Lenehan, Mrs Smith. She had everything primed in advance before the Chief Super agreed to go along with it, and she doesn't want any more agents to be killed.'

'But how did she explain this to the suspects? Are they all coming?'

'We've yet to hear from Sidney Francis, but the rest are all set. Mrs Smith can be very persuasive, ma'am. She told them that the judges were overwhelmed by the high standard of entries, and they couldn't pick a winner without seeing more of the shortlisted writers' work. Then she invented all sorts of reasons involving the judges' schedules why it had to be this weekend. She reckoned they'd be so flattered and keen to win they'd go for it, and it seems they have.'

'What if Francis doesn't play ball?' Osborne asked, stifling a burp. 'Won't that destroy the whole thing?'

'We'd still learn a lot about the rest, and that would be useful,' Flick replied. 'But yes, we do want them all to be there.'

'Tell us what's been arranged so far, Sergeant,' Palfrey said.

'The hotel's called The Pride O' Atholl.' She glanced at Osborne, expecting a reaction that never came. 'It's at the north end of Pitlochry, which is above Perth on the map.'

'It has a theatre, doesn't it?' Palfrey asked.

'Yes, but it doesn't start till May. There are a lot of hotels and guest houses in the town, and most are quiet at this time of year. This hotel's small, and had no bookings for this weekend. Mrs Smith will be able to take it over. She's been at a number of writers' retreats there outwith the tourist season.'

'The retreat will start on Friday, and everyone is asked to be there by six. They'll have sessions before and after dinner and more on Saturday morning. Saturday afternoon will be composition time, and there will be a further session on Saturday evening. Sunday morning will be reading time, while the judges look at the compositions, and there will be a winding-up discussion before lunch. They'll disperse after lunch.

'Mrs Smith has already sent out cheques for travel expenses and she'll be paying the hotel people, who have no idea what's really going on. I know she'd appreciate an immediate bank transfer.' She glanced at Palfrey.

'How much?' There was a resigned note in her voice.

'Six thousand would do for now, ma'am. She knows she'll have to keep careful records and not waste money.' Flick smiled hopefully.

'All right, but no fancy wines or silly bar bills, and if

there's any left over, she'll have to repay it. I'll authorise it this afternoon.'

'Thank you, ma'am. Here are the bank details.' She passed over a piece of paper. 'As we'll all be recognisable, it would be best if someone from Tayside Police could stay in the hotel as an ordinary guest, but I haven't approached them directly.'

'I have already spoken with their Chief Constable about our scheme,' Palfrey said. 'I can't say he sounded enthusiastic, but I'm sure I can persuade him to cooperate. We are the Met. I won't put it that way, of course,' she added in response to Flick's frown.

'They're as prickly as their blasted thistles,' Osborne muttered.

Flick said quickly, 'I thought that some of us should be on the spot, though not staying in the same hotel …'

Palfrey raised her eyebrows.

'I think I should be there, ma'am,' Osborne said. 'Fortune as well. And probably Peters. He'd be less likely to be spotted than Chandavarkar, particularly if he grew his beard. Does it grow quickly, Danny?'

'By the weekend it won't be much more than designer stubble, but I'll spray it with fertiliser.' Peters rubbed his chin then turned to Osborne, full of innocence. 'Are you going to put on a Hercule Poirot moustache, sir?'

Flick was the first to laugh. Palfrey joined in then Peters began to giggle. Osborne's scowl melted. 'Na. I'll be Sheer-luck bloody Holmes, and you can be my thick side-kick, Watson. It'll suit you.'

'Dr Watson …' Instead of putting Osborne right

about the doctor's intellect, Flick laughed again then turned to Palfrey. 'If you approve, ma'am, I'll start making the bookings,' she said. 'As a member of the public, of course. We had better try not to look like police ...'

'Easier for some than for others,' Palfrey said. 'And no five star hotels, mind. Get some quotes,' she added.

'Yes, ma'am. And it'll be useful to have Chandavarkar here as back-up.'

'I gather he's taken today off.' She sounded disapproving. 'We'd better not have another murder here in London while you're all awa' in Bonnie Scotland.' From Palfrey's mouth, the mock Scottish accent sounded strange. She shuddered then got up. 'Keep me informed, and for God's sake don't let this get too ridiculous.'

19

'Come on, Baggo, we're off to Guildford.' Flick had taken a call from Marcus Ramsay, telling her, in a strained voice, that he had discovered something that might have a bearing on Richard Noble's murder. She had briefly thought about going alone, but decided that Baggo should be there in case there were developments while she was in Pitlochry. This was her last normal day before the retreat.

On the journey, she up-dated him. His disappointment at not travelling north was obvious, and the journey passed in near silence.

But while his exclusion from the Pitlochry team made him huffy, it was the decision about what to do about Margaret Pargiter's secret that kept him quiet. He did not want to betray her confidence unnecessarily, and if Cilla knew nothing about it, the fact that one of the victims was her father did not affect the inquiry. On the other hand, if she did know, then the rest of the team needed to know it, too. Several times he was on the point of blurting out what Margaret had said then stopped himself; after all, he told himself, a reputation for being discreet was worth having.

The receptionist at Ramsay's office clearly expected

them, and ushered them straight into his room. The solicitor jumped to his feet and rushed round his desk to greet them. Was the Sergeant a little coquettish, Baggo wondered? When the two men shook hands, Baggo noted that Ramsay's grip was strong yet sweaty. The solicitor seemed nervous, but as keen to please as a puppy. Smiling and running his fingers through his hair, he phoned for coffee and biscuits. This man did not go with the room, with its leather-bound law reports, solid brown furniture, colour photographs of sports teams and a gold-framed oil painting of a lizard-faced judge.

The kettle had evidently been boiled already. Ramsay had not finished thanking them for coming when there was a knock on the door and a busty girl in a tight jumper and a short skirt carried in a tray. As her thigh brushed his sleeve, Baggo got a whiff of cheap perfume and rich coffee. To his surprise, he found this a turn-on. Ramsay made a fuss of pouring into blue and white bone china cups and offering a tempting selection of chocolate biscuits.

'As I say, it's good of you to come,' he said. 'I do hope I haven't got the wrong end of the stick here. If I have, or if there's an innocent explanation, I'll look terribly foolish, and it will be most embarrassing, not to say damaging ...' His voice tailed off. 'I rely on you to use your discretion, as much as you can, of course.' He took a deep breath and looked from one officer to the other. 'I've been going through Richard Noble's papers, including agency matters, and I've found something very odd.' His voice was low, as if he was wary of eavesdroppers.

'You probably know that Richard and Lionel Parker were the two partners in the agency. They were very successful, each doing different sorts of work. Richard did crime, as well as other things. One of the areas he did not cover, but Lionel does, is dead authors. A number of dead writers sell amazingly well, and I'm not talking about just Agatha Christie or Stieg Larsson. Well, I found this in Richard's personal, I stress **personal**, papers.' He raised his blotter and, with great care, produced a sheet of blue writing paper. 'It's a letter,' he added unnecessarily, handing it to Flick.

The writing was that of an old person, rounded characters formed by a careful but shaky hand using a fountain pen. Baggo moved his chair closer to Flick and they read it together.

Dear Sirs,

I am writing to enquire about royalties from my grandfather's book, Walks Round North Wales. He was Edwin Morris. I am the only surviving beneficiary of his will (he died in 1959) and I was surprised to see it for sale in a shop in Llandudno when I visited friends there recently. I asked the bookshop owner about it and she said it still sold quite well, and that she sent a royalty cheque to your agency on a regular basis. I have never received anything from you, and I do not believe that Mildred, my sister, did either. She passed away at Christmas, and that leaves me as my grandfather's sole surviving heir. I can prove that, if necessary.

Would you be good enough to look into this for me?

Keeping warm is an expensive business at my age (83).
I am,
Yours faithfully,
Gwynith Morris (Miss).

The address, written in block capitals, was in Manchester, and the letter was dated eleventh February, ten days before Noble's murder. Miss Morris had also given her phone number.

'Lionel was away when this came in, and Richard seems to have made some enquiries.' Ramsay continued, drawing a sheet of A4 from under his blotter. 'This was attached to the letter by a paper clip.'

In a precise hand, the dead man had noted: 'Glendower Books, Alun Glendower,' with an address and phone number. Underneath, an arrow pointed to the name and address of a Jersey-based bank, the Grouville Bank, heavily underlined. Beside that was another phone number and a name, Rob Le Broq.

'I have to ingather Richard's estate, so I felt I had to look into this,' Ramsay said. 'The long and the short of it is, the royalties were paid into an account in the name of Noble Parker with the Grouville Bank, but the only person who could access that account was Lionel Parker. I spoke to Mr Le Broq, but he wouldn't tell me any more than that. I then spoke to Waterstones and they confirmed that they sent a monthly account, covering a number of dead authors, to Noble Parker, care of the Grouville Bank, and they paid whatever was due by bank transfer, usually for a sizeable amount. Now, I've had a look at Noble Parker's accounts, and there are some entries of incoming payments relating to dead authors, but they're very, very modest, not at all detailed, and they come from a bank in the Isle of Man. Richard was the more talented agent, I always thought, but Lionel was definitely the businessman.'

'So it looks as if Parker's been moving the money round off-shore accounts and skimming the cream off the payments due to the heirs of dead authors?' Flick asked.

'And if Parker knew that Noble suspected this ...' Baggo interjected.

'Exactly.' Ramsay ran his tongue over his lower lip. 'If anyone asked, he would probably have claimed that he used off-shore accounts for tax purposes.'

'Well thank you for telling us this, Mr Ramsay,' Flick said. 'It obviously could give Parker a motive for murder. This is the sort of thing that needs to go to the Serious Fraud Office, and I'll be in touch with them today. Do you think that Parker has any inkling of your suspicions?'

'No. Unless the woman from Waterstones, or Le Broq, tells him I've been in touch.'

'Well, I'll ask the SFO to prioritise this and work with us. They'll need a warrant to search his house and the office, and I believe getting information from these off-shore banks is like drawing teeth. Meanwhile, please don't give him any hint that we're interested in him.'

'Do you think he might, you know? If he thought I'd spoken to you?'

'A desperate man might do anything,' Baggo said, then felt a kick from Flick. 'Just take sensible precautions, and I'm sure he'll think twice,' he added.

'What sort of precautions?' Ramsay ran his fingers through his hair.

Flick answered before Baggo could. 'Nothing dramatic. Vary your routine; lock doors and windows; draw curtains; if possible, avoid being absolutely on your own. He will not do anything against you unless he thinks he will get away with it and it will stop you from harming him. By giving us these,' she held up the letter and the notes, 'you have given us what we need, so it would be pointless and stupid for him to kill you. And Parker is no fool,' she added.

Baggo said, 'We are regarding this as one of the so-called Crimewriter murders, so even if Mr Noble was about to expose Parker as an embezzler, it does not follow that he was the killer.'

As Baggo paused to let this sink in, Flick said, 'But, please, I think it would be best if you said nothing to Mrs Noble. If her attitude to him were to suddenly change, it might possibly place her in some danger. Once the search warrants have been executed, we'll speak to her and take a formal statement. Full cooperation will be her best protection.'

'But when will you arrest him?'

'Once we've got evidence, Mr Ramsay,' Flick said.

'It is a bore, but justice demands it, as that gentleman would tell you,' Baggo said, nodding towards the judge's portrait. 'Please do not worry, sir. You have done exactly the right thing, and I am sure everything is going to work out fine.'

Ramsay showed them out with the nervous movements and forced smile of someone who hoped he had not made a terrible mistake.

In the car, Flick reached for her phone. 'Cooperation,' she mouthed to Baggo as she pressed the buttons. She gave Osborne a full account of what Ramsay had said, listened then shrugged. 'If the phone rings, you answer,' she said. 'It'll probably be the SFO.' She started the engine and, ignoring the speed limit, headed for London.

'I would not have expected such a man to be scared,' Baggo said as they sped through the Guildford suburbs.

'He's just out of his comfort zone,' Flick replied. 'He's not a criminal lawyer and he doesn't like going near a court.'

Baggo glanced at her. Her lips were pouting and she gripped the steering wheel hard. Interesting, he thought …

'If you wanted to kill a literary agent, this would be an excellent time,' Flick mused, ten minutes later. 'Everyone would assume it was Crimewriter. Say Parker killed Noble and the Russians killed Swanson, I wonder who might have killed Robertson. Perhaps the kinky journo did kill Stanhope after all.'

A burst of Beethoven that would have made the composer glad he was deaf erupted from her i-Phone. Baggo answered. Inspector Cummings from the SFO had a dry, unemotional voice but he sounded sincere in his apologies about the size of his work-load and the inadequacy of resources available to him. He could not drop everything to follow up a suspected embezzlement, even if it might have led to murder. What about the Crimewriter killer, anyway?

As Baggo repeated how urgent it was that Parker's records should be searched, Flick pulled in to the hard shoulder and took the phone from him.

'Oh, John, it's you. Yes, Flick... Oh fine, couldn't be better, and you? ... And your mum and dad? ... Tell them I was asking for them. Look, John, this is really serious. If this guy gets wind of our suspicions, anything could happen. No, not just destruction of evidence. I think Parker's having an affair with the widow, and she could be in danger ... Yes, really. Even if Crimewriter murdered Noble, Parker might kill to protect himself ... A nasty bit of work, I've met him, and the lawyer's scared of what he might do ... You'll have to check this out some time, and if you do it now, it's got a much better chance of being successful ... You're a star, John. I'll fax the paperwork to you when I get back to the station. Yes, quite soon. I'll hand you back to Chandavarkar. He's got all the details you'll need.'

Baggo immediately noted the warmer tone when the Inspector spoke to him for a second time. By the time they had finished, Flick had pushed the needle past ninety.

'It is important that people can rely on you to keep secrets, is it not, Sarge?' Baggo asked. Now that there was a possibility that some at least of the murders were stand-alone, he could not keep Cilla's relationship with Robertson to himself, but explaining his delay in revealing it would not be easy.

'Of course,' Flick replied, concentrating hard on the road.

'I was told a secret yesterday, and I promised to keep it to myself if I could.'

'Does it relate to this investigation?' she asked sharply.

'Yes.'

'Then you can't keep it.'

'I went to Newcastle yesterday, on my day off.'

'And?'

'I visited Margaret Pargiter.'

'Right. And?'

'Cilla Pargiter doesn't know it. That is why it is a secret, but Laurence Robertson is her father.'

Flick took her foot off the accelerator, earning a blast from the car behind. 'What? How could you think of keeping that a secret? How can you be sure she doesn't know it? What made you go to Newcastle in the first place?'

Baggo took a deep breath. Flick was now in the slow lane and she shot angry glances at him.

'On Tuesday night, after everyone had gone home, I found Cilla's book on Robertson's computer. It had been sent by someone called PP, from an e-mail address both Cilla and her mother use. I decided to use my day off to investigate. Margaret Pargiter implored me not to let Cilla know the identity of her father. I believed her that

Cilla did not know, so I kept it secret till I realised I had to tell.'

Flick swerved on to the hard shoulder and turned to face Baggo. She spoke very slowly and quietly. 'I want to know the full story. Now.'

Baggo told her fully and truthfully, apart from when he had found the e-mail containing the book. 'Please do not spread this further than you need to, Sarge,' he concluded.

'Well, thank goodness you've told me now,' Flick said, her displeasure obvious. She revved the engine and set off, ignoring the horn blast from the rear.

* * *

'It seems we have a warm suspect.' Osborne sounded less than excited as he greeted them. 'Danny's found something interesting on the CCTV.'

'It's the usual grainy rubbish, but the registration's fairly clear.' Danny Peters beamed at them.

'What is it?' Flick asked.

'The CCTV on Bayswater Road. Coming away from Robertson's murder at three minutes past six, we have the car belonging to Lesley Mortimer. The driver looks like a girl with long hair. If her photo on the board is anything to go by, it could be Cilla Pargiter.'

20

Baggo sat with his head in his hands then looked round the empty CID room. The Pitlochry team had left, none of them impressed by his delay in spilling Margaret Pargiter's secret. He feared he might soon be back in uniform. The previous evening he had met a friend from schooldays, Olly Norman, who was doing well in the Foreign Office. Years ago, he had introduced Olly to hot, spicy curries, while Olly had organised rite-of-passage, under-age, drinking sessions. Out on the town, they had rolled back the years, and, at mid-morning, Baggo still had a sore head and a churning gut. He wondered if Olly felt much better; as a schoolboy, he had always been the last to throw up.

Baggo's thoughts kept returning to Cilla Pargiter. He sensed something about her that was good. It could not have been a coincidence that she happened to be driving along Bayswater Road just after Robertson was killed, so, despite Margaret's certainty that she did not, she must have known the identity of her father. But, despite the evidence that was building against her, he could not believe that she was Crimewriter, or that she was capable of firing a nail gun into her father's back then scraping a message on his forehead. He knew Osborne wanted to pin the murders on Johnson, but if the evidence pointed clearly to Cilla, the Inspector would go with that and find some other way of getting his enemy behind bars, this time in a secure prison.

Baggo stared at the whiteboard, but inspiration failed to strike. Impulsively, he got up and rubbed out the green ink under Cilla's photo. Jane Smith had asked all the 'shortlist' to provide photos of themselves. Now the police could put a face to each suspect's name. Cilla's blurred Facebook photograph had been replaced by one that showed her enigmatic smile and the long hair that had helped identify her from the CCTV.

The phone on his desk startled him.

'Detective Constable Chandavarkar?' Fred Willetts at reception sounded unusually formal.

'Speaking.'

'I have a Mr Chapayev here. He insists on seeing someone on the Crimewriter inquiry. As Inspector Osborne is away, will you see him?'

Baggo stifled a groan then his brain began to work.

'Can I say you'll see him?' Willetts repeated.

'Yes, I will see him. Could you please get someone to show him up to the CID room?'

* * *

Osborne had his eyes closed as Flick drove their hired car off the dual carriageway and through Pitlochry. In the back, Danny Peters squirmed to find some leg-room. The Pride O' Atholl Hotel lay a couple of miles to the north of the town, just short of Killiecrankie. The old A9 was a twisty road, ill-suited to the increasingly heavy traffic that pounded up and down until the 1980s. After one double bend, a smart red and gold sign pointed left down a pot-holed drive flanked by oaks, aspens and the ubiquitous silver birch. Lower than the road, but with a fine view to the west, the hotel occupied a plateau half way down the steep, tree-lined slope from the old road to the white waters of the River Garry. Built out of grey granite as a fishing lodge for a Victorian merchant, the two round towers on the west wall suggested an importance the building had never actually achieved in an area rich in castles and ancestral homes.

'I hope I'm not staying somewhere like this,' Osborne muttered as Flick parked on the sparse gravel at the front. 'I bet it's cold as bloody charity.'

'It's got style.' Flick was fed up with Osborne's moaning. It had started at Heathrow, where flights to Scotland were unusually busy because of the Scotland-England Rugby International the following day, and had carried on through the car hire at Edinburgh and the drive north. Now they were to meet Jane Smith and the other two 'judges' as well as the officer from Tayside who would be staying anonymously in the hotel. She climbed out of the car, stretched, and breathed in cold fresh air.

'Welcome to Scotland,' Jane Smith trilled as Flick pulled open the heavy door into the wood-panelled hall. 'Come and meet Cameron and Tara.' Flick, Osborne and Peters followed her into the lounge, where a log fire and the aroma of coffee beckoned.

At the table nearest the fire, the only two people in the room stood up. Tara Fisher, the editor, looked barely old enough to have left university. Her olive skin, pale and sun-starved, and almond-shaped, brown eyes suggested Mediterranean blood. Those eyes widened as she shook hands with the officers. 'This is so exciting,' she said to Flick.

Beside her, a square-shouldered man with a face the colour of bricks, a nose like a misshapen giant raspberry and a mop of wiry, salt-and-pepper hair was less enthusiastic. 'Ye soon come to us when you need help,' he said to Osborne. 'But we'll dae what we can,' he added.

'Cammy's a Scot Nat,' Jane said, as if that explained everything.

'If you lot really want independence, you should put up candidates in the South of England,' Osborne said, sticking his jaw out. 'We'd soon vote you out of the UK.'

'And we have every confidence in the ability of the English people to govern themselves,' Cameron McCrone shot back.

Osborne scowled then grinned. He threw himself into a leather armchair, scratched his crotch and pulled out his cigarettes.

'No' in here ye can't,' McCrone said. After Osborne stomped out to the front door to light up, he shook his head and added, 'Mair's the pity.'

While Jane ordered more coffee the rest sat down. Peters smiled at Tara, but with his stubbly face he looked to Flick as if he was leering. She frowned at him but he paid no attention.

'How did you two meet?' Flick asked. McCrone was from a different planet to Jane.

Jane said, 'Harrogate, the Crime Writers' Association weekend. A couple of years ago, wasn't it, you introduced me to Lagavulin?'

'And you've never looked back.' McCrone had a twinkle in his eye.

'It's hard on the liver, but marvellous fun,' Jane said. 'We crime writers tend to get on terribly well together, not like the romantic novelists, who are at each others' throats.'

'United against our common enemies,' McCrone growled.

'Who are?' Flick asked.

'Publishers and agents.' McCrone laughed. 'Whoever your Crimewriter is, they're doing us a favour.'

'Cammy, behave,' Jane chided.

Outside, a car drew up beside Flick's, a man driving. As they peered to see who it was, the lounge door swung open and a smiling lady carried in a coffee tray. 'These are friends from down south,' Jane explained.

'Nice to see you. Make yourselves at home. I'm Liz Morrison, by the way. It's my hotel.'

'Thanks,' Flick said. 'It's lovely and full of character. Do you mind if we have a quick look round? Jane has offered to show us, if that's all right.'

'I don't mind at all,' Liz replied.

As Jane poured the coffee, Osborne returned. With him was a tall, broad-shouldered man with short, fair hair and a round, ruddy face. He introduced himself as

Sergeant Fergus Maxwell of Tayside Police. Flick noted his firm, dry handshake, strong jaw and cauliflower ears.

He refused coffee. 'I think we should get down to business before any of the suspects arrive,' he said.

Osborne nodded to Flick, who ran through the suspects, including Francis, who had not confirmed his attendance until the previous day. Then Jane outlined her plans for the weekend.

'How are you going to tell which one is the murderer?' Osborne asked.

Jane looked at him earnestly. 'Whoever is doing this must have a very strange personality, which they will conceal, but I am sure that some aspects of their quite aberrant psychological make-up will appear when they have to mix with others, compose short pieces and take criticism.'

'Jane's big on her psychology,' McCrone said.

'There's just one thing,' Maxwell said. 'I took this on with one condition, that I get away to watch the match tomorrow.'

'At Murrayfield?' Flick asked.

'Yes. I'll leave at twelve and won't be back till about seven, but if the suspects are writing essays then, there shouldn't be a problem, and I'll have a word with the local guys. They'll know to come at the double if any of you call. Anyway, the suspects will think it odd if I'm constantly drifting round the hotel.' His accent, though clearly Scottish, was not of the full-blown variety. It was a trustworthy voice, Flick thought.

Osborne shrugged. 'Don't see that it matters,' he said.

'Do you think you'll score any tries?' Flick heard herself ask.

Maxwell turned to her, eyebrows raised. 'I hope so. It depends on whether you kill the game like you usually do.'

'At least we don't get all our points, every game, from our kicker.'

'Have you ever been to Murrayfield?'

'No, but I've been to Croke Park and the Millennium Stadium.'

Suddenly hesitant, Maxwell said, 'I happen to have a spare ticket. Er, a mate couldn't come.'

Flick glanced at Osborne, who seemed to find the exchange funny. McCrone also smiled. Tara sat back, her arms folded, an expression of astonishment on her face.

'I'll get by without you - if he asks you,' Osborne said.

The redness of Maxwell's face deepened.

Flick saved his embarrassment. 'I'd love to. Thanks. And I'll pay for my ticket.'

'That won't be necessary. We have a reputation for meanness to live down, you know. You'll be surrounded by Scots,' he added.

'As long as I can shout for England.'

'Dalton and Pargiter are coming by train, and they might be here in an hour. We should have our tour of the hotel now,' Jane said.

The tour did not take long. One bedroom, which had disabled facilities, was on the ground floor next to the dining room. The remaining eleven bedrooms were upstairs. On the way up, Flick paused to admire the huge, stained-glass window throwing different shades of light over the half landing. The two unoccupied rooms overlooked the front, and had been reserved for the 'judges'. Any police activity would take place there.

'Will Liz not wonder about what's going on?' Flick asked.

'She may, but we have a good relationship, and she knows that our retreats involve a bit of coming and going. Any awkward questions will come to me.'

After exchanging mobile numbers with their new colleagues, Osborne, Flick and Peters got back into their car and located Scotland's Hotel, where they were all booked in. Osborne and Peters agreed to meet in the bar at half past six. Flick excused herself and went for a walk round the town, looking forward to the solitary luxury of a fish supper out of the paper and a Lavinia Lenehan mystery.

21

'I thought it was going to go pear-shaped after half an hour.' Fergus Maxwell brought Flick up to date as he tried to see past an early-season caravan on a slow stretch of the A9.

'How so?' she asked, sensing impending disaster.

'Rachel Lawson is some battleaxe. They were all introducing themselves at the first session, and Johnson says he's a convicted but innocent murderer who was released on parole that morning. Mrs Lawson had a fit; "I'm not mixing with murderers," "Who allowed this?" "I'm going home and anyone with any sense will come with me," and so on. Jane Smith should be in the United Nations. She took her out and had a long talk with her. Back they came and Lawson was quiet as a mouse till dinner, when she sent back her venison as it was undercooked. Actually, it was perfect, beautifully moist and tender. The food's very good, you know.'

'Don't tell Osborne or he'll gate-crash a meal. He thinks of his stomach full-time. How did you get to spy on them?'

'I don't know if you noticed, but the lounge is two rooms with the dividing wall removed. In its place they have a sliding door. It's shut as they're just using the front room at the moment, so I go in the back one and sit next to the sliding door. I can hear almost everything, but it's bloody cold. When they were closing their first session, I slipped into the dining room and got my order in ahead of them.'

'What do you make of them?'

'The wee woman, Dalton, I like. She talks to everyone, including Johnson. She fusses Wallace, in the wheelchair, and he doesn't like that because he's cussed and independent, but I suspect she'll back off him. Pargiter, who arrived first with Dalton, doesn't say much. Kinda dreary-looking, really. Johnson is one hard, vicious thug. I wouldn't like to cross him. Wallace is very bitter. I've watched him sizing up Johnson. They've both killed more than once, I'd say, and I sense a weird thing between them, almost a bond, but it's not that.'

'And Francis?'

'Oh, him. A long drink of water looking for a glass. He doesn't talk much, but when he does, he lectures. Spends all the time he can in his room. Doesn't mix. Everyone else hung about in the lounge following the after-dinner session but he bolted straight upstairs.'

'What about the retreat? How are the sessions going?'

'Fine, as far as I can tell. They get them to do exercises, like showing them a picture of a house and asking them to imagine who lives there and weave a story round the people and the house. Funny what some of them came out with. The judges didn't hold back in their criticism, that man Cammy McCrone in particular.' He paused as he overtook the caravan then looked sideways at Flick, a shy grin on his face. 'He told Francis: "Yer story widnae stand up if ye gie'd it Viagra." I don't think Mr Francis was very pleased.'

Flick laughed. 'This is crazy. I'm enjoying myself,' she said. 'How many points are we going to beat you by?'

'Oh, we'll win,' Fergus said.

'I'll pay you now for the ticket,' she said, taking notes from her wallet.

'Put it away. This is on me.'

'For heaven's sake. At least let me pay if Scotland wins.'

'All right, then. And I'll accept English notes.'

For the rest of the journey they talked rugby. Fergus had played Number Eight for Stirling County, which impressed Flick, and she was happy to meet some of his old team-mates for pints in Edinburgh's Murrayfield Hotel. 'This is Flick. The poor girl's English but she likes rugby,' was how he introduced her. When it was time to join the horde leaving for the ground, she swallowed half a pint in one, reminding herself to ask for lager, not heavy, the next time she drank in a Scottish pub.

Their seats were in the West Stand. Amid the good-natured pushing and bustle of the capacity crowd, Fergus exchanged shouted greetings with Kenny Logan and Gavin Hastings. At one point, Flick grabbed his arm, and it was a good feeling. They reached their seats in time for the anthems. Flick's voice rose above all around her for *God Save the Queen*. Booing, patchy but loud, reminded her that she was, to many there, a foreigner. She had always considered *Flower of Scotland* to be an atrocious dirge, but, sung by deep, passionate voices, accompanied by pipes and drums, it made the hairs on the back of her neck stand on end.

The match itself was a poor, drab affair, full of scrums and kicks and short on tries, but at least it could not have been closer, finishing fifteen-all. The queue for the bar at the Murrayfield Hotel was sticking out of the door. They decided to head north. 'Hope to see you again, Flick,' one of Fergus's friends called as they said their goodbyes.

The journey was quick and they talked little. On reaching Pitlochry, Fergus went with Flick to meet Osborne and Peters in the bar of Scotland's Hotel.

Standing at the bar, an unhappy-looking Danny Peters gazed into a pint glass. When he saw Flick and Fergus, he pulled a face and nodded towards a dark corner where Osborne and McCrone lolled, an armada of whisky glasses on the table in front of them.

'Felicity! Tell me we won!' Osborne's shout turned the heads of the few in the bar.

'Well, I'm not putting him to bed,' she muttered. 'Come on,' she said to Peters, and was pleased when Fergus came too.

'A draw,' she said as she pulled up a chair.

'A draw? How honourable.' He looked to his new friend for confirmation. 'So did he pay for your seat on your first date, then?'

'As it was a draw, I paid half.' Drunks had always annoyed her, but she knew she must will herself to be patient.

'So he pays for one bum cheek and you pay for the other?' Osborne started to laugh and McCrone joined in. 'Worth every penny, her bum, I assure you,' Osborne wheezed.

Gagging at the alcoholic fumes, Flick put her face up to Osborne's. 'This was not a good idea,' she said.

Osborne pointed unsteadily at McCrone. 'It's his fault. We bumped into each other by accident. Cammy has this saying, "A drink's nice, two's enough and three's not nearly enough." Unfortunately, we'd already had four when he said it.' He started laughing again.

'Yer man, here needed educating. We've gone up and doon the West Coast and we're daeing the Highlands. Will ye join us in an Edradour? It's the local drop. Very smooth.'

'No, thank you,' Flick said, steel in her voice. 'My two colleagues are going to take Inspector Osborne up to his room and make him coffee. You and I will sit here and then Sergeant Maxwell will drive you to the top of the drive of your hotel. He will go ahead of you, as you should not be seen together, and the fresh air will do you good. When you get to the hotel, please go to bed and on no account spoil this operation. If you do, someone might get killed and that person could be you. Understand?'

McCrone's bloodshot eyes focused on Flick's face. She hoped he would not respond badly, but knew she must show no weakness. He looked belligerent, then resentful, then accepting. 'So the game's a bogey,' he muttered, and slumped back in his chair.

It took more than half an hour for Peters and Fergus to get Osborne settled. By the time they rejoined Flick, McCrone was snoring loudly. With difficulty, they steered him into the passenger seat of Fergus's car.

'Thanks for a great afternoon,' Flick whispered as Fergus prepared to drive off.

'Pleasure's all mine.' The way he said it made her think he wanted to kiss her. It was a pleasant thought.

She watched his rear lights disappear round a corner then turned to Danny Peters. 'Are you up for dinner?' she asked. 'It's on me.'

22

On Sunday morning, Flick woke early and dressed. She rang Danny's room and found him showered and ready to go. 'You'd better check Osborne,' she said. A silence followed. 'Please, Danny. I did buy you dinner. And a nice claret.' He reluctantly agreed and said he would phone her back.

Ten minutes later, her phone rang. 'It could be worse. His room stinks like a distillery, but he's awake and sensible. And he's got plenty of peppermints. He's not keen on breakfast and says he'll meet us in the hall in three quarters of an hour.'

'See you for breakfast in a few minutes?'

'You bet. It's the best bit about staying in a hotel.'

Fuller than she normally was when starting the day, Flick drove the car to the front of the hotel, where a pale-faced Osborne was taking deep breaths and puffing at a cigarette. 'Good morning, Flick,' he said in a cheery voice, as if the previous evening had not happened.

By arrangement with Jane, using mobiles, the police entered the hotel and went straight upstairs while the suspects were having breakfast. From the dining room, McCrone's voice could be heard. 'Five point five metres. That's eighteen feet tae dinosaurs like me. Donald

McBean jumped that and escaped wi' his life no' half a mile frae here. Nane of Bonnie Dundee's men dared follow him.'

'Cammy's telling them about the Soldier's Leap,' Jane explained once they were in one of the front bedrooms. 'There's a walk from the end of the hotel garden to the car park. It's a National Trust property, and you can go down a steep path to the rock from where a government soldier jumped right across the River Garry to safety. 1689, I think it was, after the battle of Killiecrankie. Have you heard of Bonnie Dundee? No, well he was killed in the battle.'

'How's Cammy?' Flick asked.

'He went AWOL yesterday, but he's fine this morning. He was stuffing his face with black pudding with the others when last I saw him. Why?'

'No reason. How are things going?'

'Very well, after an awkward start. Sidney Francis got a phone call that upset him last night. I think it was about his children. He's still with us, anyway, and will fly down with the others late this afternoon.'

'Do you suspect anyone in particular?' Osborne asked.

Jane shook her head. 'We'd rather not say anything until we've seen what they've written, but we have some ideas. Tara should be up soon with their essays.'

'Essays?' Flick asked.

'"The most emotional day in my life." It can be fact or fiction, about five hundred words. I hope that will show us right inside their psyches.'

'Do they write them out longhand?'

'Good heavens, no. We asked them to bring laptops if they could, but we have a few old ones to lend out if necessary. Liz is good about letting us use the hotel printer.'

A knock on the door startled them.

'Who is it?' Jane shouted.

'Me, Tara.' Her manner hesitant, she came in carrying a sheaf of papers. 'They're all here. Cammy will be up shortly. He ordered more toast. Mr Maxwell's just behind me.'

As she set down the essays, Fergus entered quietly. He gave a shy smile that lingered over Flick then sat on a wooden chair in a corner.

As the officers waited, Jane and Tara began to read the essays. Ten minutes passed then McCrone swung the door open. He went straight up to Osborne and shook his hand. 'Good morning, old freend. How are ye today?'

'Well, Cammy. Very well.'

Flick kept silent. She went to a window that overlooked the front door. It was a stunning morning. A heavy dew glistened in weak sunlight and the trees swayed gently in the breeze. Beneath her, Rachel Lawson held the front door for Wallace then bumped him down the low step on to the gravel. They spoke briefly then went towards the drive, Lawson striding ahead as Wallace struggled to push his chair over the shifting stones.

Behind them, Dalton and Pargiter emerged wearing coats, and set off briskly across the lawn towards the bottom of the garden. As they reached the end of the grass, Francis came onto the front step and stared after them. Flick could see his chest heaving as he gulped fresh air into his lungs.

Jane tapped her on the shoulder. 'Do you mind if we leave you here and go into the next-door room to discuss things amongst ourselves? Tara's gone downstairs to order coffee and fetch the Sunday papers for you.'

The next hour passed slowly. Flick read the rugby pages while Peters took the football reports. Fergus had the news and Osborne closed his eyes. Peters soon gave up. 'Scottish,' he muttered, offering the pages to Fergus.

There was a knock on the door and Jane came in. She handed an essay to Flick. 'In view of something you said about Cilla Pargiter, this might be of interest,' she said. 'I'll leave it with you.'

Flick read it carefully.

THE MOST EMOTIONAL DAY IN MY LIFE
CILLA PARGITER

Hi! My name is Mandy and I had a twin. I've never told anyone the whole story, but I want to tell you, my reader. Your anonymity makes it easier to unburden. A bit like a confessional, I suppose, though I've never been in one.

Three years ago, in the summer, Marsha, my twin, and I had finished second year at uni. Mum was living with a man called Hector. We, Marsha and I, didn't much like him, but he was good to Mum and he took us all on holiday to Skegness. There was a restaurant, Bernardo's, where we had dinner the first night.

A young waiter called Sandy worked there. Marsha and I couldn't take our eyes off him. We liked tall, brooding men. He had incredibly sexy, hooded eyes that were as deep and brown as a pool in a mountain stream. We waited outside the restaurant till he came out, and we both chatted him up. He walked us to our hotel and we swapped mobile numbers.

The evenings were really boring. Marsha and I took turns to meet Sandy after restaurant service was over. We'd go for a walk and a snog. To make it more of a game, I'd pretend I was Marsha, so he thought he was going out just with her. We were totally identical, as you'll have guessed. We'd pulled that stunt before, with other guys. It was a right laugh, but we had to be really careful, specially when using the phone. After each date, we'd have a de-brief, so the other one wouldn't make a mistake the next night.

On the last day of the holiday, Marsha and I were sunbathing on the beach, and we started talking about Sandy. To cut a long story short, we both wanted to shag him. We knew he was up for it, as we'd both had to fight him off. It was part of our game that we wouldn't go the whole way till we'd worked out which of us it would be. There was a bay where, quite far out, there was a rock we called the Pirate Rock. We were both strong swimmers and Marsha challenged me to a race to the Pirate Rock and back. The winner would meet Sandy that night and shag him. It was Marsha's idea, and we could both do the swim, I promise. It wasn't that stupid.

It was late afternoon when we set off. I was just ahead at the rock and I turned for home. Marsha was about five metres behind. But the tide started going out, so it was tougher than we'd expected. I was fine but I heard a shout behind me. 'Cramp' was all I heard. I turned back. I swear I did, but she was gone, so I saved myself.

You won't understand how I could keep the date with Sandy, who'd heard a girl had been drowned, but never suspected it was the girl he was supposed to meet.

Marsha and I were really close. One knew what the other was thinking, feeling. It was uncanny. For the rest of that day it was as if we were back together in the womb, living yet not living. That evening, Marsha was still with me. And I knew, with total certainty, that she wanted me to keep that date. She wanted to live again through the child I would conceive that night.

I lied to Sandy, of course, said I was on the pill when Marsha and I always insisted on condoms. But not that night. Three times, Sandy and I did it. At the same place on the beach where Marsha had challenged me hours earlier. And I felt her presence. Her spirit sort of floated in the air as my body ground into the sand. Each time we did it, I tried to draw his seed deeper inside.

Marsha was born nine months later. Everyone says she's just like me, but to me she's my sister having a second go at the first twenty years, my daughter and my twin.

Fact or fiction? Flick asked herself as she stood at the window. Fergus came to stand beside her. Below, Johnson stood on the front door step, sucking smoke into his lungs as if his life depended on it. Suddenly, he froze then dropped to the ground. A split-second later there was the sound of a shot. 'He's dead,' Fergus said. 'He didn't put his arms out to save himself.'

23

Baggo smelled salt on the cold air whooshing in the driver's window, keeping him awake. He checked his speed then glanced to his right. A short distance down the Forth, the gigantic metal tubes and girders of the railway bridge were recognisable the world over. Painted a dull red, with some parts bandaged in white sheeting, it was solid, iconic, in a way reassuring. Certainly more reassuring than what Ron Doran at the car pool had told him about the much newer road bridge he was now on: 'You go over a big suspension bridge, like the one at San Francisco, only if you hear it pinging, start saying your prayers, 'cos the threads of the cables 'olding it up are breaking.'

Up till that point, Scotland had been a disappointment: small, green hills and unremarkable houses, fields and industrial sites. As he crossed safely into Fife, Baggo felt a surge of energy; he was on the last leg of his journey.

The last forty-eight hours, since Chapayev had burst into the CID room shouting in Russian and English and waving his arms to make his point, had been hectic, and it was more than twenty-four hours since he had slept, but he had the final pieces of the jigsaw in his hand ready to fit into place.

Despite the hangover it gave him, Thursday evening with Olly Norman had been the break-through. His tongue loosened by whisky, Olly had told him a lot about Chapayev. 'He's a ruthless, amoral criminal,' he had exclaimed. 'About the time he defected, a big consignment of Russian weapons, Kalashnikovs and things, went missing. No one could prove anything, but the Russians put two and two together, and we think they were right. Since then, Chapayev has done everything he can to make a nuisance of himself to the Russians, plus money laundering, arms dealing as a middle man, etcetera. He spent a lot of time in the South of France, where the Russian Mafia are strong, and we know he helped the Chechens. This book he's written is a mix of truth, exaggeration and lies. Of course, some people will take it seriously. Mind you, it's absurd to suggest the Russians killed that woman. Her death has publicised the book wonderfully. And it hasn't put off publishers. I heard someone else in Swanson's office has sold it for a bigger advance than she was hoping for. Chapayev has twisted things to his advantage. It's no surprise that the Russians wanted to keep an eye on him, and sometimes they do use South Ossetians for under-cover work if they don't want the embassy involved. Now that's a funny bunch, very secretive, don't welcome inquiries.'

With this new perspective, Baggo had waited till Chapayev's bluster had abated then told him about the retreat. 'Oh yes, Inspector Osborne has his eye very firmly on one of them, his prime suspect,' Baggo carried on. 'You can see he has written on the board that Johnson could have killed L.S., your agent. But Johnson is just a hired thug. When he arrests him, the Inspector will most definitely concentrate on the Russians, and their role in this, and he will get the truth out of Mr Johnson, the whole truth, and everyone will get to know it. You can be sure of that.'

Chapayev looked thoughtful, nodded his thanks and left. A brochure for The Pride O' Atholl Hotel, which Baggo had left prominently on Osborne's desk, was no longer there. Baggo went to the window and watched Chapayev reverse his black VW Golf out of its space with a savage twist of the wheel then drive aggressively out of the car park, forcing Palfrey to give way at the entrance. Out of habit, Baggo noted the number. 'Clean streets demand dirty hands,' he muttered to himself, gazing at Johnson's face on the whiteboard and feeling no conscience.

For want of anything better to do, he looked at the photographs relating to the Harvey Nicks murder. He went through them systematically, arranging some on his desk like a jigsaw, trying to work out why each item was where it was. Something resembling a dark, elongated sausage drew his attention. It lay on the surface of the bar, just to the right of where Swanson had sat. He found the item with the other productions that the first investigating team had bagged. A fountain pen. Using gloves, though he was sure any prints would be gone, he pulled off the cap.

At first, he thought there was no ink in it. He shook it, and clear liquid appeared on the nib. Carefully, he tried to write on a piece of paper, and left letters that were almost invisible against the white. He touched the writing with his index finger and put it to his lower lip. He felt an unpleasant, tingling sensation and rushed to the toilet to wash. When he returned, he put the cap on the pen and sent it off to the lab with a note: 'Test for fingerprints and aconite. Very urgent.'

A poison pen had been left at the scene. Now the Harvey Nicks murder had all the hallmarks of a Crimewriter killing.

The tingling in Baggo's lip had given way to a dull numbness but his hangover had receded. He thought he might risk a sandwich and some juice. As he got up to go to the canteen the phone rang. Inspector Cummings had moved fast. Armed with a warrant, he had executed a dawn raid on Lionel Parker, recovering several files and accounts from both his office and his home. After tracing and speaking on the phone to the relatives of a number of dead authors, it was clear that Ramsay's suspicions were well justified, even if the final proof, from the off-shore accounts, would be slow in arriving. Cummings was about to interview Parker, and thought it good tactics to have someone investigating Noble's murder present and asking questions. When Baggo told him Sergeant Fortune was unavailable he did not conceal his disappointment, but told Baggo to get himself to Guildford ASAP.

Before setting off, Baggo munched an egg and cress

sandwich as he looked through the Noble file. He wished he felt sharper. It was a big thing for a DC to interview a murder suspect, let alone a high-profile one, and he didn't want to make a fool of himself.

Cummings was waiting for him when he arrived at Guildford. A tall, thin man, prematurely bald and with rabbit teeth that caused him to spit as he talked, his manner was cold and precise. Baggo wondered about his relationship with the Sergeant. More old ice-cubes than old flames, he concluded.

Parker was waiting in an interview room, his solicitor, a Mr St Clair, beside him. A prosperous-looking fifty-something, he ostentatiously consulted his watch and noted the time on his legal pad when Cummings and Baggo entered the room. He looked at Baggo and curled his lip as if inspecting a bit of dead bird dragged in by the cat.

At first, the taped interview went badly. 'It is very difficult to trace the legitimate heirs of dead authors, and I have acted in good faith throughout. Beyond that, I have nothing to say,' Parker read from his lawyer's pad. If the words were brave, Baggo was struck by the deflation of the solicitous friend of the deceased and his widow. Now, his face twitched, his eyes darted round the room and his hands were never still. For half an hour, Cummings questioned him about payments he had received and payments not made to heirs but Parker kept a straight bat, either saying nothing or repeating the mantra he had been given. At length, Cummings turned to Baggo.

'Did the affair you were having with Vanessa Noble extend to sexual intercourse?' Baggo asked.

The two men on the other side of the table combusted simultaneously: 'I refuse to discuss …'; 'This is quite improper', they barked.

'It's a perfectly proper line of inquiry,' Cummings snapped, 'But my colleague might have started by asking if Mr Parker was having an affair with Mrs Noble. Were you?'

'No.'

'We have evidence you were seen secretly kissing,' Baggo said. 'I will ask once more, were you having an affair with her?'

St Clair nudged Parker and whispered something to him. Looking daggers at Baggo, Parker said, 'No comment.'

'Are you sure the late Mr Noble did not ask you about the old lady from Manchester, Miss Morris, or her grandfather's book, *Walks Round North Wales*? We do know she wrote to him, saying she had received no royalties.'

'As I said already, that was never discussed.'

'If he had suspected you of embezzling, that would have been a motive for murder, wouldn't it?'

'Please don't invite my client to speculate,' the lawyer purred.

'We all know someone is targeting literary agents, and you can't catch them,' Parker spat out.

'How many of the victims' clients have gone to your agency?' Baggo asked quietly.

'This is nonsense …' Parker said.

'That's an absurd question.' St Clair sounded genuinely angry.

'But you had three motives for killing Mr Noble, did you not?' Baggo leaned across the table, thumping it with his fist as he made each point. 'One, he might expose your dishonesty; two, you were having an affair with his wife; three, you were trying to stop him putting money into a family trust that you wanted to go towards a New York office?'

'You're pathetic,' Parker hissed.

'And you were one of the few people who would definitely have known when and where Mr Noble trained for the marathon.'

'He was always Twittering about that.'

'But you knew the lie of the land. You knew about the drainage ditch. You knew that, at first, suspicion would fall on Crimewriter. You killed him, did you not? I know you did. And did Mrs Noble help you?'

St Clair slapped the table with his pad before Parker could say anything. 'This junior officer is both badgering my client and raising new matters which we must discuss. Please suspend the interview.'

'Interview suspended.' Cummings' tone was clipped. He switched off the tape and walked out, nodding to Baggo to follow. 'You have a lot to learn. Wait here,' he said when they reached the foyer.

Ten minutes later, the lawyer emerged from the interview corridor and, ignoring Baggo, asked the desk sergeant if he might speak to Cummings. He was duly ushered somewhere.

Fed up with being treated as someone who did not matter, Baggo paced up and down until Cummings and St Clair returned. Cummings raised his eyebrows at Baggo and told him to follow.

Parker was slumped in an attitude of defeat. His face was very red and Baggo wondered if he had been crying. He had a whispered conversation with St Clair, who nodded to the policemen. Cummings switched the tape on and repeated the caution with which he had begun the interview. St Clair pushed a sheet of paper in front of Parker, who read out, in a shaky voice: 'I, Lionel Parker, freely admit that I have been embezzling substantial sums from the estates of dead authors. The money I have wrongly taken is in an account in the Cayman Islands, and I will use every effort to recover it and enable it to be distributed to those entitled to it. I also admit that I have been carrying on an affair with the wife of my late partner, Richard Noble. Mrs Noble had absolutely nothing to do with my embezzlement, and I am as sure as I can be that she had nothing to do with her husband's murder. I have taken this opportunity to set the record straight, and I am being completely honest when I say that I had nothing to do with that atrocious crime. Richard Noble was my friend. I betrayed him in two important ways, and I am truly ashamed of that. But I did not kill him, and I have no idea who did. I am now anxious to help the police in any way I can, and if I hear anything that might help their search for his killer, I will let them know.' He put down the paper and hung his head.

As Baggo watched, Cummings formally charged Parker with embezzlement, to which he made no reply. He then told him that he would be released, but must appear at Guildford Magistrates' Court on Monday.

With the formalities over, Cummings said to Baggo, 'Well, your Rottweiler tactics worked this time, I suppose. Lucky for you I suspended the interview before he confessed. St Clair's a smart cookie and he could see that we'd have plenty on the embezzlement, and by pleading guilty, recovering the money and helping as much as he can with the murder, Parker will reduce his sentence substantially.'

'I thought he should have been kept in custody.'

Cummings' mouth formed a goofy smile. 'A deal's a deal, Detective Constable. Anyway, I suppose, well done Cha … Cha …'

'Chandavarkar, sir. Do you believe him on the murder?'

'Actually, I do. He was uncomfortable when we were asking about the embezzlement, but he disintegrated completely when he saw you were serious about him killing Noble. If a smart man like that had committed the murder, he would have been mentally better prepared for questioning. He didn't want his lady-friend dragged through the mud, either. Of course, it may have been an act, but if so, it was a good one.'

'You believe Noble was another Crimewriter victim?'

'I think so, er, Chandavarkar. Well, goodbye. Oh, and send my, er, best wishes to Sergeant Fortune.'

24

As he drove back from Guildford, Baggo's concerns about Patrycja Kowalski returned. If ever she was caught, and talked about the night she left her flat, he might be in big trouble. The previous week he had inquired about her brother, Pavel. He was in Wormwood Scrubs, but Baggo's desire to find out about Patrycja was checked by a voice at the back of his head which told him to let sleeping dogs lie.

Curiosity won.

He arrived at the towers flanking the main gate of the Scrubs as visiting time ended. As they left, he watched the different people with friends or family inside. One couple looked out of place rubbing shoulders with street-hardened young mums steering push-chairs like dodgems, forty-somethings going on sixty-something, and raucous youths with shaved heads and jagged tattoos: a sleek, middle-aged man in a camel-hair coat gripped his wife's arm with stone-faced intensity. To judge by their expressions, she was coping with shame better than he was.

'I am here to check an alibi,' Baggo told the uninterested man who checked him in, and went to wait as patiently as he could.

The first impression Pavel gave was one of physical strength. Even with shoulders stooped under his prison uniform, Baggo could see that his arms and legs were thick with muscle. Toughness was another matter; a wispy beard failed to conceal swelling from his left eye to his jaw, his lip was cut and a front tooth was missing. It was a vulnerable, unhappy face.

'I don't speak to cops,' he said, his accent strong.

'I helped your sister.'

Pavel sat down but leaned back, arms folded.

'I saved her.'

No response.

'I said I was here about an alibi. You can talk to me and say you were helping someone. Where is your sister now?'

'Away. She say Paki helped her.'

Baggo forced a smile. 'Has she gone home?'

'Why you need know?'

'Things got messy.'

'Yes. She home. Never come back to bloody Britain.'

An intense feeling of relief washed through Baggo. He felt like kissing Pavel. 'How do you know all this?' he asked, his voice catching.

'Two weeks ago, mother visit. She tell. Patrycja safe now.'

Speaking slowly and clearly, Baggo said, 'I want to know everything you can tell me. If you help us, we help you. Serve sentence in Poland, soon go to open prison.'

Pavel's lip trembled as he searched Baggo's face. 'Okay,' he said.

'Do you remember Candy Dalton?'

Pavel frowned. 'Yes.'

'She helped you and your sister?'

'She say she help.'

'Did she not help?'

'Big talk, big talk. She get us away from Wolenski, to Glasgow, to Edinburgh. She find us good jobs. Pah!'

'All talk, no result?'

'Nothing happen. But we tell her things and she write down. Write, write, write. Patrycja, she tell her all tricks. I hate listen. We good people. Live good in Poland. No money, but good. We come to bloody Britain for money. Pah!'

'Did you tell Candy things?'

'I tell her things she write in big book, "bust-seller". How you slit throat, how you strangle. I …' He paused. 'You mean it, I get out of here?'

'I mean it.'

'I get her gun.'

'When?'

'Week before I arrested. End November. I think.' He shrugged.

'What sort of gun?'

'Beretta 92. I show her how it shoot, give her bullets, sound suppressor.'

'How did you get it?'

'I steal from Wolenski. Big mistake. I say I lose it, I drop in river. Accident. Wolenski bloody mad at me. Kicking. Ugh. I not know what she did with it. She say poor girl in big trouble need it very bad.'

'Did she pay you for it?'

'Promise, promise, clothes, food. She would get us to Glasgow. But money, no.'

Baggo could scarcely believe his ears, but he wanted more. 'Do you know if Candy was with Patrycja the night you were sentenced, after you got eight years?'

'Yes. Patrycja very upset. Say Candy give her sleeping pill. Slept all evening and night. Sore head next morning. Candy gone. My mother, she tell me this.'

'Is there anything else you can tell me about Candy?'

Pavel shook his head.

'You must be ready to tell all this in court.'

'No court. No.'

'Yes, court, but it may not be necessary. You have to be willing to tell. You do want out of here?'

Pavel put his hands to his eyes and nodded.

'Good man. I'll try to get you moved next week. Say nothing to anyone. Understand?'

Pavel's eyes were shiny with tears. He was like an ill-treated dog offered food by a stranger. 'Okay. Maybe you, Paki, will do as you say.'

'I am Indian. And I will do as I say.'

Pavel nodded, stood up and, fists clenched by his sides, quietly left the room.

As he drove back to the station, Baggo told himself he should phone Osborne immediately; however something held him back. On Pavel's evidence, Candy Dalton was Crimewriter, but she had a solid alibi for Robertson's killing; for that the spotlight was back on Cilla Pargiter.

25

Baggo felt tired as he sat on the edge of his bed on Saturday morning. During a wakeful period he had thought things through and had been unable to get properly back to sleep.

He spent longer than usual in the shower. He knew that his belief in Cilla Pargiter's innocence was visceral, not rational. He had met her only once, but he had also read her book and loved every page. Her prose had added so much colour and character to his image of Ancient Egypt. He was as attracted to her mind as her body. Well, nearly. And he liked her mum. And her friends liked her. That did not mean she was innocent, but before giving Osborne the evidence he had, he intended to double-check Dalton's bookbinding alibi.

'Going somewhere special, Baggo?' Willie Metcalfe called as he arrived at the station, striding briskly, his shirt crisp and his trousers pressed.

'You never know your luck, Willie,' he replied, allowing the lift door to close before the heavily-built Willie could reach it. He immediately felt bad; Willie was one of the good guys, always up for a laugh. But this morning he wanted no distraction.

In the CID room, he looked up the details of the alibi

and phoned the bookbinder. A woman's voice answered. Mr McElhinney was away at a book fair and would not be back in the shop; he did not like mobile phones and refused to carry one; this was Mrs McElhinney speaking; no, she had not been in the shop when Mrs Dalton had called on Monday evening; well, if it was really urgent, Mr McElhinney should be back home by six. Baggo prised her address out of her, reassured her that it was very urgent, possibly a matter of life or death, and promised to be with her then. He swore as he set the phone down; only Mr McElhinney could identify the woman who collected the old book. He would just have to wait. He gathered the things he would need, including the photo of Candy Dalton, and went to the car pool.

Ron Doran called the cars his babies, and he liked to know where they were going and when they would be back, specially at weekends. When Baggo told him he planned to drive to Scotland, he laughed. 'You don't expect me to fall for that one, Baggo. Who's the lucky girl? Not that you'll be taking her anywhere in a police car.' It took Baggo quarter of an hour to persuade him that he legitimately needed a car, but once convinced, Ron gave him the best car he had, plus advice on his route north. 'Now go home and get some shut-eye,' he had concluded.

But Baggo had other plans. It would be interesting to see how the Francis family were enjoying life without Sidney.

It was after eleven when Baggo drew up opposite the Tooting flat. The fine spring morning failed to lift the down-at-heel, scruffy exterior. The curtain in the front room was half-pulled and not properly hooked on to its rail, and the brass plate seemed more crooked than Baggo remembered. He got out and walked up the path. He was about to ring the bell when he heard a noise like a shout. He decided to look through the window. Treading carefully past an untended rose and across a weed-strewn patch of mud, he peered through a gap in the curtain.

What he saw shocked him, and he forced himself to stifle a yell. On the table beside the window were the messy remains of a breakfast. Both a cereal packet and a carton of milk had been knocked over, and a puddle of milk surrounded a plastic pack of uncooked bacon and dribbled over the table's edge. At the far side of the room, Harold and Rufus, in pyjamas, cowered in a corner. Harold was trying to shield Rufus while their mother lashed them with a brown belt. Through the closed window, Baggo heard her shout, 'You fucking little bastards, you fucking little bastards.'

Baggo grabbed his i-Phone and took two pictures through the glass. Matilda Francis was unaware of this, and continued to rain blows on her children, principally Harold, who used his plastered right arm as a shield. Catching his good trousers on the rose, Baggo rushed to the front door and put his shoulder to it. It did not budge. He pulled a credit card from his wallet and ran it down the side of the yale. The old housebreakers' trick worked. He ran through the hall then burst into the living room. Matilda looked up, her face contorted with rage, and aimed a blow at him. The belt buckle caught him behind his left ear. He put his head down and charged at her, knocking her to the ground and landing on top of her. Swiftly, he turned her on her front, knelt on her back, and pinned her wrists with one hand. He used the belt to secure them. Still on top of her, he used his i-Phone to summon urgent police assistance and a children's social worker.

He looked over at the two boys. Their arms round each other, they squatted in the corner, shaking and sobbing their hearts out. 'No, no,' Harold repeated, pleading with Baggo. At that astonishing moment, Baggo realised that the boy wished he had not discovered the awful truth about the family.

It took less than ten minutes for assistance to come, but it seemed much longer to Baggo. On the floor, Matilda Francis soon realised the futility of struggling She stopped swearing and her breathing returned to normal. Baggo wondered if he should let her up, but did not want to lose control, and was still astride her when a female, uniformed officer arrived.

Relieved, Baggo got up and showed her his warrant. He started to tell her what he knew then Matilda Francis' little girl voice interrupted him.

'I'm sorry, but this officer's misinterpreted what he saw. The boys were squabbling then fighting. They were hitting each other with this belt and I tried to stop them.'

'It was our fault,' Harold said, his voice tearful. 'Mum was going to give us a cooked breakfast. We were mucking about. Rufus spilled the milk so I hit him. Then he hit me with the belt. I went for him and Mum tried to stop us. It wasn't her fault.'

The policewoman turned to Baggo, her raised eyebrows inviting his response.

He showed her the photos he had taken on his i-Phone. They had come out reasonably well, despite the glass. 'I suggest you check their bodies,' he said, rubbing the lump forming where the buckle had connected with his head.

The policewoman helped Matilda to her feet and, without untying her hands, led her to the settee and told her to stay there. Then she turned to Harold. 'I'm Marjory,' she said. 'What's your name?'

'Harold.'

'Well, Harold, could we go to your room for a minute? I promise I won't hurt you.'

Reluctantly, Harold allowed her to take him out of the sitting room. They were gone for a while. When they returned, Harold was weeping. Marjory looked down on Matilda with disgust.

'This is a bad case,' she muttered to Baggo.

Soon the house was full of police and social workers. The boys were taken away and their mother was arrested and handcuffed. Baggo gave a full statement and sent his photos to Marjory's mobile. In a whispered conversation with the Sergeant from the Woman and Child Unit, he told her about the retreat and begged her to delay as long as possible the time when the father would be informed.

By the time all the formalities had been completed,

Baggo was itching to cross town to Highgate for his meeting with the bookbinder.

* * *

'There must be some mistake, officer. Mrs Dalton definitely collected that book on Monday evening.' Horace McElhinney, a sprightly little old man, full of old-fashioned courtesy, sipped his Amontillado and set his glass on a coaster protecting the marquetry table beside his chair. Baggo noted his strong, rough hands and peering eyes, the hands and eyes of a craftsman.

'What did the lady look like, sir?'

'She was quite petite, and she wore glasses. I remember her well. She was so enthusiastic about that lovely book. It's wonderful when one's work is appreciated, and I received a most effusive letter this morning from her husband, a vicar, I believe.'

'Was this her, sir?' His heart in his mouth, Baggo showed McElhinney the photograph of Candy Dalton.

The bookbinder removed one pair of glasses, replacing them with another from the inside pocket of his jacket. He held the photograph to the light. 'Let's see. Hm. No. That is not the lady I saw on Monday. She was younger, probably in her thirties, with black hair that went, you know, down the sides of her face.'

'A bob, dear,' from the sofa, his wife prompted him.

Willing himself to be patient, to take things slowly, Baggo asked McElhinney to describe his dealings involving the book.

'Gracious me. Are you sure you won't join us in a sherry? No, of course I understand. Well, Mrs Dalton telephoned me before Christmas. She had bought this book, *The King's Book of Sports*, and she wanted it restored for her husband's birthday. A fascinating book. Yes, well worth the effort. We discussed it, and she sent it to me, by post I think, wasn't it, my dear?'

'I think so, Horace.'

'I examined it and quoted her various prices for different levels of work, and she wrote back, ordering calfskin with gold lettering on the front. Well, I had a nasty cold which laid me low in January, but I managed to finish the job a fortnight ago. I wrote to Mrs Dalton, and heard nothing till she telephoned last week and arranged to pick it up on Monday between half past five and six. She was quite fussy about the time. Monday was going to be a busy day for her, and her husband's birthday was Wednesday. She did collect it when she said she would, and was very nice and grateful. She paid by credit card, but you know that.'

'Do you think it was the same woman who spoke to you on the phone last week?'

The bookbinder furrowed his brows in thought. 'I couldn't say. I assumed it was. She had a London accent, but not too broad, if you know what I mean. I can't remember what she sounded like when we spoke before Christmas.'

Baggo wrote down what McElhinney had said, read it over to him and asked him to sign the page of his notebook.

Mrs McElhinney promised to search for any relevant paper records. 'You said something about life or death on the telephone,' she said. 'But I assume this is a fraud case of some kind?'

Baggo beamed at her. 'No, ma'am. Thanks to your husband, we shall put a serial killer behind bars.'

* * *

Baggo knew that, to make the case water-tight, he should track down the woman who had been Candy Dalton's accomplice. He drove to the Mile End Road hostel, where Maggie was preparing for another busy Saturday night and was reluctant to take time speaking with him. He felt bad about threatening to alert Health and Safety officials about possible breaches of fire regulations by an organisation so obviously dedicated to doing good, but that had the desired effect, and he left with the address of Lena Vannet, a former client of the hostel with whom Candy kept in touch. Lena was aged thirty-five, with black, straight hair, and lived in a block of flats in Archway Road, not far from McElhinney's shop.

By the time Baggo had located the flat, Lena had gone out for the evening, and the very young baby-sitter said she had no idea where she might be. He wondered if he should head north and catch up with her later, but he knew that it would be safest to get her signed statement in his notebook as soon as possible.

After a quick visit to the nearest McDonald's, Baggo parked where he could see the door of the flat. Keeping warm by running the engine, and trying to concentrate on radio programmes to pass the time, he waited for Lena to return home.

It was after one that a dark-haired woman with glasses walked unsteadily across the car park and climbed the stairs leading to the flats. Baggo climbed out of the car, his joints stiff, and followed her. Lena stopped at her door, fumbled for her keys and went in. Baggo pushed his way in after her, his warrant card in one hand.

Whatever substance she had taken, Lena could still defend herself. She landed a hard kick in his balls that made him double up. 'I'm police,' he gasped.

'He is, Lena, he is.' The baby-sitter emerged from the door on the right as a baby's cry came from the door opposite.

'Well, he's got a bloody nerve following me like that.'

'This is very urgent. I have some questions for you about Candy Dalton,' Baggo said, trying to ignore the pain between his legs.

'Can I go?' the baby-sitter asked.

'Yeh. Thanks. Sorry, I needed all my cash for the bloody taxi. I'll see you all right next week, doll. Here, take these.' She fumbled in her bag and took a handful of cigarettes from a packet.

'I need your name and address, love,' Baggo said.

Shaking her head, the girl rattled off her details then left. Baggo took a seat in the living room while Lena picked up her child. She sat opposite him, quietening the baby with a bottle.

At first she was reluctant to tell Baggo anything, but became more cooperative after he threatened to tell Social Services about an obviously under-age baby-sitter and how she was paid.

'Candy said she'd visit on Monday afternoon. She's always kept in touch with me, helping me and that. We were sitting right here, having a cuppa, when she said she'd got this text and she had to go into the centre right away. She said she had to pick up some book for her hubby's birthday, and asked if I would, as it had to be done at a special time, and it was near here. She told me where the shop was and gave me her credit card and the PIN as she didn't have the cash on her. She told me to talk posh when I had to, pretend to be her and tell the bloke the book was great. I had to do this between half five and six. I was to go in her car – I can drive legally, in case you're wondering – park it in the car park near Mile End Road Tube Station and lock it, leaving the book, the credit card and the slip under the driver's seat. She handed me a twenty, to cover expenses, like. She said she'd go on the tube and pick up the car later. I got Arlene to watch Zak, and did as she said.'

'What about the car keys?'

'She gave me her spares, said she'd pick them up later.'

'Do you still have them?'

Lena paused.

'I mean it about Social Services.'

Still holding the baby, she went to a wooden box on her mantelpiece and took out a set of keys. 'Here,' she said, throwing them carelessly towards Baggo. 'If she asks, I'll tell her I dropped them in the street. Is she in trouble?'

'It's just part of a routine inquiry,' Baggo lied. 'Now, I need to write down what you've said. After I've read it over and you've signed it, I'll leave you in peace.'

Ten minutes later, he pointed the car north. The pain in his balls was easing and he was glad he had waited to see Lena before setting off.

* * *

The final miles of the drive passed quickly. North of Perth, Baggo saw why Scotland had a reputation for splendid scenery. He knew he must reach The Pride O' Atholl before the final session started at noon, and he would do so with an hour to spare. He took the slip road for Pitlochry, drove deliberately slowly through the town, and turned down the hotel drive.

When he saw a police car, with Osborne, Fortune and a big man he did not recognise standing round a body on the front step of the hotel, he hoped he had not arrived too late.

26

'What the hell are you doing here?' Osborne asked Baggo.

'I know who Crimewriter is, gov. Is that Johnson?'

'Yes.' Osborne could not keep the relief out of his voice as he looked down on his sworn enemy.

Hotel staff gathered at the front door, and a chambermaid burst into tears. 'He was a lovely man,' she wailed.

Jane, Tara and McCrone joined the group, followed by Liz Morrison, the hotel owner, who rounded on Jane.

'Jane, please tell me what's going on here. This is no ordinary retreat. I'm not daft, you know.'

As Jane stuttered, Danny Peters ran across the lawn from the direction of the road. He carried a long rifle with a metal frame for a butt. 'I found this in the bushes near the lay-by,' he said. 'Lucky I had plastic gloves with me.' When he saw Baggo, he did a double-take.

'I've cracked it, Danny.'

'Well done, mate, but too late for him.'

As Peters held it up, Fergus inspected the weapon. 'This is a Dragunov SVD, a Russian sniper rifle. It's semi-automatic but only one shot fired. A pro.' Seeing Flick's look of admiration, he added, 'I went on a course.'

The noise of wheels on gravel made them turn. From the direction of the drive, Wallace struggled to move his wheelchair towards them. He was out of breath. 'I heard a shot,' he gasped.

'What have you been doing?' Osborne asked him.

'Gov, I am sure Chapayev did this,' Baggo raised his voice.

'Chapayev? What are you talking about?'

'I can explain, but right now I am sure that Chapayev will be heading south in a black VW Golf. I have the registration here.'

'Is he one of yours?' Fergus asked Osborne, who nodded. Fergus reached for his mobile, punched in a number and spoke sharply to the person who answered. 'Maxwell here. This is urgent, so top priority. I want a south-bound car stopped on the A9. You should be able to intercept just north of Perth. Suspicion of murder. It's a black VW Golf.' He read out the number from Baggo's notebook. 'He could be dangerous. I'll hand you over to a man from the Met.'

Baggo took the phone. 'Hello, the man you are looking for is Nikolai Chapayev.' He paused while the instructions were forwarded. 'Chapayev is Russian, in his forties, with an untidy, black beard. Just under six foot. He has connections with the Russian mafia, and is very dangerous. Yes, murder. He shot a man in Pitlochry a short while ago. William Johnson. Yes. Thank you.' He handed the phone back.

'Chapayev visited me on Friday,' he explained. 'He came into the CID room and saw what the gov had written about Johnson on the whiteboard. I told him about the retreat, but did not say where it was. Unfortunately, he took a brochure of this hotel that had been lying on a desk. I realised this once he had gone, but I managed to glimpse him driving away, and noted his number.'

'Why should he kill Johnson?' Flick interjected.

'So that he would be blamed for Swanson's murder while acting for the Russians. That is the point. Everyone would assume the Russians had silenced Johnson before he could implicate them. But they have nothing to do with this. A friend in the Foreign Office told me Chapayev is a criminal: arms smuggling, money laundering and so on. Swanson's murder was one of Crimewriter's. She left a poison pen by the body. Chapayev used the murder for his own propaganda purposes and to publicise his book, just as I'm sure he plans to use Johnson's shooting. The very last thing he wanted was Johnson, whom he must have taken to be the prime suspect, to say the Russians had nothing to do with Swanson's murder.'

'Johnson was killed because of what he wouldn't say about the Russians?' Peters asked.

Baggo nodded.

'You said "she" there,' Flick said.

'Yes, Sarge …'

He was interrupted by a scream for help from the far end of the garden. Candy Dalton half-ran towards them, her clothes and hair askew and her glasses missing.

Flick and Baggo ran to help and led her, panting, to the others.

'I don't know what you're doing, but I'm glad you're here,' Dalton gasped. 'Cilla Pargiter is Crimewriter and she's just tried to kill me.'

Ignoring the noises of shock and disbelief, she carried on. 'We went for a walk to see the Soldier's Leap, and everything seemed normal. When we got there, onto that rock overlooking the river, she said, "This isn't a proper retreat. This is a police operation." I said "Rubbish", but she asked if I had been interviewed in the Crimewriter inquiry and I said I had. She said we were all suspects, and they were trying to trap one of us. And it came to me in a flash, it was her. It had to be. I must have shown it in my face, because she said, "Yes, it's me, but you're going to tell no one". Then she made a dive for me and tried to push me over the edge, but I was too quick for her. We both fell down and fought on the rock. She was determined to kill me. I've had to learn some judo for my work in the hostel, and I threw her, but she went too far and fell over the edge. I went to grab her hand as it scratched the lichen off the rock, but before I could reach her she was away.' She dissolved into tears and shook uncontrollably. 'I've killed her, I've killed her,' she repeated.

Flick put an arm round her and was about to lead her into the hotel when Baggo reached into a pocket, brought out his handcuffs, and secured both wrists. 'Candice Dalton, I am arresting you for the murders of Laurence Robertson, Denzil Burke and others. You need not say anything, but anything you do say will be liable to be used in evidence.'

'What on earth are you doing?' Flick snapped.

'It is her, and I can prove it,' Baggo replied hotly.

'Nonsense, nonsense, I'm a victim,' Dalton wailed.

'He's right, you know,' Jane said firmly. 'That was our unanimous opinion.'

'A narcissist,' Tara said. McCrone nodded.

'What about Cilla?' Baggo asked.

Liz said, 'If she fell into the pool at the Soldier's Leap, she has no chance. It's very deep, with a lot of currents.'

'She's a very strong swimmer,' Flick said. 'We must go and see.'

'Do you have a long rope?' Fergus asked Liz.

'There's an old rope some climbers left behind. I'll go and get it.'

Baggo said quietly to Osborne, 'Gov, we'll have to run to this place. I think it would be best if you were to look after Mrs Dalton back here.'

Osborne put his cigarettes away. 'That's what I was thinking, Chandavarkar.' He took one of Dalton's arms. 'We'll wait inside,' he said.

Liz brushed past them as she ran out, carrying a coil of faded blue climbing rope. 'I know the way,' she said, and ran across the lawn, Flick, Baggo, Peters, Fergus and Tara in her wake. McCrone followed at his own pace.

By the time they reached the National Trust shop, nearly half a mile from the hotel and closed for the winter, Liz was exhausted. 'You go on,' she said, handing the rope to Baggo. 'Stick to the path until you reach a big, flat rock on your left.'

The path zig-zagging downhill through the trees was

steep and rough. Baggo nearly went over on his ankle, but reached the rock first. Dalton's glasses lay on it, the brown frame crushed and the lenses shattered. He climbed through the simple wooden fence, approached the edge, and looked down and across the ravine to the other side. 'Cilla, Cilla,' he called, but heard only the roar of rushing water far below.

'There's a deep pool below here. If she survived the fall, she'd have swum to the nearest rock and grabbed it,' Flick said.

'There's an over-hang, so we won't be able to see the rocks on this side. I can't see her on the other side. If she got swept downstream to the rapids there's very little hope.' Fergus sounded gloomy.

'I am going to go down on the rope,' Baggo said.

Flick said, 'I'm lighter. I'll go.'

'I am stronger.' Baggo looked to Fergus for support.

'Can you abseil?' Fergus asked him.

'I've done it a couple of times. I know what to do.'

'We don't have the right equipment and strength is going to count,' Fergus ruled. 'Sorry, Flick.'

Fergus had assumed command. First, he tied one end of the rope round Baggo's waist then he tied the other end round his own. 'I shall be the anchor. We're going to lower Baggo down slowly. If he reaches Cilla he will grab her and we will all pull them up, like a tug o' war team.' He allocated everyone a place on the rope, Peters at the front, followed by Liz and Tara. McCrone he placed in front of himself. Flick, still scowling, was to check Baggo's progress and relay messages.

After a quick prayer to Ganesh, the elephant god, Baggo put his trust in his colleagues and leaned back over the river, his feet against the rock. Slowly and carefully, he moved down the rock face. The rope bit into his back and his hands, making his eyes water. Past the bulge of the over-hang, his feet slipped and he dangled vertically. Anxiously, he looked down at the cauldron of melted snow, now swirling, treacherous and brown. He searched for Cilla on the rocks at its edge.

She was there. She had hauled herself up into a cleft below the over-hang, so was out of the water from her waist up.

'Cilla, Cilla,' Baggo shouted, but saw no reaction. He looked up at Flick, gave her the thumbs-up, and pointed to his right. 'Two metres right,' he yelled, and was relieved to see her acknowledgement.

It took time and patience to lower him into a position from which he could wrap his arms round Cilla. By the time he did so he was frantic, and soaked from the waist down by cold, numbing water. She had not moved and he feared she was dead. Barely noticing the blood from his hands that stained her coat, he grasped her securely round the waist, and pushed back from the rocks so they swung on the rope, their legs tugged by the current. He looked up to Flick, who gave the thumbs-up.

The moan Cilla gave as they were lifted was one of the sweetest sounds he had heard. When they reached the over-hang he realised they had a problem: unless he could protect her somehow, she was going to be scraped against the rock face, and his arms would have to withstand the grazing contact with the rock and still hold on. He kicked out with one leg then the other, but could not get the leverage he needed. Eventually he managed to turn sideways so his left shoulder was punished by the rock. There were only a couple of metres to go.

Above him, Danny Peters noticed that the bit of rope passing through his fingers was badly frayed. Several strands had broken and the precious burden was hanging by only a few threads. Immediately, he went forward, grabbed the rope below the flawed section and pulled. Flick threw herself to the ground and also seized the rope. Guessing what was wrong, Fergus shouted to McCrone, who went to help Peters.

A few strong tugs and the emergency passed. Some more, and Baggo and Cilla lay on the rock like newly-caught salmon, one exhausted, the other barely conscious and moaning. Baggo's chilled hands were so tightly clasped together that he had difficulty in freeing Cilla from his embrace.

Green-suited paramedics arrived, wrapped Cilla in reflective foil, and took her away in an ambulance. Flick went with her to obtain her version of how she had come to fall. As her stretcher was placed in the back, she repeated, 'She pushed me. She pushed me.' Baggo refused treatment; he was determined to see Dalton brought to justice.

When they returned to the hotel, they found Osborne and Dalton side by side on a sofa in the lounge. Both were red-faced and looked angry. A small table near them lay on its side.

'She tried to escape, but I was way too fast for her,' Osborne explained.

While Fergus arranged for their prisoner to be detained in Perth, Baggo, wearing borrowed clothes, sat next to the fire and described how he had identified Dalton as the killer. He concluded, 'And I expect that her mobile records will show that some time after two am today she received a call from Lena Vannet. Once she knew I was onto her, she decided to kill Cilla and try to make out that she had been Crimewriter.'

'Good, old-fashioned police work,' Osborne commented.

'And Jane's psychology hit the back of the net, too,' McCrone said.

'Yes,' Jane said. 'Candy is a classic narcissist, desperate for approval, manipulative and incapable of reacting rationally in the face of criticism. We saw that several times during our workshops. And her composition was most revealing. It was a story about someone who should have been head girl of her school, but the mother of another girl started false rumours about her taking drugs, so her daughter became head girl. The protagonist arranged for drugs to be planted on this other girl so she replaced her as head girl for the summer term. The interesting thing was that gaining revenge was more important than becoming head girl.'

Tara said, 'It had a really autobiographical feel to it. I suspect she was describing what actually happened.'

McCrone nodded. 'When one agent after another

rejected even her bonking book, she wisnae going to take it lying down.'

'And her favourite classic was *The Count of Monte Cristo*,' Tara said. 'It's all about revenge, meticulously planned and carried out,' she explained.

'There's someone I must see before they go,' Baggo said.

He found Sidney Francis alone in his room, all traces of arrogance gone.

'It was me that found out,' Baggo said, then he described what he had seen and heard.

'It's been a nightmare,' Francis said. 'Matilda couldn't cope very well before the boys arrived or when they were babies, and she certainly couldn't when they started being naughty. She would do nothing, ignore bad behaviour for ages, then completely lose control, sometimes over nothing. You saw the sort of thing that could happen. So I decided to be a strong disciplinarian, insisting on good behaviour all the time. I punished them often, but it was controlled, never too heavy. I got worse thrashings myself as a boy. And it had started to work. When I went away at weekends it was partly for my writing, partly to see if she could cope on her own. And she was doing well, very well. Then you came and warned me, told me not to use the stocks.' He glared at Baggo. 'Soon afterwards the boys started being naughty again. Matilda broke Harold's arm, not me. She used a broom handle. I grappled with her, as you did, and she fell. Hence the bruise on her forehead. What will I do? What will happen to them?' He held his head in his hands.

'It is up to Social Services,' Baggo said. 'But remember this and hold onto it: you may not be great parents, but you are the only parents your boys have, and they have been consistently loyal to both of you.'

Francis looked up. 'Thank you,' he said.

'Good luck,' Baggo replied.

Downstairs, Fergus was celebrating the news that Chapayev had been caught after a car chase. Faced with a tractor pulling a wide load, he had driven into a ditch near a village called Methven. In his car there had been a Russian-made revolver and a commando-style knife. He was in custody and had been tested for gunshot residue. The officer administering the test had been optimistic.

'I think I'll drop into Perth Royal Infirmary to check on Ms Pargiter,' Fergus said as he left.

'I think you mean Sergeant Fortune,' Osborne said loudly, and was rewarded by a red flush that spread up the back of the Scot's neck.

27

It was a hot, stuffy day and Wimbledon was the centre of the tennis world. Baggo got home late and found Cilla sitting beside an open window, sipping champagne.

'The book, darling!' she cried. She poured a second glass and gave it to him. They clinked glasses.

'You've found an agent?'

'Better than that.'

'Not a publisher? I thought you needed an agent first?'

'I had the best agent I could have, my dad.'

'What?'

'You know how Dad got in touch with me without Mum knowing and we met regularly in London?'

'Yes, of course.'

'And how he said about my book, it wasn't the best time to try submitting it?'

'Yes.'

'Well all the time he had given it in hard copy to a friend who is a publisher. That friend got in touch with me this morning, and he's going to publish it! He said it's entirely a commercial decision, and he thinks it will sell.' Her voice caught. 'He said Dad hadn't told me he was submitting it as he didn't want me to be disappointed.'

'Well, congratulations. I am very, very pleased. You deserve this.' They clinked glasses again and drank.

Cilla's face clouded. 'Every time I think of Dad, I can't stop myself remembering that horrible, twisted little bitch. I'm glad she hanged herself, you know. I don't buy this "She'd have been so miserable in jail" crap. She'd have found a way to make life bearable.'

'She could not bear to lose control of her life.'

'I'll never forgive her for saying I was Crimewriter in her suicide note, that I had killed Dad.'

'You know that was never going to work. By the time we had amassed it all, the evidence against her was overwhelming. Her suicide note was the final throw of a desperate woman. Come on, cheer up. This is your day of triumph.'

'There's just one thing. I have to make one or two minor changes to the book, but they're easy.'

'Such as?'

'The opening. You remember I start with the priest being buried alive?'

'Of course. It's brilliant.'

'Well, I'm going to have to give it a build-up. Apparently people are fed up with every crime book having a murder on page one.'

ACKNOWLEDGEMENTS

While a few literary agents treat aspiring authors with arrogant rudeness, I am happy to say that I have found most to be courteous and professional in their dealings. Some go the extra mile to help newcomers, and I gratefully acknowledge the generous encouragement and wise counsel I have received from Andrew Lownie. I would also like to thank Tara Wigley for patiently teaching this old dog some new tricks. David Roberts has boosted my confidence and given me the benefit of his experience.

This is entirely a work of fiction and any resemblance to real people is coincidental. I have never been anywhere near Wimbledon CID Room and I hope no one there minds my (ab)use of their workplace. The Pride O' Atholl Hotel does not exist, and could not exist in the place I have imagined it. However, those readers who have visited the wonderful Knockendarroch Hotel, in Pitlochry itself, may notice some similarities to my creation.

I am most grateful to all at Matador, who have steered me through the publishing minefield. Special thanks go to Michael O'Shea at Tayburn for a brilliant cover design. My wife, Annie, and sons, Richard and Graham, have constantly encouraged and helped me make the transition from lawyer to writer and I cannot thank them enough.